A Kingdom of Venom and Vows

A Kingdom of Venom and Vows

HOLLY RENEE

sourcebooks casablanca

Internal design by Tara Jaggers/Sourcebooks

Published by Sourcebooks Casablanca, an imprint of Sourcebooks
1935 Brookdale RD, Naperville, IL 60563-2773
(630) 961-3900
sourcebooks.com

Originally self-published in 2023 by Holly Renee.

Cataloging-in-Publication Data is on file with the Library of Congress.

Printed and bound in the United States of America.
WOZ 10 9 8 7 6 5 4 3 2 1

For Lauren (a.k.a. LBCREADS)—
Thank you for your love of this series. You
will always be Evren's princess.

The Cleave
Human Lands

BLOOD KINGDOM
FAE KINGDOM
ONYX FORREST

CONTENT WARNING

A Kingdom of Venom and Vows contains depictions of sexually explicit scenes, violence, assault, and sexual assault. It contains mature language, themes, and content that may not be suitable for all readers. Reader discretion is advised.

Look for the moon symbol (☾) as you flip through the book, then check the back matter to discover what Holly Renee was thinking while writing *A Kingdom of Venom and Vows*.

A NOTE FROM HOLLY

Dear Reader,

When I first sat down to write Adara & Evren's story, I never imagined where these characters would take me or how fiercely they'd take hold of me.

This trilogy was always about more than magic, prophecies, & crowns. Adara & Evren clawed their way through betrayals, war, & blood to find the only thing that ever truly mattered: each other.

To everyone who fell for these two right alongside me, I cannot thank you enough. Adara & Evren have changed my life & so have you.

Thank you will never be enough.

xo,

Holly Renee

PROLOGUE

GAVRIL

My steps echoed against the old, damp space as I made my way into the dungeon.

I didn't want to be here, but my mother insisted that she be kept in the dungeon.

I could feel her as soon as I hit the bottom step, the bond between us pulling me forward even when I knew it was something I should have resisted.

As soon as I got to her cell, Leda's blue gaze met mine. She was cowering in the corner of the cell, and I watched as her hands trembled in her lap.

"How are you?" I asked gently as I pulled the keys from my pocket.

Her pupils dilated and her gaze shifted, rapidly darting around the room as if she were looking for a way out. She pressed her lips together as her body tensed with each of my movements, fear radiating from her wide eyes.

It was palpable, and I couldn't blame her for being so scared. At the same time, I couldn't help but feel hurt by the way she cowered in suspicion and dread.

"Don't touch her," a hoarse, tired voice called from the cell next to her, the same one who always tried to stop me when I visited her, but I paid him no attention.

Adara's father would serve his purpose soon enough, but this wasn't it. He was far too weak from his many years spent in a cell to even attempt to fight me.

All of them were too weak to stop me.

"Just leave her be, or I'll—" the man started, but I cut him off.

"You'll what?" I asked as I slid the key into Leda's cell door. "You'll get yourself killed before you're able to lay your eyes on your daughter again."

I stepped into the cell, and even though I could still hear him spouting his threats at me, I blocked him out as I stared at her.

I moved across the cell and dropped to my knees before her. She was so beautiful. Her long blond hair had lost its shine from the few years she had spent in this cell since my mother found her, but it did nothing to dim her beauty.

I reached my hand out to her, and she recoiled as if my touch burned her. My anger grew inside me, along with the foreign power that slithered through my veins. My fists quivered as I fought to keep control.

"I'll be going to the Blood kingdom soon." I spoke softly and reached out my hand for her again. This time, I didn't let her pull away. I clasped her hand in my own and ran my thumb over the dirt that clung to her pale skin. "I must feed from you before I do so."

I didn't tell her that I was forced to go to that godsforsaken kingdom because my brother, the man I had trusted more than any other, had escaped back there with my future queen.

He had betrayed me, and even when he returned home and tried to pretend like Adara had been taken by our enemy, I could see it in his eyes.

He had been my enemy all along.

I wished that my mother had killed him while we had the chance. The pound of flesh my mother had taken for his betrayal wasn't enough.

It never would be.

A cry escaped Leda's mouth, and she attempted to pull her hand from mine, but I held firm. "Please, don't."

Her words made my chest ache. If I could have found another way to ensure the future of my kingdom, of my power, without taking from her until she was on the brink of death, I would have done so.

But there wasn't.

Adara was the key to the prophecy, and I couldn't allow the way I wanted to protect Leda from everything, from myself, to get in the way of that.

"Don't fight me, love." I raised my hand and pressed it against her cheek. Her eyes shuttered, and her body trembled beneath my touch. "I'll make it good. Easy." I whispered the words against her lips before I met them with my own.

The kiss was gentle, pleading, but she remained stoic beneath me.

"I'm sorry," I murmured against her lips as I pulled away.

I lifted Leda's arm and slid my small dagger against her scarred skin. Her body stiffened, but I refused to let her go. My grip was firm as I ran my tongue along her wrist, collecting the blood that seeped from the cut before sealing my mouth over her and feeding from her.

I ruthlessly drained the life from her body, taking every drop of her essence into mine. As her life ebbed away, I could feel the power within me grow.

She cried out in agony, and I knew I was close to killing her as I feasted from her body.

But it was the only way to get the power I needed, the power I craved.

I pulled my mouth away from her wrist and pressed my hand to the wound. Her weak pulse thrummed beneath my fingers.

She was on the brink of death, but we would slowly nurse her back to life. It was a cycle that had to continue until I was completely ready to claim the power she held.

The power I would gain from killing my mate.

EVREN

A tingling sensation spread through my flesh like wildfire. Every nerve ending seemed to be alive with her energy, her presence felt in every corner of my being.

I could feel her blazing into my chest like a dying sun.

She had given me her magic, forced it into me without giving me the choice, and it snaked under my skin now, as frantic to find her as I was, like an invisible tendril reaching out to her.

My skin prickled with the anger of her power. It was clawing inside me like a caged animal screaming for release.

It was hers, but even with its searing rage, it felt like it was as much a part of me. The connection to my mate was still strong even through only her magic.

My heart raced as my anger was fueled from its depths.

She hadn't just forced her power into me, she had paralyzed me with it and forced me to watch my brother take her.

He took my fucking mate.

I stared at the door where he had disappeared with her as I ground my teeth together until my jaw ached. He had transported her out of my kingdom, a kind of magic I hadn't seen in many years, a kind of magic that required sacrifice.

A kind of magic that was almost impossible to fight.

Death magic.

My anger tasted like acid in my mouth. It thrummed on my tongue, white and furious and cold. It felt as alive as her magic that quivered through me uncontrollably.

But it wasn't the kind of anger that was helpful.

The kind of anger that helped me build a plan, one with the strength to carry me to the places where I would find her.

My anger was reckless. It was bloodthirsty, and I wasn't sure I could control it.

I needed to think.

Fucking breathe.

I took a step back toward the wall but fell against it, my back slamming into the hard stone.

Running my hands through my hair, I took a deep, seething breath. I needed to find a way to get her back.

I had to.

I had forced myself to be strong for so long—seen and endured so many things—but she had such a powerful hold on me. Something that made me feel so vulnerable and so fragile.

Because throughout all my years, there had never been something that could break me as easily as she could. She had the power to destroy me in ways that I never saw coming.

The chaos of voices around me jumbled together into a faint echo. They were shouting and arguing, but their words felt distant, like they were being smothered by a pillow.

My heart beat so fast I thought it might burst out of my chest. I had to force myself to inhale, to keep the ice-cold fear from overtaking me.

I looked around desperately for something to cling to, some thread of hope that might pull me back from the brink, but all I could see was her face, haunting me, taunting me.

Pressing my trembling, magic-stained hand against my chest, I tried to swallow down slow, deep breaths.

I forced my mind to think of anything that could help me, but no matter how hard I tried, all I could see when I shut my eyes was her, her gaze beseeching me.

She was my mate, and I failed her.

She had chosen me over everything. She had chosen me even though she knew the truth of me delivering her father to Queen Kaida so many years ago. The bond inside me that laced the two of us together felt taut and strained with the ache of the two of us being apart.

I had given her every reason not to, but she still chose me.

My chest tightened with a debilitating ache at the thought of losing her.

I balled my hands into fists, knuckles white and eyes closed.

I felt the stone, cold and unforgiving, behind me. The heavy brick beneath my feet was rough and worn. The smoke from the large fireplace smelled pungent and nauseating, burning my nose and curling away into nothingness. I could taste her power and feel it drip thick and slow down through my veins as if it were waiting to strike.

My breath rushed in and out of me, filling my lungs, and the tightness in my chest intensified.

I tried to focus on anything else, but I couldn't see anything beyond her.

The ground blurred beneath my feet as they staggered forward, my heart in my throat, my chest heavy and tight.

The sweat, the tears, the blood, the pain all flashed before my eyes. A reminder that I had been willing to sacrifice anything and everything for my people. To give everything I had to keep them safe.

Yet it had all been for nothing.

Because I failed at protecting her.

My anger fueled my magic, making it stronger and stronger until it pulsed beneath my skin with the same desire to know she was safe.

I felt it begin to tighten, squeezing my chest as if trying to suffocate me until I let it out. Her magic joined my own, and they started to consume me, feeding off my anger.

She had given me her magic without taking a moment to think of what the consequences would be.

Now Adara was in the enemy's kingdom, and her power remained with me.

She made herself powerless, and I couldn't stop my fury.

I couldn't allow myself to imagine a world where she wasn't mine, a world where I could never feel her skin against my own, never hold her.

Gavril had dared to put his hands on my mate, to manipulate her into going back with him, and I would kill my own blood to get her back.

I would kill him without hesitation.

I knew he had grown more powerful. I had suspected it when I arrived back at the fae kingdom, when I left her behind to make sure she was safe. The idea seemed preposterous now.

She would never be safe as long as Gavril was alive. The prophecy foretold that she would save our kingdom, but it also damned her fate. She would always be caught between two brothers.

She was our hope, but we were her destruction.

But there wasn't a force strong enough in this world or the next that could stop me from loving her.

If I could, I would do so. I would do whatever I could to make sure she was safe.

I would go to whatever end. My kingdom be damned.

I pushed forward and almost ran into Thalia who stood before me. She looked as haunted as I felt, but I knew the ghosts that hid in the dark depths of her eyes were something I would never understand.

"What's our plan?" She crossed her arms over her chest, the same stern look on her face that I had always known her to wear, yet there was the slightest tremble of her lips that betrayed her bravery.

"I'm going to the fae kingdom."

"His magic…" Her voice shook, her words laden with fear.

"I know." I nodded and looked past her to find Sorin and Jorah.

"He used death magic, Evren."

"I know," I said lowly, thinking about what my brother would do with Adara in his grasp, and a deep-rooted fear shivered down my spine. Adara's power took notice, restless inside me.

I would tear the damned kingdom down to the ground if I had to, and her magic would be as eager to do so as I was.

"We can't just march in there and take her. If he has that kind of magic, who knows what he's capable of? Who knows what he'll do to her?"

I bit down on my tongue until I tasted blood. I wanted to rage, to tell her there was nothing he could do to stop me, but deep down, I knew she was right.

The bastard had death magic, a magic I had only ever heard about but never seen, and I worried I wouldn't be strong enough to fight it.

"To get death magic, he would have had to…" Thalia trailed off, her fear palpable between us.

"Kill his mate." I met her gaze as I ran my fingers through my hair. "I was foolish to think he wouldn't go this far to get what he wanted."

"I didn't know he had a mate. Did you?"

"No." I shook my head and tried to scour my mind for anything I might have missed. "They've always been so consumed with Adara." I gritted my teeth at the thought. "I've never heard him or Queen Kaida talk of another."

Thalia's hands trembled, but she pushed them against her hips to hide the movement as Sorin made his way toward us.

"That was…" His eyes darted from Thalia to me and back again, lingering on her a beat longer. His jaw tightened and his brow furrowed as he stared at her intently, as if he were trying to convey something that couldn't be put into words.

"Death magic. We know."

"How do we fight it?" He finally broke the intense gaze he had locked on her, and his hand gravitated toward the hilt of his dagger at his side. I knew from the resolve in his gaze that my friend and captain was as ready to march into the fae kingdom as I was.

But Thalia was right. If we weren't smart about this, we would do more harm than good. We would get Adara killed.

Only death magic allowed someone to transport, but it also came with so much more. An unending power, as it was told through legend. The thought of what he sacrificed to get it ate at me.

Because death magic could become an undefeatable power.

It was legend that death magic would take as much as it gave. It was a great power, but it came at a great cost to the one who dared claim it.

A cost that Gavril would have to pay.

He was the enemy, but once upon a time, he had been nothing other than my brother. My chest ached for that past, for those memories that were now so tainted with his mother's and my father's greed.

He had become that greed. Their perfect heir who infected

everything he touched. A poison that spread through the kingdom, and I refused to allow that venom to touch Adara.

Even if she had walked into his trap so willingly. She had shaken his hand, binding the promise she made, and I had been a fool.

Her magic stirred inside me as if it agreed, and I looked back and forth between my friends. “Get Jorah and meet me in the library. We need to learn as much about death magic as we can find. We’re going to get her back, but we can’t do it blindly.”

Even as I said the words, emotions warred in my chest. There was a part of me that knew they were right, but a bigger part of me couldn’t fathom sitting here, formulating a plan, while she was there with him. While neither I nor her magic were there to help protect her.

But we were going to get her back.

ADARA

My stomach lurched as I flung out my arms, desperate to keep my balance. My vision blurred and the colors of the world spun around me. I squeezed my eyes shut, willing everything to settle. When I opened them again, I swallowed down the nausea and tried to make out where we were.

"Calm down, Starblessed, before you get sick."

Gavril's hands were like iron vises around my arms, and I could feel his strength beneath his fingertips. My body trembled, struggling against his grip as a fire of agony burned within me. My entire body shuddered in protest, every part of me desperate for relief.

I was cold and empty without my magic, without my mate. I had given Evren all my magic, and my body rebelled against me.

The smell of smoke was thick in the air, and I tried to breathe through my mouth to block it out as I looked around us. Gavril had taken us back to the fae kingdom, just outside the city, and I was shocked by the number of guards who stood around us fully dressed in their uniforms.

They hadn't just been preparing to take me. They were preparing for war.

"Let go of me." I wanted to scream, but my throat was thick and my voice barely a whisper. My vision blurred and my breathing quickened as his hands dug into my skin.

"I'm taking her to the palace." Gavril's fingers pressed against my shoulder as he spoke to one of the guards, and I glanced up into his bloodshot eyes. There was an unnatural power that thrummed through him, and his pupils dilated as he watched me.

"I said, let me go, Gavril." My voice was hoarse and weak, and the urge to summon my magic was overwhelming, but the ache inside my chest burned when nothing came. But that pain felt inconsequential.

My pain became unbearable as I thought of him.

I wanted Evren. I wanted my mate.

But more than anything, I wanted him safe.

I couldn't even allow myself to think of my father, to think of the role Evren had played in taking him away from me.

He had been a puppet then, a pawn in Queen Kaida's game, and even as my chest ached at the truth of what he had done,

I couldn't hate him for something that had happened before I knew him.

I couldn't hate him for what he did to help protect his people.

Because everything he did was for someone else.

And there was nothing I could do to stop myself from loving him. Despite everything I knew, despite the roles he played.

Gavril's hand tightened on my arm, pain lacing through my skin, and I ground my teeth as I looked up at him.

"Let's go, Starblessed."

Starblessed. The coward couldn't even say my name.

He jerked me forward until I had no choice but to follow behind him. I stumbled over my feet as he pulled me along. I was tired, the feeling sinking deep into my bones, but I didn't dare say that to him. Instead, I stared ahead as we approached the palace that I hated—the palace where I had found solace in Evren—and I tried not to let a single one of them see my weakness.

The guards parted as we reached the castle, careful to stay out of my path. I heard their whispered words of traitors and betrayal, and I felt their contempt. It was pouring out of them as visible as Evren's power fell from him.

I was the Starblessed that they all wanted, that they needed, but hated just the same.

They thought I was their savior, but I would be no such thing.

I would be their destruction.

I raised my chin, unwilling to drop my gaze in their presence. Gavril's knuckles whitened as his grip on my arm tightened and he pulled me closer to him. I recoiled as his nostrils flared. His hands were brutal against me, and his jaw clenched as we walked.

His anger was a powerful tool, and as much as I wanted him to let me go, his temper would make him reckless.

He truly thought that I belonged to him, and the thought of Evren touching me, of me choosing his brother over him, fueled his fury.

We pushed through the door, and he jerked me forward until I was forced to breathe in the suffocating heat of the palace. We had entered through the back entrance, the one I had tried to escape through what seemed like a lifetime ago, and I glanced forward at the doors ahead of us.

My old bedroom sat to the right.

The door was securely closed, and even though I never felt any comfort behind that door, every part of me ached to escape there now.

Gavril followed my gaze, and a dark laugh fell from his lips. "You actually think I would let you go back to the room where my brother fucked you as his whore?" His fingers dug into me harder, and I bit down on my lip to stop myself from crying out at the pain. "You will be staying beside me where I can keep a watchful eye on you at all times, close by so I can fuck my soon-to-be wife whenever I choose."

He pushed me back against the wall near the bedroom door, the same wall that Evren had once held me against, and my stomach ached as Gavril lifted his hand.

He gently pressed his fingers to my jaw, a stark contrast to the opposite hand, which was still holding me captive, and I flinched as his skin made contact with mine.

"You're so responsive." His gaze fell to my lips, and I turned my head away as I tried to swallow down the bile that flooded my mouth. "No wonder my brother was so willing to risk everything for you. If you fuck half as good as you fight, the two of us will be more than happy with each other."

I jerked away harshly, making his hand fall away from my face, and I watched as rage filled his dark gaze. But it was the thin red ring around his irises that made me stutter in fear.

"I will never sleep with you." My words were strong and sure, but they did nothing but make a cruel smile slip onto Gavril's lips.

"Oh, I think you will." His hand lifted, and he pressed his fingers to my jaw again as he forced me to look at him. There wasn't a trace of the softness he had been using only a moment ago. "After all, you enjoyed being fucked by my brother, and I'm sure with the right persuasion, you will enjoy me as well. Is it power you were after, Starblessed?"

He was so close now that I could smell the deep woodsy scent of him.

"I can give you more power than my brother ever dreamed of."

His words twisted through my stomach as he leaned forward and pressed his lips to my skin. I tried to jerk away but instead found myself slamming harder into the wall behind me. His teeth grazed against my skin, the sharp edges curling against my jaw.

"In fact, I can't wait to feel you around me. I'm going to fucking ruin you for anyone else, Starblessed. My traitorous brother will never want to touch you again."

I pressed my lips together to keep from retching, to keep from crying out, but I could feel the tears building behind my eyes. His anger thrummed from him like a living being, and without my power, I feared there was nothing I could do to stop him.

"You will fucking beg me for it, Adara." He whispered my name, and a chill ran down my spine at how wrong it sounded falling from his lips. "You will come crawling on your knees for me to give you what you want, and only then will I give it to you. Only then will you be worthy of the future king of Citlali."

"I won't." I shook my head against him and balled my hands into fists.

"Hold on to that fight." I could feel his lips form into a grin against my cheek. "I'm going to enjoy breaking it." He pushed away from me then, running a rough hand over his lips as if he were considering doing more, then his eyes flashed toward the hall. "Go," he demanded of me, and I hesitantly pushed off the wall as I tried to catch my breath.

He didn't need to tell me where to go. I knew this palace now, and I would never be able to forget where his room lay. The room where he took from me against my will.

I was thankful for the moment without his touch as I got my legs under me and tried to keep my hands from trembling at my sides.

It would only be a matter of time before Gavril took things further, before he forced my hand in marriage and drank from my blood. It was only a matter of time before he realized that he may have taken the Starblessed, but all my magic remained with his brother.

I wiped at my mouth as I glanced to the other end of the

corridor, and I swallowed hard as I took a step away from Gavril and the memories my former room held.

Memories of Evren that I forced myself not to think of. Not now. I would cling to those memories when I needed them most. When I felt myself giving up.

Because I knew everything about this kingdom, everything about the prince who was following behind me, would test me. They would do everything in their power to break me.

But I would not yield.

If I couldn't find the strength in myself, I would rely on the strength I still carried inside me from Evren.

"This way." Gavril nodded forward toward the hall where his room was, and the dread in my stomach became violent. "I'll give you a few moments to gather yourself, then the queen would like to see you."

Everything inside me stopped as I looked back at him. As fearful as I was of Gavril, he had nothing on his mother. She was where my true fear lay.

"I'd like to get some rest."

Gavril bit down on his lip as his gaze trailed down my body. I turned away from that look quickly and continued to push forward toward his room.

"You have a lifetime for rest here in this kingdom, Starblessed. Eletta will help you get ready to meet with my mother. She'll help you change from that fucking dress my brother put you in." He sneered, and I clung to the deep black fabric that still shone against my skin.

Eletta. Eletta would be with me.

"And what would you like me to dress in?" I stopped near his door and balled my hands into fists in the fabric of my dress. "What would impress you, Your Highness?"

Gavril grinned and took a step toward me. I shouldn't have goaded him, but I couldn't control the fury that burned within me.

"I know you think this temper inside you will anger me, but you're wrong." His gaze dropped to my mouth, and my breath caught in my throat. "It only increases my desire to make you bow down to me." He lifted his hand as if he were going to touch me again, but he nodded to the door just down the hall from his instead. "That is your room for now. You will not leave unless you are told to do so."

My jaw clenched as I stared at the door. I moved away from him and to the room he had given me. I didn't glance back in his direction as I clasped my hand around the ornate handle and turned. I just wanted to sleep and be away from the nightmarish world I now lived in.

I wanted to be alone where I could try to figure out what the hell I was going to do. How the hell I was going to get back to Evren.

The room was small. The bright walls and the light wood furniture were the exact opposite of what I was used to. So different from everything that was Evren.

Everything about this kingdom was so different from all that he was. I didn't know how he had survived here so long. How he had played the role they all thought he belonged in.

They had been so wrong.

"Adara."

I jumped and spun at the sound of Eletta's voice. She stood at the edge of the washroom door, linens draped over her arms and worry clouding her eyes.

"Eletta, you scared me." I pressed my hand to my pounding chest and quickly closed the door behind me. It was just the two of us alone in the room, but I knew better than to let my guard down.

"I'm sorry." Her gaze dropped to the floor. "I ran you a bath." She glanced back to the washroom, and her next words were more hesitant. "The crown prince would like you to cleanse yourself before you're presented to the queen." I frowned at her, and she offered me a shake of her head. "He's not asking this of you, Adara. The queen has demanded that you be brought to her as soon as he rescued you."

"And I'm not going." I laughed, and the sound rang out with every bit of bitterness I felt inside me. "Your prince didn't rescue me. He took me from my mate." I turned and started toward the bed, but she followed me quickly.

"The dark prince? Starblessed..."

"I've told you before not to call me that," I spat, and I hated that I felt so angry with Eletta. She had done nothing to me other than be a part of this kingdom.

"Adara." She sighed and set the linens on the bed. "I'm sorry. I will do whatever I can to make you comfortable in your new room."

I clenched my fists as I turned to her. "This isn't my room, Eletta. This is a cage."

"He hasn't hurt you. He wants to protect you from his brother." Eletta's voice was so soft, so sure, and I couldn't stop the bitter laugh that escaped me.

"You don't know your crown prince at all if you truly believe that." Anger vibrated through me where my power was missing. "He's a monster."

Eletta jolted backward as if I had hit her, and I wondered if she was truly that blind to those she served.

"No." Her voice shook with her denial. "No, he's not."

I shook my head and turned from her. "You can go." I dropped onto the bed, and I was glad for the fabric against the soreness that still radiated from my body. Nausea still roiled in my stomach from whatever magic Gavril had used to bring us here, from the sight of his troops ready to fight my mate, my kingdom.

"I'm not leaving you." Her voice was firm. "I'm here to help you get ready for the queen."

"You're here to help me bathe for the man who stole me from Evren." I lifted my eyes toward the ceiling, wetting my lips. "I think I can handle that on my own."

"I was instructed by Gavril not to leave you alone." Her voice was small, hesitant, and when I looked back to her, I could see her own doubt marred across her face.

"Oh yes. What a savior your prince is." I stood and began pulling my dress from my shoulders. I stepped out of it as she watched, and I couldn't stop myself from bringing the fabric to my nose. I breathed it in, my eyes falling closed as the scent of Evren overwhelmed me.

The smell of him still clung to the fabric the same way he

was engraved in every part of me, and I could feel moisture pooling in my eyes as I thought of the horror on his face when he saw me take his brother's hand. He promised that he would never let his brother touch me again, but I had taken that choice away from him.

Gavril had used my father against me. He had taken my every weakness and played me exactly how he wished to.

And I had done nothing but fall into his trap.

"Did you see that army out there?" I nodded toward the window on the far side of the room. "Do you think that entire army is stationed just outside these walls because he wanted his betrothed back?"

"He's gone crazy since he found out you were taken." Her eyes were wide with conviction.

"No." I shook my head and held out my right hand. The one that held the scar where he had stolen from me. "He went crazy because he knew my power was taken from him." I stared down at my inky black-stained fingers, and I wished that I could pull my magic from myself and let my darkness fill the room around us.

I wished I could show her I was exactly like the man she feared so much.

"He wants me because he wants my power, and he will take it from me against my will." I turned and glared at her. "He will take from us all, Eletta. That's what Gavril does. He takes." I shook my head and pressed the dress to my face one last time before laying it at the foot of the bed. "He takes until there is nothing left."

"You don't know that," she whispered, her gaze dropping to

the ground as I closed my eyes. "You don't know what he's been through and what he's had to endure." Her words were soft, but I could hear her belief in them. "He's the only one who can protect us from the Blood kingdom." She shook her head. "You just can't see that."

"The Blood kingdom?" I moved past her and into the washroom that was billowing with steam from the bath she drew. "You are fearing the wrong kingdom. You are as brainwashed as he wants you to be."

"What?"

"The Blood kingdom is my home." I turned to look at her once more with my fingers digging into the wood of the door. "And the Blood Prince is my mate. If you are to fear anything, it should be me. You should fear what I am willing to do to get it all back."

EVREN

My eyes were glued to the crumbling pages of the book before me, the ink fading and barely legible. I stared down at the words *death magic,* and I couldn't bring myself to look away. I had been searching these ancient texts for hours and had yet to find any real answers.

Everything we knew of it was from legends that spoke of its power. Death magic came at a price. It brought great power to the one who possessed it, but it also ate away at one's soul.

Killing one's mate would destroy it.

My brother didn't care what he ruined in his path to gain as much power as he could. He was driven by an insatiable desire for it, and he would destroy Adara if that was what it took for him to fulfill the prophecy.

He would destroy everything.

Rage stirred in my belly, starving me of the air in my lungs, as I thought of his greed. Having the power of death magic wasn't enough for him. Gavril wouldn't stop until he knew no one held the power to defeat him.

And Adara and I together were the only ones who held that power.

Without her fate, his rule can't begin.

His death magic didn't matter without her because I would destroy him.

"This is useless." I slammed the book shut with a loud crack and shoved my hands into my hair. My chest ached as I stared around the small room, and my breath felt trapped in my lungs.

Thalia looked up from the book she was currently scouring, and her gaze darted back and forth between Jorah and me.

"I think I found something." She pushed the book to the center of the table, and Jorah and I both stood to see better. "We've all heard that death magic comes with certain powers. The transporting, death touch, but it appears that there is much more to it." She turned the page quickly and ran her finger beneath the words that marked the page. "In order for someone to gain the full powers of death magic, they must make sacrifices. They must give up a part of their soul that they can never get back."

My eyes slammed into Thalia's as she briefly met my gaze before looking back down at the book in front of her. I heard my heart beating, a dull thumping in my ears.

"His mate," I finished for her, and she nodded before looking back at the book. "What other powers can he gain from that?"

"I'm not sure yet." She shook her head as if she were as frustrated as I felt. "I need to do more research. This text talks about all-consuming power."

The door to the library shot open with a loud boom, startling all three of us, and I could feel my and Adara's magic thrumming inside me, ready to strike before I could even look up to see the threat.

"Sorin has sent for you," one of my guards rushed out, and his eyes bounced between the three of us. "There are fae soldiers in the city."

Anger wrapped around me, suffocated any logical thought, and I stormed toward the guard as I barked out at him, "Where?"

"Just outside the palace. The captain has gone ahead."

I stormed past him, and I knew that both Thalia and Jorah would be following close behind me without ever looking back.

We had tracked every one of the fae soldiers that had arrived with my brother, and they had all transported back with the coward. For them to be here now meant that more had arrived.

I checked the daggers that lay against my chest as I headed for the door. I didn't know what we would be facing once we stepped outside, but I hated how unprepared I felt for my brother's plans.

I had expected him to fight for her, but not like this.

The sound of screams hit us as soon as we stepped outside, and my power began pouring from my fingers before I could stop it. Black smoke swirled around me as I watched the people of my kingdom running in fear.

"Bring them inside the castle." I barked out the order at the guard who had come for us. "Get as many as you can in the palace and bar the doors."

He nodded his understanding, and I stormed away from the castle. I saw the relief on some of my people's faces as I passed, but I didn't have time to offer them such comfort.

The fae soldiers had dared to come to my kingdom, and they would all pay dearly for that decision.

I came across the first soldier as he held one of my people in his grasp with a sword in his other hand. His eyes flashed with fear as he saw me, and it didn't matter that he was one of the men who had been a part of my guard when I was still in my father's kingdom.

His loyalty to me then meant nothing now.

I shot my power out toward him, the black smoke moving so quickly that it was barely visible, and the soldier's arms fell away from the woman as he clawed at his neck. But it was no use.

My magic wrapped around him and cut off his airway without effort. There was nothing he could do to stop me. Nothing he could do to save himself.

His body fell to the ground with a loud thud, and I moved to the next.

"Head to the castle," I heard Thalia call from behind me, and the woman took off quickly with tears streaking down her cheeks.

I continued to push forward, my power fueled by the life of the soldier I had just taken, and I searched for the rest of the men who had invaded my kingdom.

I could hear the deep clanging of metal as I moved through the streets, and as I turned the corner toward the Olde Vine, I took in a sharp breath.

There were at least a hundred fae soldiers infiltrating the streets, and I spotted Sorin as he lifted his sword and tore through one of them before moving to the next.

Blood spattered against his chest, but it didn't slow him down. These men were his enemies as much as they were mine. They had made enemies out of all of us the moment they stepped into my kingdom and took Adara from me.

I pulled one of the daggers from my left side and let it fly from my hand. I barely watched as it lodged in the fae soldier's chest before I let more of our magic slip through my fingers and take out the soldier at his side.

Jorah called my name, and I looked up just in time to see one of the soldiers powering toward me with his sword in the air. There was so much anger on his face, so much betrayal.

They had all once seen me as their leader, their captain, who they followed blindly into any situation, and all they knew now was that I had turned on them.

I didn't have any room for guilt, even if a trace of it did sit heavily in my gut. I lifted my hand in time to allow my power to escape, but Thalia was already on the man, her own power knocking him to the side before her dagger slammed into him.

She had a vicious look on her face. Every bit of fear I had seen when Gavril had arrived had completely disappeared as she protected this kingdom that she loved from the kingdom that she hated. ☾

She looked every bit the warrior, but I knew the truth. She was first and foremost a friend, and that venom in her eyes was for Adara, who was also taken from her.

And Thalia knew better than anyone how bad the fae kingdom could be.

Even when I had gone back, when I had left Adara behind in my home, the things they did to me would never compare to what they did to Thalia.

I could still taste copper in my mouth as I thought about how my father and brother had both stood there while they watched Queen Kaida unleash her pain on me.

She had wanted answers, she wanted my mate, and I had refused to give her anything. Queen Kaida hated to be refused.

She hated it almost as much as she hated me. The bastard son of her king who was born to do nothing but ruin her plans. That was how she had always seen me, and I had spotted the poison in her eyes the moment I was first brought to the fae kingdom by my father.

She only wanted me there because she thought she could train me, turn me into whatever she wanted, but I refused to allow her to break me.

Regardless of how much I allowed her to believe otherwise.

She had thought that she had molded me into the weapon she needed, the weapon to surge her son into power, and for many years, she had.

I had been the sword she drove between the kingdoms until I truly saw the evil that lay beneath her veil.

Because Queen Kaida was pure evil, regardless of the excuses she used to justify her actions.

It was her face I pictured as I let my power flow through my fingers with a growl and took out the next ten soldiers who moved toward us.

I heard the gasp that left Thalia's mouth, but I didn't let it stop me. I typically tried to rein in my anger, the power that coursed through me and craved taking the life from any of these fucking men who had stepped into my kingdom, but I lacked that control today.

They had taken my mate, and I wanted nothing more than to destroy them all.

The sound of their bodies hitting the ground echoed around me, but I didn't stop. I kept pushing forward, toward my second-in-command, and I could hear the sounds of Thalia and Jorah fighting with those around me.

I would stop at nothing until I got her back.

And these men would pay for what side of this war they chose to be on. They were my enemy. They had always been my enemy, and I refused to forget that fact as I stared into their familiar faces.

My power shot out from me, killing more men without thought, and I could feel my power strengthen inside me as it ripped the life from their bodies.

I had almost made it to Sorin's side. He was tearing down as many soldiers as I was, and I could see the hate that filled his eyes. These men were responsible for taking Adara, and Sorin took that as seriously as I did.

He was a loyal second-in-command, but more than anything, he was a loyal brother to me. Much more of a brother than Gavril could ever be.

Sorin gripped a soldier by the collar of his shirt and lifted him close to his face as I approached. His dagger was already in his right hand, and I knew Sorin was seconds away from slicing through the man and taking his life.

But there was something in me that hesitated when the soldier's familiar eyes flicked back and forth between me and my captain.

"Captain, please." His voice shook with fear, and I could taste it on my tongue. His terror fueled me because there would be no mercy when it came to Adara.

"Don't waste your words on me." I pulled the dagger from my side and twisted it between my black fingers. "You should be praying to the gods now for forgiveness for what you have done."

The soldier's eyes widened. "You don't understand what he's done. You're not prepared to fight him."

Sorin hesitated, his eyes sliding to me for only a second, but we both knew we needed to hear what this man had to say. We were unprepared, and any knowledge of what my worthless brother had planned would help us.

But I hated giving this soldier that power.

"And what has he done?" I asked him lazily and watched as his chest rose and fell rapidly under my stare.

I wanted to take my dagger and carve it into his skin. I wanted to force the words from his lips until he had no choice but to tell me everything I wanted to know, but I didn't want to become the monster that my brother and his queen made me out to be.

The monster they tried to create.

This was my kingdom. My people were the ones being

harmed, and they needed to know that I was here to protect them.

"He has death magic."

I let out a sarcastic laugh and looked bored as I stared down at him. "You think this is something we don't already know?"

The man shifted, his hands clinging to Sorin's, which were still holding him, and he was trying to buy time to save his life. But there was nothing he could do or say that would save him at this point. He had attacked my kingdom. He had attacked my people after the man he served stole Adara.

"I've never seen..." He shook his head rapidly. "I've never even heard of a death magic like this before. He has power that cannot be matched."

"And how did he get this magic?"

"He has sacrificed." The man looked around us. "He sacrificed the people of his kingdom, of the palace. It is said that when he feeds from the life of his mate, of the Starblessed who was promised, his power grows and shifts."

"Adara is not his mate," I snapped, my anger barely leashed.

He stuttered over his next words. "He has his army surrounding the kingdom, but that isn't all that protects it. He has some sort of enchantment, and no one can get in and no one can get out."

"What kind of enchantment?"

He shook his head quickly and looked at Sorin before looking back at me. "I don't know. The only way we've been able to get in and out of the kingdom is by him transporting us. Even his soldiers can't get past the barrier he's created."

I heard a crash of metal and looked to my left just in time to see Thalia slam her small dagger into the chest plate of the soldier in front of her before she hit him in the head with the butt of the knife. He fell to the ground, but she was already moving on to the next. "So you have no useful information for me? No way for me to get into the palace?"

"No, Captain. There is no way to get in there. There is no way to get to the Starblessed."

I rolled my head as his words coiled around me. "I am not your captain. I am the crown prince of the Blood kingdom, and I have no doubt that I will get her back."

The man's eyes flashed with fear once again just before Sorin's dagger sliced across his throat.

ADARA

I wasn't sure how long I had been in the fae kingdom. I tried not to sleep for fear of what would happen if I did, but my body was exhausted, and I continued to fall in and out of sleep before jerking awake to check my surroundings.

There was no window in my room, and I knew that was no accident. I was Gavril's prisoner despite him putting me in a fancy room and pretending that I was nothing more than his betrothed. I was his prisoner, and he was going to treat me as such.

I had just dozed off again when there was a soft knock at the door, and Eletta stepped inside before I could even utter a word. She closed the door behind her, and her gaze raked over me before I saw her wince. She tried to hide it, but I knew. I must've looked as awful as I felt.

Giving Evren every bit of my power drained me until my body felt hollow and sluggish. It weighed me down like a stone, leaving me weak.

"You need to eat." She carried a tray to the bed, and as much as I wanted to refuse her, my stomach growled at the smell of the savory stew in front of me. "And you need to bathe. The queen is requesting you again."

My fingers tightened around a piece of crusty bread that lay on the tray, and I allowed my eyes to meet Eletta's.

"Is the queen too good to see her prisoner in the state they stole her? Should she not see what her son has done to me?"

Eletta swallowed roughly before walking to the small closet and pulling out a soft white dress. She laid it across the front of the bed before running her hand over the skirt to make sure there were no wrinkles.

"She has requested you in the throne room within thirty minutes' time." She ignored my question altogether, and I let my anger with her seethe.

"I can bathe myself." I took a bite of the bread before dipping my spoon into the stew and taking a large bite.

Eletta looked around the room as if she was unsure what to do, and for a moment, I felt sorry for her. Had I not just been the girl who knew nothing but the lies I was told? How could I expect her to know the things that I did when she had spent her lifetime under the king and queen's rule?

"If you'll fill the tub, I will be ready in time."

She let out a sigh and clasped her hands together before quickly moving into the washroom.

I ate every bite as I listened to the tub filling, then Eletta leaving the room. She hesitated by the door before she slowly closed it behind her, but I would not allow her to help me. I would not lean on anyone in this kingdom.

I bathed quickly and pulled on the dress Eletta had set out for me. When I stared in the mirror, it was almost comical how different I looked. This variation of Adara was so different from the version I was with Evren.

I looked like the lost girl who first came to the fae kingdom. As I stared at myself in the mirror, I reminded myself of who I was. I was the Starblessed that was promised. Not to Gavril. I was promised to Evren, the crown prince of the Blood kingdom, and I would not cower in front of these people.

I would not let them see my weaknesses, and I refused to break regardless of what they did to me. *I would not break.*

I opened the door and stepped out into the hallway. My hair was still wet and pulled back in a simple braid, something that I knew the queen would hate, and Eletta barely met my eyes as I started down the hallway toward the throne room. I didn't let her see the way I shuddered as I passed Gavril's bedroom, the place he first took from me, and I clasped my hands together to stop the trembling as we finally stepped in front of the double doors of the throne room.

Raising my chin as the guards opened the doors, I stepped inside without being beckoned. The queen's eyes tracked me immediately, and there was a grimace on her face that made me both fearful and smug at the same time.

Gavril sat at her side on the throne, but the king was nowhere to be found.

It didn't matter. The queen was the one who truly ruled this kingdom. It was her wrath that I would face. Hers and her cruel son's.

I stopped in front of them, but I didn't dare bow before them. They both waited expectantly, and after a moment when neither of them spoke, I opened my mouth before they could. "I was told you summoned me." I dipped into a small curtsy dramatically and lifted my skirt. "And what can I do to serve my captors?"

"Captors?" The queen spat out the word. "The bastard prince stole you from our side. He was sworn to protect you, and instead, he betrayed his kingdom. He is a traitor. He was your captor."

Even though I knew I had given Evren every ounce of my power, I could feel a trickle of it warming inside me with my anger. Deep in my gut, it called to me, and I wished I could call it forth now to destroy the queen and everything she stood for.

"You will not speak of my mate in such a way again. He is the crown prince of the Blood kingdom. He is the rightful heir to the throne on which your son now sits, and you will address him as such."

There was so much venom in my words, and an audible breath left the queen's mouth. Her eyes widened as she tried to hold her ground and hide her fear.

"I will speak of him how I wish to." The queen glared at me, and I knew that she was unaccustomed to being challenged. Gavril was his mother's puppet, and I had no doubt that he and his father likely never went against her. No one did. "It would appear the bastard prince did more than just use you as his whore. He gave you a backbone as well."

My jaw tightened at her words, but she wasn't finished.

"That was dangerous of him. You would think Evren would have told you what happened to traitorous people in my kingdom who think they are above our rule."

My stomach hardened, and I searched her face. "He is above your rule."

She grinned, the look terrifying, and stood from her throne. "Yet when the traitor returned without you and thought me foolish, his skin bled as easily as yours will."

I jerked backward, and her grin widened. I knew that Evren had been harmed when he returned to the Blood kingdom, but I hadn't thought…I hadn't even considered that it was by the queen's hand.

"What did you do to my mate?"

"Cling to that word, Starblessed." She moved closer to me until the overpowering smell of roses hit my nose. "You will need every bit of power you think it gives you while I remind you where you belong."

She circled around me, and I jumped when her fingers trailed over my braid. She *tsk*ed, clearly unhappy with my appearance, but she continued around me, and her gaze met her son's for the first time since I entered the room.

"Do you think you can handle the Starblessed on your own, or should I accompany you while you feed from her?"

"No." That same tendril of power stirred inside me, and I shook my head as I took a step back.

"It isn't a choice, Starblessed." The queen looked back to me. "We don't have the luxury of waiting for you and Gavril to be wed any longer."

I choked out a laugh. "I'm not marrying him, and he's not feeding from me."

The queen's hand tightened into a fist, but it was the only sign she gave of her anger. "You will do whatever you are told, Starblessed."

She looked back to Gavril before she stepped away from me, and I watched them both as the queen passed by the thrones and slipped through a door at the back wall.

Only Gavril and I remained in the room, and I dug my nails into my palms as I watched the prince stare at me. His hand rested on his chin, and he leaned back in his throne as if he was completely unbothered by me standing before him.

We stared at each other wordlessly before he finally stood and took a step toward me.

I swallowed hard. "What kind of pet would you like me to be, Gavril? Because that is all I will ever be to you. I will never be your queen."

Gavril's lip lifted in a sneer, and he took another step forward. "Are you sure, Starblessed?" His eyes slid over my body and dipped to my exposed cleavage. "I could drop to my knees before you when I feed from you. I could soothe every bit of the burning with my tongue. Is that what my brother did to win your loyalty?"

His words sent the fire in my gut raging.

The prince reached out slowly, and I cringed when his hand

touched my face. He brushed a finger over my lip, and I wasn't prepared when he pressed against my flesh roughly until a bite of pain coursed through me.

"I could make you forget my brother's touch altogether if only you'd let me."

"That will never happen."

His thumb trailed down my chin, and I tried to jerk out of his touch, but he held firm, controlling. He leaned forward, and I clamped my lips closed when his mouth came within inches of my own. "You won't have a choice."

He pressed his mouth against mine roughly, and I jerked my head to the side to try to get away from his touch. His lip curled into a sneer as he examined me for a second before he slipped his hand into my hair and tugged harshly. He used the hold to tilt my head back, and I cried out in agony when he used his teeth to scrape down the length of my throat.

My heart thundered, and I struggled to catch my breath as I pressed my hands against his chest and tried to shove him away from me. But he was too big, and I had no energy left to fight him off.

"You will beg me for it by the time we're finished, Adara." He drew back his hand, and he curled his fingers around my hair so tightly that I whimpered in pain. "I can make this as painful or as pleasurable as you want. It is up to you how this will go." Gavril snapped his fingers, and the doors to the throne room opened.

I didn't have to turn around to know that his guards had entered behind me. My heart thundered in my chest, and I could feel my panic rising inside me. Gavril was going to feed from me against my will. He was going to feed from me, and he had no idea I had no power left for him to take.

That was the truth I clung to as two guards stepped up beside me, each one taking one of my arms in their hands. I didn't fight against them. There was no use, but I also didn't look away from Gavril.

If this was what he wanted, then he would watch every second of what he did to me. He would have to look into my eyes and see my hatred staring back at him.

The two guards pushed me forward until I had no choice but to follow their lead, and I was shocked when they pushed me down against the throne Gavril had been sitting on only moments before. Both of them still held on to my arms, pressing them down against the throne, but their effort was wasted. I had no strength left to fight them off.

Gavril stood in front of me and pulled a small dagger from his side. It was ornate and looked about as worthless as he was, but I knew it would cut me just the same. He stepped toward me, and I jerked my arm away from the guard, which threw him off-kilter. I did nothing but simply thrust my wrist out toward Gavril while I stared at him with every bit of venom I possessed.

"Not there." He shook his head as he stared down at the black mark of endless night and stars on my wrist. "I will not allow my lips to touch the same place my brother took from you."

I ground my teeth together as I pulled my wrist back into myself. "Your brother didn't take from me. I gave. And there's nowhere on my body you can touch that hasn't already been claimed by him."

There was a sneer on his face, but he tried to mask it with a smile. "Do you really think giving me the details of how you were my brother's whore is going to save you?"

"I'm not telling you that to save myself." I pressed my thighs together protectively as his gaze dropped down my body. "I'm telling you so you know who I belong to."

The guard at my side shifted nervously, but Gavril simply laughed. "You belong to me, Starblessed. I was the one who brought your father to you. My brother was the one who took him from you in the first place."

I clamped my eyes closed because I couldn't think of my father. Not now, not when I knew he had been treated so much worse than anything they would ever do to me. But Gavril's words were a blaring reminder of what they had taken from me, what the queen had taken from me. It may have been Evren's hand that had taken my father, but it was the queen's rule. It was her orders that forced him to do things he would never have done on his own.

The fury inside me took over, and I could hardly control it as I stared up at him. "He will kill you."

"Your father?" Gavril laughed, but I shook my head.

"My mate."

There was a flash of anger on his face as he stepped closer to me, reached out, and pressed his hand against my cheek. I reached up to stop him, but one of the guards snatched my hand back before I got the chance. Gavril caressed my skin like that of a lover, and bile rose in my throat as I stared up at him.

"My brother was always good at convincing others to believe

exactly as he wanted them to. It would appear that you have fallen exactly where he wanted you to lie. With your legs open and your loyalty to the enemy strong."

I tried to control my anger, but it raced through me, desperate to attack. I felt hollow where my power used to be, empty without my magic, but my anger filled up the space before I could stop it, and I reared back and spit in Gavril's face before he could utter another word in my direction.

The sneer on Gavril's face brought a smile to my own, but fear sank deep in my gut as I watched every ounce of his facade melt away, leaving nothing but the pure evil prince I knew him to be staring back at me. He wiped his hand down his face, looking as unbothered as he had been just a moment before, and his grip tightened around the dagger as he moved closer to me.

"Where do you think my mark on you would bother Evren the most?" He pressed the tip of the dagger into my knee before pressing his own between my legs to force them apart. He ran the blade along the length of my leg, dragging my dress along with it, and I wanted to scream.

I begged that tendril of power I felt earlier to do something. To do anything. To explode inside me and become more than what it was. I wanted to fight him, to throw him off, but all I could do was swallow the cry that built in my throat as I stared at him. I would not let him see my fear. I would not allow him the pleasure.

"Where is my brother's favorite part of his whore?"

His gaze trailed along my bare thighs. I tried to clamp them together, but I did nothing more than press them harder around his leg.

"The others before you told me that Evren had a thing for thighs."

His dagger pressed harder, digging into my skin, and I bit down on my bottom lip as pain sliced through me.

"But others"—he raised the dagger higher, dragging it over my dress, up my stomach, until he pressed it just at the top where it lay against my breast—"told me that Evren was a fool for breasts."

I tried to block his words. I didn't want to think about Evren's past lovers. Not now, not ever, and Gavril knew exactly what he was doing. Trying to break me. Break my spirit, my body, everything he could get a hold of, but I released my lip and stared straight ahead. I refused to give him anything.

"But I think we should start here." Gavril's hands dropped and gripped my hips before jerking them to the edge of the throne.

My dress was still high against my thighs, and I felt completely exposed to him. The move had shoved his leg farther between my thighs, and I felt it pressed against my pussy.

Panic clawed at me, but I didn't know how to stop him. To stop this. Gavril dropped to his knees for me while still pressed between my legs, and he widened my thighs even though I tried to fight against him. He pressed a soft kiss against the inside of my thigh, the one opposite the one that now held Evren's mark. His lips had barely left my skin before his dagger replaced it and sliced through my flesh.

I couldn't stop the cry that left my lips. It was too much, the pain too severe, but Gavril didn't care. His mouth met my bloody thigh, and I tried to jerk my arms away from the guards as his mouth tightened around me and he drank the blood from my body.

He was taking from me as he did once before, and though it hurt, there was no power for him to take. I could feel none of my power leaving my body, and my eyes closed as he continued to take. Draining and draining, searching for what he wanted most but would not find.

His hands tightened against my thighs, fingers digging into my flesh, but I didn't react to the pain. I kept my eyes closed and prayed for it to end. I thought of Evren, of his face, of his smile, of everything he would do when he found me again. I let myself think of nothing else as I blocked Gavril from my mind, and my chest ached.

"What have you done?" Gavril's booming voice called out to me from between my thighs, but I still refused to open my eyes. "What the fuck have you done?"

I finally blinked up at him as I felt him rise from where he had knelt before me, and I didn't let him see anything on my face. It was nothing but dead emotion staring back at him, and I would give him none of my truths.

"What could I have done, Your Highness? I am nothing but a whore, remember?"

Red smoke poured from Gavril's fingers, magic I'd never seen him use, but I knew he wasn't in full control. Whatever Gavril had done, whatever power he had, it was not his to control.

And the lack of my power in my blood forced something to snap inside him that he had been clinging to.

"Take her to my room." He wiped my blood from his mouth with the back of his hand, the trail of red smoke following his movement. "If you want to act like a whore, you'll be treated as such."

EVREN

The people of my kingdom were frightened, and fear hung in the air where there had been none before.

Many of them were still in my palace, and I scrubbed blood from my hands as I stared out over the kitchens where the staff was preparing food for all those who had stayed.

"Ninety-four." Sorin's voice was rough and tired, and I knew that number hurt him as much as it did me.

Ninety-four.

The fae soldiers who infiltrated my kingdom had killed ninety-four of my people. My hands balled into fists, and I could barely control the power that surged through me with my anger. They had killed ninety-four of my people, and still, all I could think about was her. What was he doing to her?

"I'm going to my father's kingdom." I turned to my best friend, and his eyes were two burning embers, flickering with a mixture of rage and worry.

"And what will we do about what the soldier told us? If Gavril has enchanted the border like the soldier said?"

I stared down at my hands before looking up at him. "I have both my and Adara's power inside me. I will find a way to defeat any magic my brother could possibly possess."

"And if it's a trap?" Thalia walked up to us, and I noticed the way she let her body lean into Sorin and accept some of his comfort after what we'd just done.

All of them—Sorin, Thalia, and Jorah—had killed almost as many men as I had, and taking that many lives took a toll on your soul. It didn't matter how many had come before it. It still ate at a part of you that you'd never get back.

"I don't care." I shook my head and let out a growl. "I can't just sit here while she's there with him. While he tortures her."

Thalia's pupils widened, and her breath caught. A wave of terror seemed to wash over her, and she closed her eyes, waiting for it to pass as Sorin's hand tightened on her hip. "Adara is much stronger than you give her credit for. She can handle whatever Gavril throws her way. What she can't handle is us storming in there with no plan and making things worse than they already are. If we have any chance of getting her back, we need to be smart about it."

I pushed my hands through my hair, but I knew she was right. As much as I hated it, if it were any of them, I would tell them the same thing, but that didn't make it easier to take.

Jorah moved to the other side of me and pressed a crust of bread into my hand. "Eat," he ordered me and nodded toward the bread. "You're not going to do Adara any good if you run yourself to death. You need to eat, you need rest, and we need to come up with a plan."

I looked down at my hands and at the piece of bread, and I stared at the red blood that still stained my palms. I was still covered in the blood of my people, of our enemies, and I knew that by the time this was over, I would be covered in much more.

I took a bite of the bread and let it settle in my mouth. It was almost stale, but I didn't care. I ate the rest of it, took a deep breath, and tried to let my anger calm.

"I'm going to go bathe." I looked up at my friends, and there was so much worry and concern staring back at me. "Then we'll meet back in the library."

They nodded, and I walked away before any of them could tell me again that I needed to rest. I couldn't rest when Adara was in the hands of my enemy. I couldn't do anything except think of her and pray to the damned gods that Gavril hadn't touched her.

I didn't know what he would do when he discovered that she no longer had the power he so desperately craved. How would she protect herself?

I pushed into my bedroom and shut the door behind me before leaning against it. Despite the power that coursed through me, I was exhausted. I could feel the loss of Adara all the way to my bones, and it created an ache there I knew wouldn't go away until I had her back.

I pushed off the wall and moved toward my bed. I toed off

my boots, mud falling to the floor, and I fell back onto the bedding that was still rumpled from the last time Adara had been in it. I took a deep breath, breathing in the scent of her, which still clung to my sheets, and my chest ached.

Every part of me ached.

I could still taste her on my lips, her kiss, her body, her blood. My ears longed for the sound of her voice, and my throat burned with the longing to make her laugh, for her sweet voice to fill my home.

I would get her back. Even if my death was the cost. Adara would not stay a prisoner of the kingdom that wanted to take everything she had. She would be free of the burdens the blessing of the stars had bestowed on her, and I would use every breath in my chest to make sure of it.

She was my mate, and she would come home.

ADARA

It had been hours since the guards locked me in Gavril's room. My hands were bloody and aching from the way I had pounded on the dark wood to be let out, but it was pointless. There was no one in this kingdom that would help me.

It was me and me alone.

I pulled the heavy ornate chair into the corner so my back was against the wall, and I stared out at the door as I steeled my gut and wiped the tears that fell down my cheeks.

I needed to be strong to survive this. I needed to find a way to escape and go home.

It was hours before the doors to his room finally opened, and I refused to let Gavril see the weakness in my eyes as he closed them behind him.

Gavril had a tall glass with an amber liquid in his hand as he approached. I stared at him, trying to see if there was any humanity left inside him. Any sign of a human in those cold, dead eyes.

"I thought you might be thirsty." He pulled a stool from near his desk and moved toward me. I tensed, and his eyes softened. "I'm not going to hurt you, Adara."

His words didn't matter. I could still feel the throbbing pain in my thigh where he had taken from me hours before.

He sat down next to me and scooted himself so close that the scent of him overwhelmed me. His scent was a fog, a dense cloud around me. His musky smell filled the space, and I struggled to breathe.

He moved languidly, like a serpent, each movement slow and calculated.

His face was just a few inches from my own, and his eyes were a startling shade of cerulean. They did little to hide his anger. He looked at me, his face softening as he took me in.

"I would like to go back to my room."

Gavril stared at me for a long moment without saying a word. His gaze trailed down my body, achingly slowly and tortuously, and I squirmed in my seat when his eyes fell to my thighs.

My white dress was covering me, not a trace of skin visible, but he could see the blood that now caked on the fabric.

The blood was a dark ruby that had ruined the fine fabric just as easily as Gavril had ruined me.

"We need to get you cleaned up." His hand reached out toward my thigh, and I jolted away from him.

The sound of his voice filled me with dread, his words crashed between my ears, and my heart began to beat faster. I did not want him to feed from me again. I didn't want him to touch me. We both knew that I no longer held the power he craved.

I was useless to the prince in front of me.

He reached out with a gentle touch before his hand gripped around my calf, squeezing, sending a sharp pain throughout my body.

"Let me care for you, Adara."

A sick laugh bubbled out of my throat as I tried to pull my leg away from him, but his hold on me was firm.

"You care for nothing other than yourself, Gavril."

His face tightened, and his hand reached for my thigh. My skin screamed at the thought of his touch. Sweat beads coated my brow, and chills streaked down my spine. My eyes shut for a moment, and I tried to remind myself of my strength.

I imagined Evren's face in my mind. I focused on his dark hair, the smirk on his face that I loved to hate. My stomach warmed, and I tried to cling to that feeling.

"Look at me." Gavril's voice was rough and demanding, and I blinked my eyes open to look back at him. "You don't know me, Starblessed. Maybe we should get to know each other." He moved his hold to my knee, and I clamped my legs together to stop him from moving any further.

"I know everything I need to know about you."

"From my brother?" He laughed, and his fingers tensed against my thigh. "Did it ever occur to you that the Blood Prince would say anything he wanted you to hear to keep you at his side?"

I blocked out his words as I stared at him with every bit of hatred I felt for him. "From Thalia."

"Ah, Thalia." A small smile formed on his lips, and my hands ached to smack it from him. "I hadn't realized until I came to save you that the other star girl was in my brother's kingdom. Another thing my brother stole from me."

"She's not a star girl," I practically growled at him. "She has a name."

His smile only widened. "She wasn't as particular about names during her time here as you are."

"I'm sure all the scars on her body had something to do with that."

His jaw tightened as he studied my face. "You are desperate to make me your villain, aren't you?"

"I think you've handled that perfectly on your own."

His hand slipped from my knee, and he ran it along his jaw as he studied me. "I'll be whatever you need me to be, Adara, but you are mine."

I shook my head, and his hand shot out and gripped my chin roughly.

His eyes narrowed further, his lips set into a grim line. His gaze fell to my lips, and he watched as I pressed them together and tried not to cry out from the pain of his grip.

I didn't know how long we sat there like that, but his touch was bruising, punishing. It only seemed to intensify as he moved closer to me and his breath rushed out near my ear.

Chill bumps raked against my skin, and I held my breath.

"You are mine." Each word felt like a physical blow that slashed against my body. "You can deny this and try to act brave. But the truth is written across your cheeks. I can see it, Adara. You are so frightened of me."

Neither of us moved, but the world was spinning around me. He was breathing in my scent, and I was simply trying to catch my breath. His scent was so dense, so overpowering, and I swallowed hard against it.

"You are to be my wife, Adara. You will learn to obey me." His words were sharp and damning.

"He'll come for me." I spoke through a painful, tense jaw, and I tried desperately not to look at him. Gavril pressed his mouth against my lips, and I wanted to pull back, but his hand was demanding my obedience.

He pressed his tongue against the seam of my lips, and I opened just enough to let him inside. The deep groan that left his lips had my stomach churning.

He slid his tongue against mine, and I tried to keep my body calm as he took what he wanted from me. I pressed my lips against his, sucking his bottom lip into my mouth, and when the next groan of pleasure fell from his lips, I bit down until I tasted his blood on my tongue.

He shot back from me, but he didn't lessen his grip on my chin. He held me firmly in place as he stared at me with venom in his eyes and his red smoky power dripping from his hands.

"Don't fucking play with me, Adara. You will regret it."

"You made me bleed." I lifted up my skirts to show him the bloody wound on my thigh. "It seemed only fair that I do the same to you."

His thumb traced along my chin, gently, almost lovingly, and he ran it along my bottom lip as if he were tracing his own blood away.

"We're done talking." His voice was hard, harsh, and it sent the blood in my veins rushing to my ears.

He pulled back from me, and I was finally able to take in a breath of air. I stared at him, his eyes and his face, but he gave nothing away.

He ran his hand down his face as he stood and looked down at me. He seemed to be at war with his own thoughts, but then a grimace took over his lips, and he reached down for me. He pulled me toward him with a firm hold on my arm.

He wasn't careful or gentle as he jerked me to my feet, and I swallowed hard and forced my eyes away from his. He hauled me toward the large bed that sat in the middle of the room, and I dragged my feet against the floor.

"I'm not staying in here."

He wasn't listening, though. He pulled me harder, my tired body unable to resist his commands, and he pushed me forward until I sat on the bed before him.

"I said I'm not staying in here."

"Move." He nodded toward the head of the bed and crowded my body with his own. "You either get up there and lie down, or I'll do it for you."

"No." I shook my head, and my hands shot out and pushed against his chest.

"You don't have a fucking choice, Adara." He gripped my hands in his and stopped me from hitting him. "Get in the bed." His voice was an animalistic growl, and when I stared up at him, I noted the thin red ring that formed around his eyes.

"Don't touch me." I jerked my hands away from him and crawled up in the bed to get as far away from him as I could.

His knee hit the bed, and he crawled in behind me, but I was surprised when he fell back against the mattress and laid his arm against his forehead.

I curled myself into a ball, taking up as little room as I could manage, and I watched Gavril for a long time as his breathing evened out and the fire in the hearth settled to a low thrum of heat.

He didn't move to touch me, but I didn't trust him. I stayed like that for a long time, watching my enemy as I tried to keep my eyes open, but eventually sleep became too hard to resist, and it claimed me.

ADARA

I jolted as I awoke and searched the room, but I was alone.

I took a deep breath and looked down at my body. I was still wearing the bloodied dress from the night before, but now an ivory blanket was draped across the length of me and kept me warm.

That fact made my stomach churn. Gavril had cared for me in my sleep. Had he touched me?

There was a small knock at the door, and Eletta entered slowly with a tray of food in her hands.

"Good morning, Adara." She moved toward me and set the tray of food on the bed at my feet. "The crown prince ordered me to make sure you were fed this morning."

I grimaced at her words, but the scent of the meat, eggs, and pastries on the plate made my stomach growl.

"And what else has he ordered?"

She swallowed hard as she looked toward the door. "You are not to go back to the room he provided. I will be seeing to you in the prince's room going forward," she said hesitantly, as if she were frightened.

"What a noble prince you serve," I said sarcastically as I pulled myself up in the bed. My leg ached as I sat up, and I winced from the pain.

"Are you all right, my lady?"

"Oh, yes." I pulled the blanket down my body to reveal the soiled dress to her. Her face blanched as I lifted my dress and let her look at the wound on my thigh. "Your Highness has been the most caring betrothed."

"We should…" She stuttered over her words. "We should get that looked at."

"I'm fine." I dropped my dress back down against my skin and reached for the glass of water on the tray. I downed every drop of it in one go, and Eletta watched my every movement.

I pressed the glass back on the tray before diving into the food. My stomach was empty and my body weak. As much as I wanted to refuse anything from Gavril, I would be foolish to do so.

"Thank you for bringing this to me." I didn't meet her gaze as I picked up the fork and plunged it into the thick slice of ham.

"The prince…" She hedged, and I looked at her, pulling my eyes away from the food. "He's asking that you meet him in the library. You're to be there in an hour."

"He's asking?" I asked as I raised an eyebrow. "I thought the prince did nothing but demand."

She stopped to give me a look that would have made me laugh under different circumstances. "Anything the prince asks for is a demand."

I turned my face back to the plate of food because I knew she was right.

"What is the…?" I looked up at her, and I didn't know if I could trust her with my questions. But she was the only chance I had. "The red power that Gavril has. Where did it come from?"

I tried to wrap my brain around it. Had he fed from someone else that gave him this power? Was it something he had taken from me the first time he did so?

Eletta's gaze shot to the door before looking back at me with wide and pleading eyes that reflected her fear, though she said nothing.

"That is not a question for me." Eletta's voice was pained—like words were being wrenched from her mouth.

"Why not?" I watched her carefully. I studied her for any signs of the truth.

"Because the prince wouldn't want me talking about it." There was a quiet trepidation in her voice that spoke of her fear of the royals who she normally spoke so highly of.

She looked back to the door as if she worried he would return at any moment, and the next words were out of my mouth before I could stop them.

"I'm sorry." I reached my hand out and touched her arm. "Gavril isn't here. You can speak freely to me."

She swallowed hard, and I held my breath, waiting for her to speak. "The prince will be angry with me if I talk about this."

"What is going on?" I demanded, though my voice was but a whisper. "What has he done? Has he been feeding from someone else?"

She looked down at the bed and then finally to my face again. "His magic…it's forbidden." Her words were so quiet I had to strain to hear them. "He has death magic."

The world around me went silent as my mind tried to process what she was saying.

"Death magic?" My hands started to shake as I looked at her, and she met my gaze as she nodded. "What does that mean?"

I had never heard of death magic before. My knowledge of most magic in this world was limited, but it wasn't something I had even heard in legends.

"I don't really know." She shook her head softly. "We've heard legends of death magic growing up. About how it twists and changes the person who claims it. It is rumored to destroy one's soul for giving up something so precious." Her words were obviously difficult for her, but I watched her face for any signs of deception.

"What has he given up for this magic?" I whispered as I tried to wrap my brain around what she was saying. There was no way any of this was possible.

She nodded her head. "I'm not sure, but there are whispers that he's given up his mate."

"What?" I sat up straighter as dread filled my gut. Gavril had a mate?

Eletta clamped her lips together and looked back to the door once again as her hands trembled. "I will not talk about this anymore."

I shook my head and stood from the bed. I almost swayed on my feet, and I immediately pressed my hand against the bed to keep me up. Even the night's rest and the food I had just eaten weren't enough to make me feel halfway normal.

Not after the news she had just delivered.

"Can I at least go back to my room to get something to wear?"

"No." Eletta's words were soft as if she was worried she would upset me. "Gavril had clothes brought into his closet for you. You are to bathe and dress in here."

She didn't wait for me to answer her. She simply moved toward the washroom and started filling the bath as I tried to wrap my head around everything she had just told me.

If Gavril truly had this magic that she spoke of, if he had a mate, what would that mean? Would Evren be able to fight him to get me back?

Would the two of our powers be strong enough to fight someone cruel enough to consume the other half of their soul?

Eletta helped me bathe and dress, and I couldn't help but notice the way she paled as I winced when my leg hit the warm water.

The wound was still aching as I stepped into the dim library and braced myself for whatever was to come. I prayed to the gods that Gavril wouldn't feed from me again today. I wasn't sure that I could handle it. Especially not after what I had just learned.

I held my breath as I stepped into the room and passed a

few stacks of books. I had been there many times before, and the smell of the old books flooded me along with the memories of Evren. Of the way he had touched me in this very room.

My hands ran over the spines of the books, and I paused as I noticed Gavril. He smiled at me from where he sat in one of the large armchairs that were situated around the room. He didn't have a book in his lap. Instead, he sat there quietly staring up at me as I studied him. His smile didn't reach his eyes. Something dark hid in the blue depths.

His mate was all I could think about.

He was dressed in a pair of dark trousers with a dark blue shirt that matched his gaze. His hair was brushed back, and his face was cleanly shaven. He looked like the crown prince that I knew him to be. Nothing of the days that passed had taken a toll on him.

He leaned his head back as if to get a better look at me. "How did you sleep?" He ran his hand over his jaw as he watched me, and it made my back straighten in panic.

"Horribly."

He let out a soft, bitter laugh. "It's okay for you to admit that you slept like the dead in your future husband's bed, Adara." He sat up straighter and leaned forward. "Your mate will never know." He spat out the word *mate* as if it offended him.

"I slept like the dead because you tried to drain the life from me."

His lips formed into a sinister smile at my words. "I could fuck the life out of you too if you want."

I jolted back, and he stood until he was crowding my space.

"But I suppose we should wait until we're wed. Then I can show you exactly how you're meant to feel when we consummate our marriage."

"I'm not marrying you, Gavril." I let out a heavy breath and wrapped my arms around myself.

He watched the movement, and for a moment, I thought he would pry them away.

"Our wedding is in a week." He smiled at me like he was imagining me in a white dress walking down the aisle to him. "It will be the wedding that seals the fate of our kingdom and a day to remember."

I hated him. I hated the way he spoke of me like I was nothing more than a prize he planned to claim soon.

"Why are you doing this?" I asked quietly, but my anger burned on my tongue. "Is this about the prophecy?"

"I want you." He said the words like they were nothing, but I felt them slice through me. "I want your magic you're keeping from me. I want your body. I want your mind. I want you to look at me and never again think about my brother. I want him to be helpless against me."

"That will never happen." I started to shake my head, but he gripped the back of my head firmly in his hand and forced me to look up at him.

"By the time I'm finished with you, you won't be able to remember his name, let alone any silly thoughts you have of him."

"With your death magic?" I regretted the question as soon as it fell from my lips.

He didn't answer me. Instead, he pulled me close and forced

his lips against mine. His kiss was harsh and demanding, and I tried to turn away from him, but he gripped the back of my neck. He held me in place as I felt the warmth of his power run through me. It left my skin feeling cold and numb, and chill bumps rose all over my body.

Everything about his power felt wrong.

It felt otherworldly, and I tried again to pull away from him. His kiss fell away, but he didn't loosen his grip. He pressed his forehead to mine, and his lips brushed against mine as he spoke. "Yes. With my death magic. But I think we should discuss your magic, Starblessed. Where is it?"

"I don't know. Where is your mate?"

The red ring of power that I had seen before consumed his gaze, and the wrath he stared back at me with instilled a fear in me unlike any I had ever felt before.

"You will not speak of my mate."

"I want to leave."

My voice shook as the words escaped me before I could stop them, and I was rewarded with Gavril stepping back. He took a deep breath before he spoke, and it was filled with the bitter scent of disappointment.

"You are never leaving this palace again, Starblessed." He ran his fingers through his hair. "It seems that you're tired, Adara. Maybe you should head back to our room for rest before meeting with my mother."

"But I'm already here." Queen Kaida's voice sounded from behind me, and I turned quickly, giving my back to Gavril as I prepared myself to face her.

"Mother." Gavril nodded his head to her almost in a bow, and bile climbed up my throat at the sight.

"Leave us, Gavril." The queen didn't look at him as she spoke. Her gaze was settled directly on me. "Let us ladies speak alone."

"Of course." Gavril moved to my side, and I stiffened as he leaned down and pressed his lips to my cheek.

The queen watched his every move, and I watched her. I didn't look away from her for a single moment.

The queen was as beautiful as her son, her body curved with an ageless grace.

She wore a silver dress, her hair cascading around her shoulders and down her back as it held her crown. The one she wore today was a delicate gold band that encircled her head with a red stone as its central piece.

Her lips were in a tight line and painted with a deep red, pomegranate, like the blood of people she had spilled.

How many lives had she ruined? How many lives had this queen destroyed with nothing more than an order that fell from her lips?

"Where is your power?" the queen asked as she watched me. There was no hesitation in her question. There was only one thing she wanted from me.

"I have no power." I shrugged simply, but that did nothing but make a fire burn in her eyes.

She stepped closer to me, and I stepped back in turn. A smile crossed her lips at that. "I underestimated you, Starblessed. I thought you little more than a farm girl who we plucked from a field, but it seems you have much more fire in you than I would have thought."

“I get it from my father.” I steeled my spine and watched as her eyes narrowed slightly. “Did you not see that same fire in him when you tortured him for the last two decades?”

“I rarely thought of your father, let alone saw him.” The queen laughed. “I am the queen of Citlali. Do you really think I have time to be bothered with such people?”

“Yet you have time to be bothered with me?”

“You are to be the next queen,” she bit out, and that control that she held so tightly began to slip. “You are to be the most powerful queen the fae kingdom has ever seen. You and my son will be unstoppable.”

The queen’s gaze locked with mine, but I didn’t look away. Instead, I made sure she knew that I wasn’t afraid of her. “What is it that you want? You already have your kingdom. You are already queen.”

“Yet there is another.” She cocked her head slightly and studied me. “Queen Veda rules her kingdom as if she is as powerful as me. She has shared my husband and birthed him an heir.”

“And what? You’re jealous of her?”

The queen’s harsh laugh was startling. “Queen Veda has nothing that I envy. I simply want to destroy her.”

“Why?” The question was stupid. I could see the greed in her eyes staring back at me.

“Because this world belongs to us.” She waved her hand around. “There is only to be one true ruler over it, and that ruler will be my son.”

“Is that what you told yourself when you killed Gavril’s mate?” I took another step back as her eyes widened in surprise.

"Where are your powers, Starblessed?"

I stared at her before looking past her toward the door where one of her guards was entering.

"It would appear that I have secrets, just as you have yours."

"Queen Kaida." The guard bowed his head. "The king is asking for you."

"Have him wait." The queen offered me a smile, but there was nothing friendly about it. "The Starblessed and I have much more to discuss."

"I'm done speaking to you."

"No." She shook her head gently. "You aren't." She moved around me, circling where I stood. "I'll ask you again. What have you done with your powers?"

"I don't have any." The lie tasted bitter on my tongue, but I would never tell the queen the truth. It would do nothing but fuel her vengeance for Evren.

I started to walk from the room, but her hand reached out, and her nails dug into my upper arm. I stood there frozen, not moving, as the queen's perfume burned into my nostrils. It was thick, cloying, and the longer she held me, the more I felt like I was suffocating under its weight. The scent was flowery, but it also carried a hint of something I couldn't quite place. Like burnt sugar and sulfur, sickening and sweet, but too thick for the smell to ever be pleasant.

"We are having a ball to celebrate your return in two days' time." Her nails dug in harder, drawing blood. "I would suggest you find the magic my son once tasted in your blood before then."

I turned my head and met her hard gaze. "And if I don't? Will I end up like his mate?"

Queen Kaida's face was hard, the lines around her mouth, her brows, and her eyes deep and etched with malice. She didn't cower from my stare, and the longer she held me, the more I could feel her aura seeping into my skin until I felt as if I couldn't move. My feet were planted to the floor, and every muscle in my body locked.

She was resolute, but her words were like glass being crushed under her hand. "Then I will do everything in my power to destroy that mate of yours." Her eyes flicked back and forth between mine, watching. Assessing. "We will drain the life from him while you watch. I don't give a damn if he is the son of my king." ☾

EVREN

We found very little information about death magic in our tomes.

Almost nothing to go on, but I couldn't stand around and wait any longer. There was no telling how strong my brother's magic had grown.

My chest ached with the weight of my guilt that Adara was under his rule while her own magic resided with me.

I began stuffing supplies into my saddlebags and tossed a canteen of water in Sorin's direction. He slid it in his own saddlebag before grabbing more supplies from the table.

I lifted my bags and draped them over my shoulder, and when I turned around, I almost ran into Adara's father, Dareen.

The man was frail, still so weak from what they had done to him for years, and I could hardly meet his gaze without guilt eating me alive.

"I'm coming with you."

I pressed his hand against the table and used it to help support his weight.

"No," I said gently but firmly. There was no way I was taking her father back into that kingdom. Even if he wouldn't be a hindrance to getting her back, Adara would never forgive me for it.

He had just gotten out of that hell, and I wouldn't send him back.

I refused to.

"You can't stop me," Dareen growled, and the already great respect I had for the man increased.

"You're right." I nodded my head and adjusted my bags on my shoulder. "But you're not in any shape to fight. I am going to get your daughter back. I will give my life if that's what it takes to do so, and you will be a hindrance."

The air around us grew tense and heavy as his grip on the table tightened and his jaw clenched. But I saw a flicker of understanding pass across his face as he slowly nodded in agreement.

"I know that you spent many years with them." He shook his head as he looked past me. "I know that's your father, but I'm not sure if you truly know what they're capable of."

Dread filled me and turned my stomach. "I do know what they're capable of. Especially my father and the queen. I saw my fair share of their cruelty during my years as their captain, and I will never be able to earn your forgiveness for delivering you to them."

His gaze met mine, and he searched my depths as if he could see to my very core.

"I'm not talking about me." Pain marred his face, and he leaned against the table. "I'm talking about the girl."

I was confused by what he meant. "Adara?"

"No." He shook his head. "The girl who was in the dungeons with me for many years. Leda."

I had never heard that name before. I had no idea who he was talking about.

"What girl?"

His brows pinched together in furrowed anger, his mouth agape and eyes narrowed. A wave of dread seemed to pass over his features.

"Gavril's mate."

The two words felt like lead being slammed against my chest. It was true. He was doing the unthinkable to obtain power that no man should possess.

"Is she dead?" My voice shook with fear that I hated. If he had killed her, then he may be truly unstoppable.

"She would be better off if she was." He met my gaze, and his pupils flared. "The things they have done to that girl are worse than death. Queen Kaida has kept her alive as a toy to dangle in front of her cruel son. He would visit her down in the cells, but even as his mate, the girl hated him. She hated him for what he had allowed the queen to do, for what they had planned."

"The death magic?"

"Yes." He nodded. "The queen never spoke of it, but Gavril would whisper his apologies to her in the darkness of her cell.

He thought the other prisoners couldn't hear, but Leda's cell was next to mine. I would do my best to comfort her after he left."

"Did he…?" I didn't know what I was asking. *Assault her? Take from her? Abuse her?* Of course he had. He had kept his mate, the person he should have cared for more than anyone else in this world, as a prisoner.

Dareen shook his head, and his gaze darkened. "I don't know everything they did to her. She would never talk about it after they were gone. I couldn't see her through the stone wall that separated my cell and hers, but sometimes she would reach her hand through the small bars until she could touch mine. Her hand was always caked in blood and cuts. He had taken from her. I just don't know to what extent."

"I thought he had to kill his mate to gain the power?" I thought over all the pages I had read about death magic, and they were all the same.

"To gain it fully, he does." He nodded and his gaze shuttered. "But bringing her so close to the brink of death again and again gave him enough power to lay waste to his enemies if he so chose. He would whisper to Leda that he would spare her as long as he could as she cried. Killing one's mate gives one an evil power that should never be seen by this world, but torturing her, inflicting that kind of pain over and over, it fed him just enough power to satisfy his greed without taking her life."

Rage filled me. It oozed through my pores, seeped into my cells, and brought out a darkness in me I tried to keep at bay. Every part of me contracted and ebbed with the flow of my fury.

I knew we had to be smart about how we got Adara back,

but guilt clawed at me for doing so, for not cutting down every member of Gavril's kingdom until there was no one left who could keep her from me.

"Don't leave her." Dareen pinned me with his gaze and made it clear that this was a demand. "You do not leave Adara or Leda behind."

"I won't," I promised, although I didn't know how I was going to manage to save either of them. But I knew if it came down to it, I would choose to save Adara. I would always choose her.

I looked over at my friends. Sorin and Thalia were both packed and ready for our journey to Citlali, and Jorah stood with his hand on his sword as he watched us.

"Protect the kingdom."

Jorah bowed his head slightly, and I knew he would do everything in his power to make good on his word. He would protect this kingdom with his life just as I would.

"Let's go." I looked back to Sorin and Thalia. "We have a long journey ahead."

ADARA

It had been two days since the queen left me in the library. Two days since she threatened Evren, yet there was nothing I could do with her threat. I had no way to pull my power, no way to give her son what she wanted.

Gavril had left me alone most of the time, only coming back to his room at night after I'd fallen asleep. He would crawl into the bed I lay in, but he hadn't touched me at all. For that, I was thankful, but I couldn't rest.

Especially not when I noted the dried blood on his hands and lips night after night.

Eletta flitted around me, pinning my hair into curls and adding a silver crown to my head with the twin moons in the center of my brow. The dress I wore was a crisp white that clung to my body and shimmered endlessly, and as usual, the queen made sure my star mark along my back was on full display.

I looked in the mirror in front of me with hollow eyes and stared at my sunken cheeks where Eletta was applying rouge. I could hardly recognize the girl who looked back at me.

As the days stretched by, I could feel myself withering away. The hollowness in my gut that I thought was simply from the loss of my power grew and grew, and I knew it longed for much more than my power. Every part of me ached for Evren.

I could live without my power for the rest of my life, but I could do nothing without him.

The door to Gavril's room opened, but I didn't look up as he entered. I knew it was him.

No one other than he and Eletta had entered this room.

He moved farther into the room, and Eletta hurried out of his way as he stood behind me and stared into the mirror. He watched our reflections carefully, and I tried not to meet his gaze.

"You look lovely, Adara." He reached forward and ran his hand along my shoulder, and I couldn't stop the shudder that ran through my body at his touch.

My heart hammered in my chest, and my bones throbbed in the same rhythm. "This is what you wanted." I looked at him in our reflections and raised my chin. "Am I not the girl you promised to showcase tonight?"

His brow furrowed, but he quickly smoothed out his features as his fingers tightened on my shoulder. "Tonight is the celebration of your return, Starblessed. The entire kingdom is to celebrate the return of their future queen."

I stared up into his eyes as I clenched my jaw. "Does the entire kingdom know that I'm a powerless future queen?"

Gavril's gaze darkened, and he didn't answer me for a long moment as he stared down at me; then his touch moved along my back. He ran his finger down my spine, tracing the star mark, and his hands were gentle, the soft caress of a lover.

"My kingdom will hear no such thing." His hand stopped just below the small of my back, and chill bumps invaded my skin. "Your power is here. I will just have to try harder at coaxing it out of you."

"I have no power, Gavril. Just let me go." I hated how weak my voice sounded, how desperate.

"That'll never happen."

I turned on the stool until I could face him fully. I wanted to make sure he heard every word that left my mouth. "Then I will fight you every step of the way. I will never stop fighting you to get back to him."

That red ring appeared around his irises, just as the red smoke of his magic dripped from his fingers and wrapped around my hands. I tried to struggle against it, but the power pinned my hands to my sides in an iron hold.

"What the hell, Gavril?"

"There are far too many important people here tonight, but it would appear that you have too much spirit." He leaned forward and ran his hand along my cheek. I jerked out of his touch, but it didn't stop him. "Allow me to break it for you."

He pulled a small dagger from his side, and my gaze searched the room until it landed on Eletta standing in the corner. There was shock and terror in her eyes staring back at me, but she did nothing to stop him. There wasn't a single word uttered from her lips that would stop the prince from taking from me. And I decided at that moment that I hated the girl.

"Please don't," I begged him, but Gavril wasn't listening to me.

He took my wrist, the opposite of the one that held Evren's mark, and he held it firmly in his hand as he pressed the blade to my skin. He only made the smallest cut there before he quickly closed his mouth over it, and I felt the bite of his teeth against my flesh as if he thought it would hold me still.

His magic grasped me tightly, holding me firmly in place, but I still thrashed against it. I fought against him, and I cried out as pain sliced through me. Him feeding from me felt so different, and I didn't know if it was due to my lack of power or because I'd experienced feeding with Evren.

Because nothing would ever feel the same as him.

I blinked my eyes closed as the only thing I felt was pain.

Gavril drained and drained me until I felt like a wilting flower. I could feel my strength leeched from me, and even as I tried to cling to it, it slipped from my fingers like sand.

The heat of his breath was like a brand on my skin, and when he lifted his mouth away from my wrist, the fire that had ignited in my gut to fight him was left in a pile of ash. He wiped his mouth with the back of his hand, and for the first time since he entered the room, I noticed his attire. He was dressed in black pants and a rich blue jacket that had the crest of his kingdom on his chest. There was a golden crown set upon his head, and he looked every bit the prince that ruled this kingdom.

There was no questioning who he was when he entered the room tonight; his appearance demanded respect, and I knew that these people would give it to him. He had done nothing to earn it, nothing to gain their loyalty, but fear ruled far more than loyalty ever would.

"Clean her up," he demanded of Eletta, and she scurried toward me with a cloth in her hand. I didn't meet her eyes as she knelt before me and pressed the cloth to the fresh wound on my wrist. Her hands trembled against mine, but I would not be sympathetic toward her fear.

"I think..." She hesitated. "I think she might need sutures."

Gavril straightened his jacket and looked down at the lady-in-waiting. "Put a small bandage on her wrist and then cover it with jewels. I want no one to see the mark."

Eletta hurriedly did as he asked. She wiped away the blood from my wrist before pressing the cloth down harshly to stop the bleeding. There was so much pain that sliced through me, but I didn't look at her to see if she had noticed.

Once the blood stopped rushing to the surface, she grabbed the bandage and wrapped the thin white material around my wrist three times before tying it in a small knot. She let my wrist go, and it fell to my side limply as she rummaged through the small desk, frantically looking for something to hide the evidence of Gavril's cruelty.

She wrapped five small bracelets around my wrist. Each one

was covered in jewels clear as water, and they reflected every bit of the light that shone against them. Gavril watched her work, and when he was satisfied with what she had done, he reached his hand out and grabbed me around my upper arm.

He lifted me until I had no choice but to stand, and he pressed a kiss against my cheek. "Come, Adara. There are many people that are expecting us."

He pulled me from the room, his grip tight and unyielding. I floundered beside him, my feet dragging as I stumbled toward the ballroom. My thoughts were muddled, and my head swam like I was no longer in control of my body.

If Evren saw me now, he would be ashamed of what I had let Gavril turn me into. If Thalia saw me… I winced and tried not to think of my friend. Tried not to think of how much worse she had it here.

But it was the thought of Thalia that I clung to as we walked through the double doors when someone announced our arrival. She would tell me to fight. Thalia would scream at me to get up off my ass and fight. She would have demanded it of me until I was so furious that I had no choice but to answer her command.

But right now, I couldn't find it inside me. Gavril had drained the fight from me just like he said he would.

This was just a game to them, and I had no choice but to play my part. If he wanted to show me off to the people of his kingdom, then he would show off the shell of a girl that he had created. No one would be impressed with the Starblessed that he paraded around tonight.

Gavril pulled me toward the dance floor, and I was surprised when he reached around me, placing his hand on my back and pulling my body into his side.

"See?" He started moving us along the floor, and my eyes drooped for a second. I was tired, so very tired. "We can have so much fun tonight, Adara."

He brought my hand to his lips and kissed along my knuckles. I looked out to the side and watched as people from the kingdom watched me curiously. Could they see what he had done to me? Could they tell I was nothing more than a prisoner to their future king?

"I'm dizzy." I barely managed the words as he spun me around the floor. I looked up at the ceiling and stared at the chandelier.

The crystals blurred and danced in the light, and I watched their movement even as Gavril's hand tightened around my back as he tried to force me to look at him. I leaned back further into his hold, and I felt weightless as he moved us along the dance floor.

I heard whispers around me, but I didn't care what any of them were saying. I hoped they saw the truth of what I was.

I prayed they watched me in Gavril's arms and knew this wasn't where I belonged.

Because even drowsy from his feeding, I could feel it through every part of me.

I barely noticed the song end, but Gavril's body stopped moving against mine, and I blinked up at the chandelier as it still swirled above me more slowly than before.

"Stand up, Starblessed." Gavril's words were a hiss between his teeth, and I lifted my head to finally look back up at him.

There was a sneer on his face, and it made a smile grace my lips.

His voice cracked like a thunderous explosion, and I flinched. "They are watching you, and you will show them you are worthy of me."

I didn't meet his gaze at first. I stared at his chest as my anger started to clear some of the fogginess from my head. "Worthy of you?" I let out a soft laugh and finally looked up to meet his eyes. "It is you who is not worthy of me."

He stared down at me, and for a moment, I couldn't hear or see anything on the dance floor besides the two of us and that sickening red ring around his eyes.

"Yet you think the bastard prince of my father is?" He lifted his hand and pushed some stray hair out of my face. I knew what it must have looked like to those around us. It was the touch of a lover. The careful attentiveness of my betrothed.

But that ring around his eyes burned brighter with his words, and his fingers on my back dug into my skin.

I felt the pain and fought against the need to cry out. "I think he wouldn't have broken me the way you have. He wouldn't use me like this."

Gavril laughed, the sound a threat, and he moved his mouth closer to me. "The only thing my brother has done is use you, Starblessed. You are just too foolish to see it."

Suddenly, I felt a viselike grip wrap around my waist as he jerked me into his chest, and his lips collided against mine. There was no warning and no gentleness in the way he kissed me. His mouth was brutal against mine, and I reached forward and tried to shove him away from me.

I pressed against his chest, but it was no use. He didn't budge. One hand held me firmly while the other moved to the back of my neck and slipped into my hair. He gripped my hair in an iron hold, forcing my head back until he had better access to my mouth.

When his lips released mine, I gasped for breath. I felt swollen and bruised from his assault on me, and I didn't know how much longer I could handle this. I looked up at him, and his eyes were almost taken over by the power there. He looked at me with the hunger of a beast, and I jerked free from his touch.

I turned away from him, my head still spinning from everything he had taken from me. I stumbled forward until I was able to reach out for support, my hands digging into someone's chest. I didn't know who it was, but I held on to them to stop the room from spinning.

I heard the whispers around me, and I knew people were staring at me. Looking at me like I was some sort of plaything for their prince.

Was this what they wanted in their future queen? Could they not see how desperately I didn't want to be here?

Closing my eyes for a moment, I felt the world rush around me, and I tried to breathe through the nausea that clawed at my gut.

I heard Gavril laughing behind me. "Sorry about that, Frederick. It would seem the Starblessed was in the mood to celebrate and went heavy on the drink."

I heard his words, and I flinched. I wanted to find my magic so I could rip his eyes from his head. I wanted to show him he didn't control me. I wanted to show him that I wasn't what he was making me.

Yet it would not come.

I blinked up at the man I was still clinging to, but I didn't recognize him. His hair was a rich dark brown like mahogany but speckled with white, which showed his age, and his eyes narrowed on me as he reached forward and pressed his hands along my arms to hold me steady.

"I think the queen-to-be might need to sit down, Your Highness." His voice was like velvet, deep and smooth, and he smelled of leather.

There was a softness in his voice, but I didn't trust it. Not with what I knew about the people of this kingdom. They wanted me because they wished for the day the royal family would be made stronger with my blood. I knew my presence here strengthened them against their enemy. Against Evren.

I leaned away from him, but he didn't release his hold on me.

"I will take her from here." Gavril laughed again, and I felt his hand wrap around my midsection. He pulled me backward until my back pressed against his chest, and the man in front of me finally released me from his hold.

But his gaze tracked my every movement.

"She looks different from the last time we saw her," the man said absently as he ran his hand over his clean-shaven jaw.

"Does she?" Gavril's hand pressed against my face, and he tilted my head back in his direction so he could look down at me. His hand dwarfed my face, but his hold was soft against me.

My heart began to beat faster and faster as I stared up at him and watched that red power slither around his pupils.

Could these people not see it? Did they not fear it as I did?

Was I the only one who could see the monster held prisoner behind his mask?

"She looks like the perfect Starblessed to me," Gavril said softly, his fingers trailing along my jaw. "She looks exactly like what our people need." There was a threat in his tone, and I felt my fear clawing up my throat.

He wouldn't show his power here. Not with so many people around. But I didn't doubt he would the second we were alone again. I felt his hold tighten, and I knew he wanted to show me what would happen to me if I didn't do exactly as he wanted.

"Do you think the bastard has ruined her?" The man whispered, and I felt Gavril stiffen behind me. "It is rumored throughout the kingdom that he made sure that she is no longer pure for our future king."

I couldn't breathe, couldn't think beyond the man's words or Gavril's rigid hold against me.

"I will be the only one to touch her." His voice was hard, and I felt his hold on my midsection tighten, digging into me through the dress. "The only one," he said it again. "The Starblessed belongs to me, and no one will speculate on what condition she will be in when she is presented to the kingdom." His voice lowered to a whisper, and his words were menacing. "Do you understand?"

All the color drained from the man's face as he stuttered his next words. "Of course, Your Highness." The man backed up a step. "I didn't mean to imply otherwise."

"Of course you did." Gavril released his hold on me, and I almost fell forward before his hand took mine. "But you will pay dearly if you are ever to speak it again."

Gavril didn't wait for the man's reply. He simply hauled me toward him and toward the dais on which his parents sat. My head swam again as he pulled me behind him. I squeezed my eyes shut as I clung to his hand.

"Get yourself together," he hissed at me. "You're about to be presented to the queen and king."

I didn't know if it was his words or his magic, but the world rushed around me, and the room spun harder as I opened my eyes.

Gavril didn't seem to notice. He simply dragged me behind him until we were standing in front of the king and queen who were seated in golden thrones. They were dressed in rich clothing, and golden crowns sat upon their heads. Both were watching me with the same hunger as the people in the room.

But no one looked as ravenous as the queen.

Gavril's hold on my arm tightened as he pulled me to the base of the dais. He whispered harshly into my ear, "Do not embarrass me." He jerked me forward until the toe of my shoes hit the base, and the people in the room dropped to their knees as the king and queen stood before us.

The queen's face was severe as she looked down at us, but it was the king's voice that boomed low and resonant through the room, rolling back and forth over the crowd.

"We are pleased to welcome the Starblessed back to Citlali." He motioned his arms toward me, and the crowd of people cheered at his words. "She is the symbol of the great war our two kingdoms have waged against each other. She is a symbol of what the Blood kingdom is willing to take in their thirst for power." The king roared over the cheers, and I felt Gavril's magic swirl around me as bile rose in my throat. "But thanks to my son, the heir to my throne, she is back where she belongs."

Their cheers rose to a fever pitch, and Gavril's magic exploded over my skin. I looked down as his red power swirled and danced along every inch of me, and when I looked back up, the people stared back at me with insatiable longing.

They claimed Evren had a thirst for power, but that greed they spoke of was all I could see in their eyes.

"Look at how his power has grown with her at his side." The king looked down at me, and for the first time since I stood in front of him, his gaze met mine. "She is a part of the kingdom forevermore, and once the two of them wed, I will have an heir to my throne stronger than any leader we've had in hundreds of years."

The room exploded, and I felt Gavril's power snake over me again. It was brighter this time, almost blinding, and it made it hard to breathe. When it receded, Gavril was standing in front of me, his hands clamped down on both of my arms as the king stared down at his son—stared at both of us.

Everyone was staring at us, and I felt suffocated by this game they played. I choked on the way they tried to fool these people into thinking they were the royals they deserved.

When the truth of what they were was far more terrifying.

But none of these people who surrounded us seemed to care

to look beyond their masks. I was the only one who knew how closely the royals resembled monsters hidden behind a thin shield of human skin. These people were fools for believing in them.

They were fools for watching Gavril's power grow and not cowering in fear of what their ruthless prince would do.

I looked back up to the king, but my vision swam again as the glittering room moved around me.

"I think I'm going to be sick," I whispered aloud, but I wasn't sure if Gavril could hear me.

If he could, he didn't indicate it. He kept his grip on my hand as he looked around the room. Everyone was still watching us, but their faces passed me by in a blur.

"It's time to go," Gavril said next to my ear, and I gasped and attempted to pull away at the feel of his breath against my skin.

He dipped his head toward his mother and father, and I took a step back. I just wanted to get out of here. I wanted to lie down. I was desperate to think of nothing but Evren and let my dreams of him wash away this awful feeling inside me.

The room began to spin and swirl like a tornado, the colors of the floor and walls darkening with each turn. I was focused on the ground in front of me, watching my feet as if I were standing in quicksand. I could no longer see the king or queen, the man next to me, or anyone else. I felt like I was falling.

Gavril's hands tightened around me, and I felt him press me into his chest. His arms were the only thing holding me up, and I couldn't bring myself to care how it looked to the others.

He led me from the ballroom. I wasn't sure if we had already passed the doorway into the hall when he bent at the knees and lifted me in his arms.

I didn't want to be held by him, but I couldn't deny the relief I felt when my feet left the ground.

Burying my face in his shoulder, I held on as nausea churned in my stomach. I tried to focus on thoughts of Evren, but my mind was too foggy to focus on anything except the way I felt, the way the room moved, and the way the air left my lungs in short bursts as I tried to hold it all in.

I had never felt like this from being fed from before, but my body was rejecting Gavril as much as my mind did. I wasn't sure if he had simply taken too much from me or if it was this magic of his that my body reacted to so poorly, but I cringed at the thought of him ever taking from me again.

Gavril carried me down the hall, and I tried to refuse when the guards opened the doors to his room. But I couldn't find the words.

My head lolled back into his arms, and darkness bled in and out of my vision.

He pushed into the room and set me down gently on the bed. I was expecting his anger, but his hands were careful as he made sure I was stable before he leaned away from me and stood.

"I want to go back to my room." My words sounded weak even to my own ears, but I watched Gavril grimace before dropping to his knees before me.

I tensed as I watched his every movement, and I felt desperate to get away from him as he lifted my foot in his hand and slowly pulled my shoe off.

Gavril watched me with calculated reserve, his jaw set, lips closed, and eyes shuttered. He set one of my shoes to the side before pressing my foot back to the ground and lifting the other in his hands.

I shivered at his touch as he worked my shoe from my foot. His fingers tensed against my ankle, his thumb rubbing over the sensitive skin there as he stared up at me.

"Let me help you get ready for bed." His hand skimmed up the bottom of my dress, and I could feel that spark of magic deep in my gut.

It was elusive and intangible, like a phantom I couldn't grasp.

Yet it was there, and I found solace in that fact. I could feel its presence, though it remained just beyond my reach, taunting me and making me feel both comforted and frustrated at the same time.

But I knew Evren held it safely inside himself, and he would use it and every bit of power that he possessed to get me back.

There wasn't a trace of doubt inside me.

But it was hard to hold on to that faith when Gavril's hands were on my skin.

He bunched my dress up until it reached my thighs before meeting my gaze. His eyes were soft and should have been comforting, but I found no comfort in the man before me.

I would never be so foolish.

"Can you lift?" he asked, his voice soft and smooth with only a bit of a rasp that hinted at the emotion he was hiding.

I didn't answer him. I simply pressed my hands into the bed and lifted my hips while he pulled the skirts of my dress from beneath me.

I couldn't hold myself long, and when I sat back down on the bed, Gavril stood and headed toward his closet.

I was silent as I listened to him rummaging through the small room, and I could feel tears clouding my eyes.

He came back holding one of his white shirts, and he dropped it on the bed beside me before gathering my dress in his hands once again. He pulled it over my head without uttering a word, and I pressed my arms against my chest.

I was bare before him, wearing nothing but the undergarments Eletta had put out for me, and the cold night air prickled at my skin as Gavril stared down at me.

"Here," he said before clearing his throat. He held up the shirt, and I tried to take it from his hands. "Let me help you."

"I can help myself."

He scoffed. "You can barely keep yourself upright, Adara. Let me dress you before I put you to bed wearing nothing but what you have on now."

He arched a brow at me, a challenge, and I slowly let my arms fall away from my chest and lifted them as he held the shirt in my direction. He carefully helped me into the soft fabric, his skin barely touching mine, and I sighed in relief when the shirt swallowed me.

Gavril stepped away from me, and I took a deep breath. But everything around me smelled of him. I attempted to stand up on my own, but I wobbled on my feet and fell back onto the bed.

"Stay," he commanded before he walked toward the door and turned the lock. The sound rang out through the room, and I could feel the panic rising up inside me.

He pulled the hem of his shirt up and over his head, and I met his gaze. I shouldn't have. I knew I shouldn't have. But I couldn't look away from him. He was cruel, but he was also beautiful.

He kicked his shoes from his feet before he stepped back into his closet and left me alone with my thoughts.

This was the man I had always been meant to marry. This was the monster my mother had so willingly given me away to, and I knew that he had spent his life becoming a master of fooling people.

His mask was ironclad and rarely slipped.

But I could see past it. His mask seemed to slip more frequently with me than with others, and I knew it was because I was the only one fighting him. He tried to hide the man he was deep down from everyone else, but it seemed to pour out of him when he was with me.

He was a monster, and I was his prey.

I didn't know how much time had passed when Gavril finally returned. But I watched as he walked toward me, and there was something dark in his eyes that hadn't been there moments before.

His jaw was set and his gaze unflinching. There was desire there, but there was also anger and power.

It was the look of the man I feared.

He walked toward me, and my heart raced. I had no doubt that he could see the fear in my eyes as he raised his hand toward me.

He brushed my hair back behind my ear and rested his hand against my cheek. His eyes searched mine before he leaned forward and pressed his lips to my forehead.

"Sleep," he demanded of me before crowding my space, his knees pressing against mine. He slipped his hands beneath my arms and lifted me higher in the bed until my head hit the pillow.

He climbed into the bed behind me, crawling past me to get to his side, and he lifted the blankets up until they covered my body.

I stared up at the ceiling as I listened to him breathe. I didn't dare look over at him, but I could feel him looking at me.

There was a silence between us that weighed on me heavily, and I wondered if Gavril could feel it too.

I tried to stay awake, to stay alert, but that weight dragged me under. I blinked my eyes open, but it was no use. I was so very tired.

"You are mine now, Adara," I heard Gavril whisper somewhere in the back of my mind, but I was too far gone to care about his words. "No one will ever question that you belong to me ever again."

I felt the heavy weight of his hand wrap around my middle; then I felt nothing at all.

EVREN

My chest felt like it was in a vise, squeezing tighter with every inch closer we got to the fae border. We had been inside the Onyx Forest for hours, and I felt desperate to get closer to Adara.

My heart beat faster as I recalled the words her father had said. The fear that had already filled me had only grown more intense now that I knew the true horrors that my brother was willing to do.

I had promised Sorin and Thalia that I wouldn't storm into the kingdom when we got there, but I could feel my and Adara's magic growing within me like a wave about to break on the shoreline, eager to unleash its power.

Her magic felt as desperate for her as I was, but I would have given anything to touch her, to lay my eyes upon her for even a moment to know she was safe.

Thalia cocked her head to the side, and I tracked her gaze into the dark forest. I saw nothing there, but Thalia went stock-still at my side.

She had felt something, and the magic around her body began to spark, to grow. She was taming it, holding it back, but I could feel it just the same.

A snap of a limb sounded through the woods, and everything around us went still. The birds stopped chirping. The wind that had been blowing through the trees stopped. Everything froze.

Thalia dropped from her horse and let out a low growl, the sound rumbling deep in her chest, but the moment it slipped from her mouth, a nymph slipped through the trees and into our line of sight.

The same nymph I had seen with Adara when she had attempted to run.

A smile formed on her lips, and my mare brayed and backed up a few steps. The nymph felt otherworldly, and even my horse couldn't contain its uneasiness around the being.

The nymph's frail body was barely noticeable, her skin covered in green moss and damp leaves. She bled into the trees as if she were one of them.

She stood along the roots of a giant tree, and as she moved, leaves and twigs snapped underneath her feet. They made crackling sounds like embers turning to ash.

I climbed down from my horse and grabbed the reins to hold her steady, but I refused to turn my back on the nymph.

"What do you want?" Thalia's hand rested on her dagger, but she had yet to pull it out.

"The true heir has come," the nymph said in a voice that didn't belong to this world before bowing deeply before me. "He has come to save our queen."

Thalia looked back at me for only a second before her gaze slammed back into the nymph's. Sorin still sat upon his horse, but his back was rigid. His jaw was clenched as he watched Thalia as carefully as he watched the nymph that stood before us. His muscles were tight, ready to spring into action at the smallest sign of a threat.

"You know she was taken?" I let the question slip from my tongue, and the nymph smiled. Her lips were caked in the same moss that covered her frail body. She looked as if she might snap under her own weight.

"Of course we know." She blinked up at me. "All the creatures of the forest know of our queen."

I had traveled the Onyx Forest many times, but I had never seen the creatures of the forest that she spoke of. The first time I saw the nymph with Adara was the first time I had seen any creature that didn't lurk in the darkness.

"And you know she's being kept in the fae palace?"

I didn't know how much the nymph actually knew, but I would try to get any information out of her that I could.

"I know our queen was taken by the one who devours." The nymph moved carefully farther back behind the tree until her body was shielded behind the dark bark. If I hadn't been looking carefully enough, I wouldn't have been able to notice her at all. "I know that his magic will destroy us all if he is not defeated by the true heir."

Her words made a chill run down my spine.

"And how do I defeat it?"

The nymph blinked up at me, and I could feel her retreating farther back into the woods. "Save the queen." She stared at me with eyes of the deepest black I had ever seen, and my frustration grew. "You must save our queen before she becomes his."

I needed more, but the nymph was slipping farther back into the dark forest.

My heart raced as I watched her slowly disappear, and I dropped to my knees before I could think my actions through.

"Please help us."

The nymph stopped, her hand clinging to the tree as she watched me carefully, but she didn't respond.

"The death magic that he possesses, I don't know if I can beat it. I don't know that I can save her." That honesty from my lips ate at me. I didn't want to need her help, but I would take it regardless.

I would do whatever it took to get Adara back.

"You have the queen's power inside you, do you not?" The nymph searched my face as she cocked her head to the side.

"I do."

"Return it to her." She looked at me, unblinking. "She is strong enough to defeat him."

"He has a magical barrier around the palace."

"Her power is stronger." She slipped farther back into the dark forest again.

"Come with us." My fingers dug into the damp ground as I pleaded with the nymph.

"You do not need me." She shook her head gently. "When you reach the barrier, let her power go. Let every ounce of it pour from you, and her magic will find her. The queen will save herself."

ADARA

It had been two days since the ball.

Two days sitting in Gavril's room with only Eletta visiting me to make sure my needs were met.

She brought me three meals a day although I barely ate. My stomach still churned from memories of the ball, that feeling that had taken over every part of me, and I could hardly stomach the food she brought to the room.

Gavril had been gone most of the days, and I only knew he returned because I could feel him slip into the bed behind me. I hated that moment. I loathed how easily he thought that he belonged there behind me.

But more than anything, I hated how slowly my strength began to come back to me.

I had just gotten out of the bath when Eletta entered the room with a white gown in her hands. It shimmered like a thousand stars in the sky. The fabric was sheer and only the small crystals were visible, and I stared at the garment for a long moment as she hung it from the closet door and turned back to look at me.

"What is that?" My voice trembled, and I hated the pity in her eyes as she met my gaze.

"The gown is for your wedding to the crown prince." Eletta's hands bunched at her sides, and she looked down at her feet and away from me. "The whole castle is preparing."

"Today?" There was something in my gut that hardened. Something that I had been clinging to each passing second since I'd been here. It was a hope for what was to come, a hope for who was to save me, but in that moment, it slipped through my fingers. If I were to be saved, I would have to do it myself.

I feared that Gavril's magic was too strong to fight. If Evren couldn't get to me, how would I ever be able to get out on my own?

Because even with every ounce of hope slipping out of my grasp, I still held firmly to the truth that Evren was my mate, and I loved him.

I forced myself to remember those facts as my fear consumed me.

"I am to get you ready." Eletta grimaced, and sadness took over her face.

I turned away before she met my eyes.

I went through the motions with Eletta, letting her do my

hair and cover my face with rouge, but with every passing second, the anxiety and anger inside me burned deeper and deeper.

I was angry with Gavril for bringing me here. I was angry with him for trying to force my hand into this marriage. I was also angry with myself because I was the one who had agreed to come. I had agreed because I knew the moment he had taken Evren that they would have killed him.

Evren was only good to them dead, but they would use me. Gavril would use every ounce of life I had inside me, and that was the only card I had to play.

My life over Evren's death.

Thoughts of my father ran through me. What did he think when I left with our enemy? When I had to willingly give myself over to the man who had been responsible for torturing him? Did he feel as betrayed as Evren must have?

I stared down at the scar on my wrist, which was still fresh and throbbing from where Gavril had fed from me as Eletta clasped more bracelets over the wound. She didn't say a word as she worked, but her normally deft fingers fumbled over her task.

Eletta helped me into the dress, the weight of the fabric heavy around my hips and falling to the floor in a mass of fabric.

Tiny crystals covered the length of the fabric shimmering in the light of the fire, and I knew that I probably looked exactly like the Starblessed they wanted me to be. This was the mask they painted on me, a mask that forced me to play the part of the girl that would save their kingdom, but I would do no such thing.

If Gavril was to marry me, I would do nothing but fight him. I would do everything in my power to destroy anything he worked toward, and I didn't care what I had to sacrifice to do so.

"Would you like to see?" Eletta motioned toward the mirror, and I stood before it and took myself in for the first time.

To those of this kingdom, I had to look like the Starblessed that was promised, but if only they looked deeper, they would see the dark circles under my eyes, which Eletta had tried to cover. The way my weight had dropped significantly since arriving in this kingdom.

If they removed the jewels from my wrist and the fabric that covered my thighs, they would see the scars from their ruler, who took from me and attempted to force my obedience. If they looked even harder, they would see a heartbroken girl who was just trying to survive.

That was all I could see staring back at me. I no longer recognized this girl. I saw my mother in the brown eye staring back at me, but I didn't dare look into the blue one. That color belonged to my father. And he had survived this torture for years. I would be ashamed to look into what he had given me and see what I had become.

There was a soft knock at the door, and Eletta's gaze flew up to meet mine in the mirror. "It's time."

She moved to the door and pulled it open. A burst of cool air entered the room. I rubbed up and down my arms as chill bumps crawled across my skin, but it was no use. Nothing would warm me from the cold this kingdom brought.

Nothing but Evren.

I followed after Eletta, but I moved slowly, tracking my steps and looking through doorways.

There was nothing I could see that would provide me a way out. No escape from this palace. I reached forward, grabbing Eletta's hand in mine, and she swung back to look at me with her eyes wide.

"Please." I looked around the hall, but the guard in front of us was barely paying us any attention. "Please, Eletta. I cannot go through with this."

The color drained from Eletta's face, and there was a ghost of hesitation in her eyes. That spark of hope that had died out flickered back to life as I looked at her. I bit down on my lip and prayed that she would help me.

Eletta looked over her shoulder toward the guard before slowly looking back at me. "I…I can't." She shook her head, and her hand trembled in mine.

My words caught in my throat as I tried to take a deep breath, but I knew where her loyalties lay. I knew where her fear did.

"Of course." I straightened my shoulders and moved past the lady-in-waiting without saying another word. There was pity written all over her face. It would do me no good.

Her pity was useless to me, and we both knew it.

I headed toward the throne room, but the guard motioned for me to go down the long hall. I had never been to this part of the castle before, and I hated feeling so unprepared for what was to come.

But I moved forward in the direction he sent me. I took slow, calculated breaths and tried to keep myself calm as I heard the chatter of a crowd somewhere before me.

We reached the end of the hall where more guards gathered, at least a half dozen, and I looked around at each of them and met their gazes.

I steeled my spine and prayed for the girl who Evren knew me to be to finally show her spirit.

"You were all once loyal to your captain." I watched some of them blanch while anger crossed the faces of others. "Has that loyalty to Evren completely gone?"

It was silent for a few moments before one of them finally found the courage to speak.

"Our captain betrayed us. There is no loyalty left for the bastard prince."

I nodded my head and linked my fingers together as I tried to keep myself calm.

"The true heir of your kingdom," I corrected him and watched as that anger morphed into fury. He bared his teeth as he stared at me, but I continued, "None of you deserved him. The bastard prince, as you call him, was loyal to you all even in his betrayal of this kingdom. His fight is with Gavril, and if he loses, then you men will know nothing but betrayal from the one you serve for the rest of your lives."

I knew that these men would have lost their loyalty to Evren, but I at least expected to see some hesitation in their gazes. There was none.

All that was staring back at me was pure hatred for their former captain.

"He's already lost." The bold guard took a step closer and peered down at me with a sneer. "I heard that the soldiers the crown prince transported into the Blood kingdom created a massacre before the traitor was able to stop them."

The blood in my veins ran cold. These men had gone into Evren's kingdom, into our kingdom, and they had massacred our people?

"What did you just say to me?" I growled, and my hands formed into fists at my sides.

The guard backed up a step, and his face lost its color. His eyes darted from me to his fellow guards.

I could feel the bloodlust rising inside me. I wanted to taste the blood of this fool, of everyone who had dared raise a hand against the Blood kingdom, my kingdom, and hurt the innocent people there.

My thoughts went to the man who danced with me at the Olde Vine. And Mina. *Gods, please tell me she was safely in the palace when this occurred.*

The guard's hand rested on the hilt of his sword, which was sheathed in a leather scabbard and attached to his belt with a black leather strap. His fingers were rough, probably from years of gripping the worn handle to unsheathe the sword to take innocent lives.

But those hands shook with his uncertainty as he faced me.

His voice was harsh but quiet. "The bastard prince has already lost, and it is Gavril, the prince of Citlali, who will rule over us all."

The spark of power in my stomach caught aflame, and I could feel it burning inside me.

It slammed into me, stealing my breath, and it didn't stop

until that hole in the pit of my stomach where my magic belonged was full. I closed my eyes as my magic raced through me, and I took a deep breath.

The heat in my stomach rose through my limbs, and I felt it burning beneath my skin, an oil spill erupting from the earth, its flames turning everything in its path black and smoking.

That fire, my magic, begged me to destroy each and every one of the guards in front of me, and I would have done so had it not been for the ornate set of double doors opening in front of me.

There was a gasp from the crowd as the shimmering of my dress bled out into the garden, and Eletta hurried to my side and pressed a giant bouquet of flowers into my hands.

Black smoke wrapped around the delicate white flowers, engulfing them in my power, and just as the music started streaming through the small garden, I stepped into the light of the sun.

The delighted gasps of the guests changed to ones of fear as everyone looked at me, but I only looked at him.

The crown prince stood at the end of the long aisle, which was covered in white flowers. He wore the finest red jacket with a golden sash and a large golden crest of his kingdom on his chest. But it was the oversize crown that sat atop his head that made the magic pouring out of me feel uncontrollable.

I gasped at the feel of it, and I didn't understand. I had pushed every bit of magic I had into Evren, but this magic was mine. My heart raced as I thought about what that meant. Evren was close.

Gavril's eyes widened the moment he saw me, his mouth slightly agape. I wondered if he could feel the magic that slithered under my skin.

I suddenly felt the urge to unleash my power on the prince, to make him pay for everything he had done to me.

For everything they had done to my kingdom.

Standing before him, I heard the priest hiss when my dark power came near him. But I didn't care about his fear.

"Adara." Gavril said my name, but his voice was strained and filled with his panic.

"Did you send men to massacre my kingdom?" The question rolled off my tongue and tasted of ash.

I was burning from the inside out, and if I didn't release some of this magic soon, I worried it would consume me.

My vision began to blur, and I felt a thin sheen of sweat on my forehead. My magic was growing, crawling beneath my skin. I could feel it tugging at me, like a tide pulling at my feet.

"I see you found your magic." That red ring around Gavril's irises glowed brighter than I had ever seen it before, but I couldn't find it in myself to be frightened by it.

"And I see you have stolen yours." I cocked my head to the side as I watched him. "Tell me, prince, did you feel any remorse at all when you killed your mate to gain that power?"

The prince's face twisted into an angry sneer as the magic pulsed around him. A gentle breeze moved past me, and the scent changed, a subtle hint of death and decay as if Gavril's magic ate away at his life.

"My mate is none of your concern." He stepped closer to me, and I was acutely aware of everyone's eyes on us. "She is mine just as you are."

She is mine. I stared up at him in surprise. Was his mate still alive?

Gavril's magic crawled against my skin like a plague, trying to consume my own. I could hear it whispering to me, telling me that any magic I held was no match for him.

But it was wrong.

Blistering heat and fire burned my fingers, and I dropped the bouquet of flowers at my side. "You will never take from me again."

"That's enough." Queen Kaida stepped down from her dais, which had the perfect view of where we were to wed, and her harsh face was laced with anger. "You are to marry my son." She looked pointedly at the priest. "Please continue."

"There is no need." My voice was a harsh command, and the magic pulsing through my body felt like a great beast begging to be set free. "There is no magic that could make me marry him." I took a step toward the prince, and he did the same. "No magic could bind me to you."

I took another step forward, and the crystals of my dress weighed me down. Gavril's magic came near me, and the burning inside my stomach became unbearable. It was a roaring flame, the fire flooding my veins and causing my ears to ring.

"You belong to me." His voice was harsh and hot. "You will always belong to me."

My magic shot out from my hands without my control and into Gavril. I didn't stop until it poured out of me, casting the entire palace in my dark magic. I felt Gavril's magic tug against my own, but it snapped beneath my will. I watched as the crown prince landed on his ass before me, and I tried not to smile as the strangers he had invited to our wedding began to scream.

Blood dripped from his nose, but he quickly wiped it away as he climbed back to his feet and stormed toward me. His hand gripped my arm like a vise, and my skin burned from the magic in his fingers. His eyes were a swirl of red, and the magic was so thick that it became suffocating.

The guests cried out in alarm, and the music stopped. Guards poured from the doors, and I could hear everyone scrambling to get out of the way.

"Get your hands off my mate." Evren's voice boomed through the garden, a demand not to be mistaken, as he stormed through the double doors with a blood-soaked sword in his hand. Sorin and Thalia both stood at his sides, the same vicious look in their eyes and bloodstains on their clothes.

My knees threatened to buckle, and tears clouded my eyes. Evren was here. He had come for me.

He was death and blood and power. All of it was wrapped up in a beautiful, dark package. He stared at me, and I watched as his face softened.

"Princess." My name fell from his lips, and my chest ached with my longing for him.

"What are you doing here?" Queen Kaida moved to my side, and the softness on Evren's face morphed into something they all should have feared.

"I was invited, remember?" Evren held the invitation they had sent to his kingdom between his fingers, and a small laugh bubbled up my throat.

Gavril's hold tightened on me, and I cried out at the way his skin burned against mine. He pulled me to him until my body was shielding his own before he finally spoke. "Brother, I think we made an agreement the last time we spoke."

"We did no such thing." Evren stepped down the aisle, and Gavril's magic poured from him.

Evren watched the red smoke carefully before his eyes met mine. Those beautiful dark eyes of his caused a deep ache in my bones with how badly I missed them.

"You and Adara agreed for her to come back to your kingdom with you. Her debt has been paid."

"She is mine, brother." Gavril's voice started out even but grew in volume, and Evren's face darkened.

Gavril's magic held power, but I could feel his body tremble against mine.

"I will only tell you once more to get your hands off my mate." Evren's voice was a low boom, like a warning of the storm that was to come.

"Son." I heard the king from behind me, and it was the first time I noticed he was still there.

I turned my head to take in the man who had turned so easily on his own son. "Don't you dare speak to him," I hissed the words between my teeth, and he jolted back as if they shocked him.

"I see you brought the other little Blood whore with you."

I turned back to face the queen as her words found their mark, and I watched as she ran her gaze up and down Thalia.

My magic surged inside me, feral in its need, and I ripped myself out of Gavril's hold. Air hit the spot he had just been touching, and the pain was almost unbearable. I reached for Gavril's dagger at his side, and his magic shot out at me as if it meant to trap me in its mist. But I moved away quickly before it could dig its deathly talons into me.

I reached out for Queen Kaida, and even though my hand trembled around the dagger, there wasn't a trace of doubt in my mind.

"Gavril!" she screamed out for her son, but it was too late. My hand and the pommel of the dagger collided with her jaw, and she dropped to her knees before me.

My magic swirled around us in a storm of my fury, and no one could touch us. Not Gavril as he tried to get to his mother or even Evren as he tried to get to me.

It was me and this woman who had played such an intricate role in almost every dark moment of my life.

"Never speak to my friend like that again." I gripped her jaw in my hand and forced her to look up at me. She was the queen, yet she deserved no respect from me.

"The Blood whore?" The queen's voice was cold, but I felt nothing but my own power. "I guess it is fitting that you two would become friends since you are the same. She was never worthy of my son either."

I could feel the magic pulsing through my veins, the flames burning inside me. "She is worthy of far more than your kingdom could ever give her."

Queen Kaida laughed, the sound making my stomach turn. "My kingdom gave her more than she ever deserved. Your father too. I wonder if he regrets the years of torture he endured just for you to become the bastard's plaything."

I didn't have time to think about my next move before

Gavril's dagger lodged in his mother's chest. Her deep red blood poured out around my fingers and ruined the perfect dress she had put me in.

"I'm certain he'll never regret it as much as you will." I pushed the dagger harder into her chest as her hands scrambled to get hold of mine. Her eyes were wide with panic, and blood trickled from her mouth as she gasped for breath.

I released my hold on her, and I watched as the woman who had caused me so much pain crumpled in front of me. The life in her eyes seeped away with the blood in her chest.

I felt a hand, Evren's hand, cup the back of my neck as my magic swirled around us. My fury was finally being released. "I'm sorry," he whispered. "I'm sorry I took so long to come back to you."

My magic fell around me like the final crash of a cascading wave, and my hands shook as I dropped the dagger to the ground. My vision was clouded over with every emotion that bombarded me, and I reached up for Evren, even with blood covering my hands.

"Evren." His name was a plea on my lips. "I'm sorry."

"Don't." I felt his hand cup the side of my face, and I reached out and clenched his shirt in my fist. A jolt of electricity shot through me, and I dug my fingers into the fabric until my heart hammered against my chest.

I took a deep breath, one I had been suffocating without, and even as my adrenaline and magic still raged through me, I felt myself calm with him near.

"Princess," he whispered, and his hand tightened in my hair.

I shivered with the sound of his voice, an ache of desperation that had been growing inside me finally surfacing. My need for him overwhelmed me, my body humming from the torturous thought of never seeing him again.

I was Evren's mate, and his strong hold on me reminded me of all the things I was, of what I should have been. I was his mate, the future queen of the Blood kingdom, and I was the Starblessed that would determine the fate of this world.

"Both Gavril and the king are gone." Sorin's voice was even and commanding as he spoke, and I looked away from Evren long enough to see my friend.

"They're gone?" I pulled back from Evren, his hands digging into me as he tried to bring me back to him. "Where would they have gone?"

"I don't know, but the girl is gone too. There is no one left in the cells. We need to leave now. The guards are already starting to break through my barrier."

The sound of Thalia's voice stole my breath as my gaze met hers, my best friend, and a small sob of relief broke from my lips.

A wave of emotion washed over her face. Her eyes, usually so vibrant, had softened to a glassy hue, but they narrowed as she looked around her. I couldn't imagine the pain she must have felt at being back at this place, yet she had come for me regardless.

I moved away from Evren, his hands trying not to let me go, and I pushed forward until I pulled Thalia's body against mine and wrapped my arms around her.

The surprise of the embrace stole the air from her lungs, and she dug her fingers into my back as we clung to each other. The steady thumping of her heart pressing against mine was the only sound in that moment.

"Are you okay?" My voice was muffled against her shoulder, and she nodded her head against me.

"I am now. Are you?"

I squeezed Thalia tighter, and she winced as if I had hurt her, but the way she looked into my eyes assured me that it was nothing but our desperate attempt to make sure that we were both okay. The pain of our hold only reminded us that we still had each other.

Sorin cleared his throat, but I didn't let her go. "We need to leave. Now. Before they find their queen."

I heard the sounds of the guards' fists and swords pounding, and I looked out the double doors to see Thalia's blue magic forming a shield around us.

I stepped away from Thalia, and guilt crept into my chest. The moment was broken by Evren's hand on my arm, insistent, drawing me back to his side. I raised my gaze to his and saw the warmth in his eyes.

I looked down at Queen Kaida's lifeless body at our feet. Blood still seeped from her wound.

"Princess." Evren's voice was the only thing that brought me back into myself, and I looked away from the queen to look back up at him. "We must go."

I nodded and gathered the long skirts of my dress into my hand as I clung to Evren, and I followed him as he led me from the now empty gardens toward the back of the palace.

"Thank you for coming for me, for saving me."

Evren shook his head as he pulled me forward. "You saved yourself, princess. All I did was give you your magic back. We were helpless until you destroyed Gavril's barrier around the palace with a blast of your power." His hand tightened in mine. "Now come."

I didn't let go of his hand as I followed his every step, and Thalia kept her shield firmly in place until we moved through the passageways of the palace, Sorin killing two guards who tried to block our path. Chaos was consuming the fae kingdom, guards scurrying to protect their king and prince who had abandoned them.

Evren kept his hand in mine, and he shielded me every step of the way as we dodged the guards as best we could and escaped the kingdom.

ADARA

Evren didn't stop until we reached his horse. He, Sorin, and Thalia climbed on their horses quickly, and Evren reached down and pulled me up until I was settled in front of him on the saddle.

He kicked his heels into the mare, and we were off, the ride harsh against my bare thighs beneath my dress. But I didn't dare complain.

I was with him, and I could handle any pain it took to get back to our kingdom.

The journey was grueling; time seemed to slow as we rode, Evren's strong arms keeping me safe from the jolting of our galloping horse. Exhaustion seeped in, but I refused to give in. Evren was determined to get us back home, his grip tightening as we raced against the ever-darkening sky.

My hands trembled in front of me, clinging to the saddle, my arm still stinging from Gavril's touch. Evren's hold on me never wavered, and the safety I felt in his arms was overwhelming.

His breath was heavy, its warmth pushing and pulling against my skin as I felt the rise and fall of his chest with each heave. His heart raced against my back in a rhythm that matched my own. The wind rushed past us, rustling the dark leaves of the Onyx Forest, and I clamped my eyes shut, letting go of everything but being in his arms.

"We need to stop," Sorin called from beside us, his voice rushing out of him with the exertion from our ride. "The horses won't last at this pace."

"No," Evren's voice rumbled behind me. "I'm not stopping until we reach the safety of our kingdom."

I forced my heavy eyelids open and glanced over at Sorin. His eyebrows were furrowed, and his lips pressed together in concern.

I felt the heat of Evren's hand on my own as I twisted to look at him over my shoulder. His gaze was tense, with deep creases from his eyebrows to his mouth. I took a weary breath and said, "I need a break. I'm not sure if my body can take any more." It was true, but I would have powered through if not for the worry in Sorin's expression.

Evren's face softened as he peered down at me, and the horse slowed almost immediately. My legs ached against the movement, but I didn't look away from him.

"You should have said something earlier." His gaze darkened, but I shook my head and leaned forward to press my lips against his.

The kiss was brief but searing, and I didn't want to move away from him when he finally pulled away and brought the horse to a stop.

"Over here," Thalia called out to us, and Evren led the horse in her direction, deeper in the woods.

I could feel the exhaustion in Evren's body as we stopped, but he helped me down from the horse before pulling me back into his arms.

He hadn't released his hold on me since we left, and I didn't argue because I had no interest in leaving it.

Evren handed the reins of the horse off to Sorin, and he quickly led the horses to the small stream of water once Evren pulled his things from the saddlebag.

He laid a small blanket on the ground before pulling me down to sit on it, and he opened a small canteen of water and held it in my direction. I took a small sip before handing it back to him.

The night air was heavy and oppressive, and my lungs burned as I tried to catch my breath. The jeweled bodice of the wedding gown I was forced to wear scraped against my skin, and the moonlight glinted off the intricate beading. The heavy fabric was meant for royalty, but in the middle of the dark forest, I felt ridiculous.

Evren didn't seem to care, though. He took a long pull from the canteen before pulling me back into his arms. My back pressed against his chest, and he ran his nose along my shoulder. Chill bumps skated over my skin, and I twisted to peer up at him.

He looked so angry, so conflicted, and I raised my hand to smooth out the deep crease between his brows.

"We're together." I whispered the words that were only meant for him and me, and he nodded once.

We were together, and nothing else mattered.

The moonlight hit his face just right, and I reached up to take his face between my hands, pulling his lips down to mine. The kiss was sweet, a soft caress that didn't last nearly long enough.

My hands were still caked in the queen's blood and my dress was soiled, but Evren didn't seem to notice either.

A shiver rushed through me as Evren's hands moved up my arms and shoulders. He squeezed my sore arm, and I winced. Evren sucked in a breath and released my arm, gripping me by the elbow and turning my arm so he could get a better look.

My arm looked burned from where Gavril had touched me, his magic branding me.

Evren's fists clenched so tight his knuckles turned white, and his lips curled into a sneer. His fingers traced lightly against the skin around the burn. Every muscle in his body tensed. "I'm going to kill him."

His rage clouded around me like smoke, and I choked it down.

"I'm okay, Evren." I laced my hands through his hair and tugged on the strands until he was forced to look up at me. "I'm okay," I repeated, because he didn't look convinced.

The words didn't alleviate the tension in his body. Instead, he pulled me toward him until I sat in his lap, and my legs straddled him. His hand smoothed over my back, never leaving me as I stared up into his dark eyes. His hands were rough and calloused, but his touch was featherlight against my skin.

His magic poured from his fingers and skated over my injury. There was a moment of pain before my body recognized his magic and calmed. The burning skin was soothed, and as I looked down at my arm, a small scarring of his magic formed.

The heavy beat of my heart slowed, and I leaned into him.

"You need to get some sleep." He lifted his hand away from my arm and pushed some hair out of my face. "We will only be stopped for a couple hours at most before we get back on the road."

"And you?" My hands pressed into his shoulders, and I could feel his tense muscles beneath the fabric.

"I'm going to watch over you."

"You need to rest too."

But he quickly shook his head at my words as if weighed down by them. "Not tonight." His hand caressed down my cheek gently and lingered there. "I'm going to watch over you," he repeated.

I knew there was no arguing with him. No denying the intensity in his gaze.

Evren's guilt bled out of him—guilt for not stopping me, guilt over my father—and there was nothing that I could do tonight that would make him think differently.

He pressed more firmly against my back until I was forced to lay my head against his chest. I could hear the deep, steady beat of his heart beneath my ear, and the heavy sound lulled me to sleep even as I tried to fight it.

"Evren?" My voice was laced with sleep and barely understandable.

"Yes, princess?" Evren's hand still caressed my back, up and down in gentle strokes.

"You have nothing to feel guilty for, but I still want you to know that I forgive you."

His body stiffened beneath me, and that soft beat of his heart picked up.

"For my father. For everything."

His warm hand rested gently against the small of my back. I waited but heard only silence in response. His presence soothed me, the comfort it provided calmed my racing thoughts, and eventually I drifted off to sleep in his arms.

EVREN

Adara was still exhausted. Her body rested against me as we rode forward into our kingdom after hours and hours of riding through the night.

Sorin had spotted no signs of Gavril or his men following us, but we had no powers to track him with the death magic he now possessed.

When I had seen the red smoky magic fall from his fingers while he held on to Adara, fear had coursed through my veins like poison. I didn't know what he was capable of, but I knew that I didn't trust him.

Not him, my father, nor the queen. The queen whose life was taken by Adara.

Gavril's eyes had blazed with a seething fury as he watched Adara thrust his dagger into his mother's chest. His fists clenched with unbridled rage, and his face contorted with a deadly intensity.

And I knew that this war wouldn't end without his death or my own.

"We're here," I whispered against Adara's ear, and she blinked her eyes, which she had been desperately trying to keep open.

Her body relaxed deeper against mine as she looked up at the palace before her, at our home.

I climbed from the horse before reaching up and gripping my hands around her waist. I pulled her down from the horse, and I couldn't stop the way my teeth ground together at how light she felt in my hands.

Whatever my brother had done to her, it had taken its toll. Deep, dark circles formed under her eyes, and her cheeks had sunken in.

It did nothing but make the guilt eat at me harder.

She had been there suffering while I held her power inside me.

I held her in my arms as I moved toward the palace entrance.

"I can walk." She smiled up at me with tired eyes.

Of course she could, but I couldn't take my hands off her. I needed to touch her to know that she was here, that she was mine.

If I let go of her for even a moment, I worried that she would disappear.

"Just let me." I peered down at her as I walked into the palace.

My mother stood in the main room as we approached, but I avoided her completely as I headed toward my room. I could see the relief on her face, relief that I was home, relief that I carried Adara alongside me.

But Adara was still the Starblessed to her. She was still the girl who would fulfill our prophecy, and that thought filled me with rage.

But it was Mina who blocked my path and searched Adara's body with narrowed eyes. "Oh gods. Is she okay?"

"I'm fine, Mina." Adara gave her a soft smile before placing her hand on Mina's cheek.

Mina lifted her own, pressing it against the back of Adara's and leaning into her touch. "I'm happy you're home."

Adara swallowed hard before she answered her. "Me too."

"She needs to get some rest," I said as I adjusted my hold on Adara. "It's been a long night."

"Of course." Mina dropped her hold on Adara's hand before wiping at her cheeks. "Let me know if either of you need anything."

She moved out of my path, and I continued down the hall to our room.

I pushed my door open before stepping inside, and I didn't stop until we reached the washroom. I used my magic to quickly start filling the tub with steaming water before I carefully sat Adara on her feet, and she looked around as if she had been homesick for this place all along.

It was a look that made my chest ache and my fist clench at my side. I felt desperate to return to the fae kingdom and burn it to the ground. I didn't care who was innocent. That kingdom had taken her from me, and I wanted to ruin every part of it.

I reached around the back of her with trembling hands, and I quickly undid the laces of her bodice. The weight of the gown made it fall from her frame almost instantly, and she reached for my hand before stepping out of the fabric.

I dropped to my knees before her, slowly pulling her undergarments down her legs, and I paused as I noted the long unhealed scar on her thigh.

Adara quickly dropped her hand to the wound as if she could hide it from me, but I pushed it away. My brother had done this to her. My own blood was responsible for causing her this harm, and I would kill him for it.

I dragged the undergarments over the scar, careful not to hurt her before I leaned forward and pressed my lips against the angry red line.

"I'm okay." She repeated the words she had said to me earlier, but she wasn't okay. She had been harmed.

And I would hate myself for the rest of my life for allowing it to happen.

"You are not okay." I kissed the scar again as I pulled the undergarments to her feet and helped her step out. "I'm so sorry, princess."

I kissed the wound again, and I felt her tense under my lips. She stood before me wearing nothing but the jewels on her wrist, and I reached forward to remove them.

Adara pulled her wrist away from my touch, and her gaze shuttered as she gently shook her head.

My jaw clenched tight, my teeth feeling as if they might snap, and I reached out for her wrist again and pulled it toward me. This time, she let me, but her wrist trembled in my hand.

There was so much fear in her, fear that hadn't been there before, and my heart hammered in my chest as I imagined what they'd done to cause that fear.

My magic thrummed inside me with the thirst to destroy anyone who had created it.

I unclasped the three bracelets one by one, and my anger only intensified as the still bloody cut on her wrist was revealed beneath. She stared down at the wound, and I could see how badly it affected her.

I ran my fingers over the cut, careful not to hurt her, and I let my magic flow through me and into her. Her spine straightened as soon as she felt my magic touch her skin, but as the black of my power bled into her skin, she sagged in relief.

I didn't stop pushing it against her until both the wounds on her body healed and both scars were replaced with a mark of my own. If I had known they were there last night, I would have healed them then. It wouldn't take away what he had done, but I never wanted her to look down at her body and hate what she saw.

When she looked at these scars, I didn't want her to think of him. I wanted her to think of me and how my love for her was something I had waited a lifetime for.

I would have waited a hundred lifetimes to get to her.

I pressed my hands against her hips, running my fingers over her smooth skin, and she grasped my shoulders with her still trembling hands.

"You are so beautiful." I looked up at her, and her cheeks flushed as she stared down at me. "Every part of you is perfect."

I leaned forward and pressed my lips to her bare stomach. My body was on fire, and I wanted nothing more than to bend her over this tub and bury myself deep inside her. But that wasn't what she needed from me right now.

And I would give her anything she needed.

Every part of me belonged to her, to use as she demanded.

"Let's get you in the bath." I rose from my knees and dipped to pick her up in my arms. She wrapped her arms around my shoulders as I slid my hand beneath her knees and cradled her against my chest.

I slowly eased her into the water, and she moaned as the hot water surrounded her. I laid her head against the back of the tub before I stood to grab a towel.

But she stopped me with her hand on mine before I could manage a single step.

"Get in with me. Please."

There was no denying her. I had never been able to.

I quickly threw off my clothing, and she leaned forward in the tub, leaving room for me behind her. I climbed in and groaned as soon as she leaned back and pressed her back to my chest.

The feel of her body against mine was overwhelming. I ran my fingers up and down her arms because I couldn't get over the feel of her. She was here. She was mine, and she was here, and my breath caught in my throat at how badly I had missed her.

It had been suffocating me, starving me of life, and with her here before me, I could finally breathe.

I pressed my nose into her hair and took a long, deep breath.

We were both silent, just happy to live in the feel of each

other, and her fingers trailed up and down my thighs as if she was trying to commit my body to memory.

I reached up and gently pulled the small clips from her hair, which were still holding it in place, and her dark hair tumbled down her back and against my chest. I pressed my fingers into her scalp, massaging and touching every inch of her I could.

"That feels good," she moaned and leaned harder against me.

I kissed the top of her head before pressing my lips to the shell of her ear. She cocked her head to the side, giving me better access, and my lips followed the path down her neck.

My heart hammered in my chest, and I knew she had to feel it against her. But I couldn't calm myself down.

She was the most spectacular thing I had ever seen, and just sitting here in the tub with her, being allowed to touch any part of her, was a blessing I would never take for granted again.

Reaching forward for the soap, I lathered it into a small cloth. I rubbed it along her neck, and the sound that escaped her mouth made my cock jump against her.

I took my time, slowly running the cloth down her arms and hands before moving on to her chest. I rubbed the cloth down her breastbone before moving it around her breasts at an achingly slow pace.

She arched back into me, her body begging me for something I was dying to give her, and she whimpered as I pressed the fabric against her nipples.

I didn't linger there long. I trailed the cloth down her stomach, and I grinned as she huffed in frustration.

I cleaned her midsection thoroughly before moving the cloth

over her hips. Her lips opened the smallest bit, her body begging me for more, and I avoided her center altogether as I moved down to her thighs.

I worked the cloth over both of her legs, washing away every trace of the fae kingdom from her body, and she slowly rocked against me.

I reached forward, taking both of her thighs in my hands, and I pulled them apart until either thigh rested on mine. She was spread open for me, her pussy begging for my touch, but I took the cloth and ran it along the inside of her thighs at an achingly slow pace.

"Please, Evren." Adara cocked her head to look back at me, and the desire in her eyes was almost enough to break me.

She wanted me, and nothing in this world or the next would ever have that kind of hold on me.

"What do you want, princess?" I whispered the words against her lips, and she craned her neck until her mouth pressed firmly against mine.

"I want you," she whispered. "I want to remember nothing but you."

A growl ripped from my chest, and I couldn't control the way I wanted her. It was all-consuming, my desire for the beautiful creature in front of me, and I knew that it would be my demise.

She had the power to destroy every part of me if she so chose.

I ran my hands down her body, one cupping her breast while the other sank lower. I rolled her nipple between my fingers, and she arched into my touch.

Watching her was intoxicating. I felt drunk off my need for her, and I groaned low in my throat as my hand lowered and lowered until I pressed into her center and felt her wetness against my fingers.

She tensed as my fingers trailed over her clit, and I tried to block out the fear that anyone else had touched her. If my brother had forced himself on her in this way, I would torture every inch of him until he was begging the gods to take his life.

Adara must have felt the tension in my body because she looked up at me before reaching up and wrapping her hand around the back of my neck. She pulled me down until my lips met hers.

"Only you," she murmured against my lips between her kisses. "It's always only been you."

The territorial groan that left my mouth filled the small washroom, and I sank my fingers inside her. She gasped, and I swallowed the sound into my mouth.

I wanted everything she would give me, every whimper, every sigh of pleasure.

They belonged to me, and I felt greedy for them all.

I squeezed her nipple between my fingers as I moved my palm against her clit. I thrust my fingers into her, slowly at first, then faster as her body began rocking against me and telling me exactly what she wanted.

Everything inside me screamed to be gentle with her, to allow her to take the lead, but there was a bigger part of me that was desperate to claim her. To remind her that she was mine and I was hers and that no one would ever take her from me again.

"Gods, I will never get enough of you." I rocked my hand harder and curled my fingers inside her.

Her hand on my neck tightened, the pain from her grip only spurring me on, and I lifted my knees, spreading her legs farther.

"I love every part of you. Every inch," she whimpered, and it felt like a hit from the most intoxicating drug. "I have never wanted anything more in all my years."

She kissed me again as my hand moved harder and deeper inside her.

Her body was tense, a ball of nerves dying to release, and I was desperate to give it to her.

"That's it, princess." I moved my hand from her breast down to her thighs, and I widened her farther, pushing her ankle over the side of the tub. "Give me what belongs to me. I thought I would die without the taste of your pleasure."

She whimpered, and her body went rigid against me.

"Tell me this is mine." My hand worked harder, coaxing her pleasure from her body. "Tell me who it belongs to."

My voice was a growl, but I couldn't control myself. Every part of me was desperate, was feral in my need for her.

"It's yours." She rolled her hips against my hand, chasing that crash we both knew was coming. "I belong to you."

My fingers moved harder inside her, and she cried out as her release raced through her. She tried to clamp her thighs together, but I held them apart with my own as I slowed my touch and coaxed every drop of her pleasure from her body.

Her body slowly relaxed, sinking further against me, and my cock was rock-hard beneath her. I pressed a gentle kiss to her shoulder, and I loved the taste of her on my tongue.

I loved everything about this girl before me.

She turned against me, her body rolling against mine, and her hands tangled into my hair at the back of my head. She brought her mouth to mine, and she kissed me slowly before she sucked my bottom lip into her mouth and bit down.

My cock jumped, and I could feel her smile against my lips.

“I need you,” she said so softly I almost missed it.

“You have me. For this lifetime and any that come after.” I stared at her and pushed her hair out of her face. Her star marks were burning bright against her cheeks, and I was in awe of her. Of her beauty, of her strength. She didn’t realize what she possessed. She had no idea the power she held over me.

But I could feel it with every fiber of my being.

“I need you inside me.” She moved, straddling my hips, and water sloshed around her and hit the floor outside the tub. “Shit.” She giggled, and my chest felt like it would explode.

I gripped her hips in my hands, helping her get settled against me, and I thought I might die when she reached beneath her and ran her small hand up and down the length of me.

She bit her lip as she watched herself work me, then she peered up at me with a hooded gaze as she lifted onto her knees and pressed me against her center.

I pressed my head back against the back of the tub as I tried to stop myself from thrusting up into her like I was dying to.

She sank down on me slowly, the pace driving me mad with need, and my hands tightened on her hips until I was worried I was hurting her.

“Gods, Adara,” I moaned and closed my eyes.

“No princess?”

I opened my eyes, and she cocked her brow, a damning smile playing on her lips.

"You will always be my princess." My hips surged into her, and her eyes rolled into the back of her head. "I'll call you whatever you want me to."

"Hmm." She hummed and started to move against me. "What else would you like to call me?"

She was teasing me, and the playful smile on her lips made something loosen in my chest.

"There are many things I'd like to call you." I caressed her hip with my thumb, and she moved harder against me.

"Like?" Her word was breathless.

"My wife."

Her gaze slammed into mine, and those wide eyes were the most beautiful sight I had ever seen.

"My queen."

She rolled her hips against me, and my thumb moved to her center. I rolled my finger against her at the same pace she had set, and her pussy clamped down around me.

"Gods, yes." She let her head fall back, and she was fully exposed to me. I leaned forward, taking one of her breasts into my mouth, and I rolled my tongue against her nipple. "I will be anything you want me to be," she murmured above me, and her words only spurred me on. "I am yours for whatever you want."

I let out a curse, and pleasure tightened in my lower stomach, and I knew I would come if she continued to say those words to me.

I leaned back again, my fingers dug into her flesh, and I helped her lift off me until I pulled her back down hard. Her eyes rolled in her head, and I continued the movement over and over until we were both staring at each other and gasping for breath.

Her body took over, lifting and dropping back down onto me, and I rubbed her clit as I thrust my hips up out of the water to meet hers.

She pressed her hands against my chest, using the leverage to ride me, and when her nails dug into my flesh, I knew I wasn't going to last.

"I'm going to come, princess." My voice was rough and filled with the pain of holding off my pleasure.

"I want it," she moaned and worked herself harder. "You belong to me, and I want it."

I leaned up, claiming her mouth with my own, and I kissed her roughly as our hips met.

I bit down on her lip as her sex clamped down around me. I pressed my thumb harder against her, and she cried out against my mouth, her nails digging into my shoulder as her pleasure crashed through her. I came inside her with a loud groan, and I thrust up into her, deeper and deeper until I felt every drop of her pleasure wring from her body.

I leaned back against the tub, my body spent, and she followed me. She laid her head against my chest, her body fitting perfectly against me, and my cock jerked inside her.

She let out a small giggle at the feel of it, and I let out a deep breath as I ran my hands up and down the length of her spine.

I couldn't stop touching her, the feel of her under my fingers soothing something inside me that nothing else could touch.

We stayed like that for a long moment until the water went

cold, and I feared that we'd freeze before either of us was willing to move.

"Never again." I let the words slip from my lips, and they sounded so full of anger.

"What?" she asked as she lifted her head and rested it on her arm against my chest.

I rubbed my wet hands along her face and over her head. I pushed her hair away from her face and leaned down to press my lips against hers.

It was meant to be a simple kiss, but the way she reacted made me feel desperate to take her again. I kissed her urgently, my hand tightening in her hair, and when I pulled away, that same need shone in her gaze.

"I will never let you go again." I told her the most honest truth that I would ever give her. "Gavril will have to kill me."

"I'm not going anywhere." She shook her head in my hand.

"Promise me," I demanded of her, and her pupils flared. "No matter what we must sacrifice, it will never be each other. Not ever again."

She was quiet for a long moment before she nodded. "I promise. Never again."

I leaned forward, wrapping my arms around her, and I stood from the tub, carrying her with me.

"I told you I can walk." She laughed, but I didn't care.

I carefully set her on her feet before grabbing a towel. I ran it along her body, drying the water that clung to her skin before I wrapped it around her. I wrapped another around my hips before I took her in my arms again and headed toward my bed.

I knew there were many people waiting to see us, waiting to talk to us about what had happened in the fae kingdom, but none of them mattered in that moment.

It was just her and me, and everything else could wait.

ADARA

Evren and I walked down the hall hand in hand.

I wasn't sure how long we had slept, but I hadn't felt so rested in a very long time. Evren had wrapped himself around me, his body cocooning mine in his warmth and safety, and the darkness of the night pulled me into sleep quickly.

My body still ached, and I could feel the ghost of Evren between my thighs. He had wanted to stay there, to forget the rest of the world until we were completely sated, and I wanted that too.

But thoughts of my father, of him being here, ate at the back of my mind, and I was eager to see him. Eager and nervous at the same time.

Evren's hand wrapped around mine settled something inside me, and I followed him step for step as he led us through the palace.

We made our way to the dining room, and I was surprised at the number of people sitting around the table as we entered. Sorin, Jorah, and Thalia were all chatting as they ate, and Queen Veda sat at the head of the table, quietly watching all of them.

But it was my father at her side, my father, who looked far more human than the last time I saw him, that drew my attention.

Thalia jumped up from the table, moving to me so quickly that she almost knocked me over, and she drew me into her body with a tight hug. She let out a deep breath, a breath of relief, and it settled deep in my gut.

She finally let go of me, and she reached out and smacked Evren playfully in his chest. "Don't you dare keep her locked away like that when we just got her back."

Evren rubbed at the spot she just hit with a smile on his lips. "I would say I'm sorry, but I'm not." He pulled me back toward him and wrapped his arms around my middle before pressing a gentle kiss to my shoulder.

"Well, she's mine for the rest of the day." Thalia grinned at me as she crossed her arms, and gods, I had missed her.

"Not going to happen," Evren said nonchalantly, and Thalia's eyes narrowed.

But I looked past her to stare at my father. He still held a fork in his hands, but he was no longer using it as his gaze settled firmly on me.

"Excuse me." I moved out of Evren's hold, and he let go of me easily as he tracked my gaze.

I walked hesitantly toward this man I didn't know but who looked so much like me. He stood quickly as I approached, his chair scraping against the floor, and he looked as nervous as I felt.

He was my blood, my father, yet I knew nothing about him.

And he knew as little about me.

Still, there was something deep inside me that was drawn to him. This man had sacrificed his life for my own, and I knew that truth deep in my gut.

"Hi," I said awkwardly, and he wiped at his mouth with the back of his trembling hand.

"Adara," he whispered, his voice gruff and filled with age. "I can't believe you're standing before me."

"I know." I shrugged my shoulders, and I could feel everyone's eyes on us even though they were pretending not to eavesdrop.

I started to turn to Evren, seeking his strength, but my father quickly moved toward me, and it caught me off guard as he wrapped his arms around me. He squeezed me against his thin body, and my breath rushed out of me.

"Gods, it's really you." He took a deep breath, breathing me in, and my chest tightened as his hands trembled against my skin.

"It's me," I whispered so quietly that I wasn't sure he heard me, but his hands pressed even harder against me as if he worried I would disappear the moment he let me go.

I felt the same.

He was my family, but he was also a stranger. He was a ghost of the father I thought I had lost, and I didn't want to let him go. ☾

We stayed like that for a long moment, just holding on to each other with a desperation that I knew we could both feel, and when he finally pulled away from me, his eyes were clouded with unshed tears.

His frail hands ran over my face, taking me in, and he smiled. "You look so much like me."

"That's what I've always been told." I laughed softly, and his smile deepened.

I felt a hand press against my back, Evren's hand, and he smiled down at the both of us. "Let's eat." He nodded toward the table, and my father slowly let go of me as we pulled out the chairs.

I smiled at my father as I took the seat next to him, and the light in his eyes soothed something in me.

"Welcome home."

I was caught off guard by the sound of Queen Veda's voice, but I gave her a tight smile as Evren wrapped his hand around my knee under the table and gave it a gentle squeeze.

"Thank you." I nodded in her direction, and Evren slid a plate of food in front of me.

"We have much to discuss." The queen wiped her mouth with her napkin, and I tensed. "There is so much to come."

"Not this morning," Evren practically growled from beside me.

"We don't have time to spare." His mother seemed clueless about the way Evren's body had tensed and his gaze darkened.

"Adara just got home after being in that hell of a kingdom, and she just got her father back after not having him for almost two decades. I think we have plenty of time to spare before you demand more of my mate."

"It's okay." I forced a smile even though the last thing I wanted was to talk to his mother about anything, let alone the consequences we all knew we were about to face. I just wanted to bury my head a bit longer. I wanted to bury myself in the safety of Evren and pretend like everything outside of him and me didn't exist. "We can discuss whatever we need to."

The queen looked between Evren and me before her gaze finally settled on me. "With Queen Kaida dead, the fae kingdom is likely to bring the war to us much faster than any of us suspect."

I straightened, my back rigid, as she mentioned Queen Kaida's death so easily, as if it hadn't been my hand to stab the blade into her chest. Guilt clawed at my stomach, eating away at the calmness Evren had given me, and I couldn't stop the way my heart hammered in my chest.

"Queen Kaida's death would have come sooner or later." Thalia looked at the queen, and her voice was stern. "If it wasn't by Adara's hand, it would have been mine. Let them bring the war. I will protect Adara and this kingdom no matter the cost." Thalia looked at me, and there was such an intensity in her gaze. "It is my greatest honor to call you my friend."

I swallowed hard, emotion clogging my throat, and Evren squeezed my knee. "As it is mine." I barely managed to choke out the words as I nodded toward her.

My father smiled up at me, and my chest warmed until the queen spoke again.

"Regardless, it will make them move faster. We don't know the extent of the power Gavril possesses. What he's capable of."

"Death magic." I reached forward and grabbed my cup of water. "Eletta told me of his mate."

"You saw her?" Sorin asked, and my father stiffened beside me.

"No." I shook my head, and there was a part of me that felt guilty for never trying to find her. "I assumed he had already killed her."

"They kept her in the cell beside me." My father cleared his throat, and I stared down at his trembling hands. "Gavril would take from her until she was on the brink of death to gain his power, but he always stopped. I think he was saving the poor girl's life until he needed her most."

Sorin's words from the palace haunted me.

The girl is gone too.

"He took her when he escaped." I asked as I looked up at Sorin.

It wasn't a question, but Sorin still nodded his head at me. "There was fresh blood in her cell, but Leda was gone."

Leda.

I hadn't even considered her name. It hadn't occurred to me that he could have been torturing her the entire time I was in his palace. "Gavril kept me in his room."

Evren went rigid beside me, but I continued.

"He left me alone in there most of the time, but sometimes when he'd crawl into the bed at night, his mouth and hands would carry traces of blood."

Evren's hands tightened into fists, and his black magic rolled out of his fingers and gently around his wrists. He was still in control but just barely. His anger was palpable, and it was eating away at him.

"He was feeding from her still?" Sorin looked carefully between Evren and me.

"I don't know." I shook my head and pressed my hand to Evren's thigh. "I never saw him take from anyone other than me."

Sorin and Thalia looked back and forth at each other, and Jorah leaned forward. "I read in one of the old texts that he must kill her to gain full control of the death magic. If she's still alive, then the magic he's gaining is tearing at his soul. He's caught in a limbo of the power and his mate."

"Gavril will go to whatever end," I told them. "He will not stop until he has me back at his side, as his queen, or he's dead. Mate or not, he's adamant that he needs me to fulfill the prophecy. He will not stop until he rules all."

"Then we kill him," Sorin said it as if the answer was that simple.

"I don't think it will be that easy." I shook my head. "I don't know the extent of his power, but I know that he'll use everything he has against us."

Everyone was quiet for a moment before the queen asked, "How many times did he feed from you?"

"Twice that I remember. The second time was worse than the first. He took too much, and my body rejected his magic. I hardly had control of my mind."

Evren's chair scraped harshly against the floor.

He didn't look at me as he stood and dropped his napkin to the table. "If you'll excuse me, I need a bit of air."

He pushed out of the room, his long strides moving quickly until the door clicked shut behind him.

I stood, unable to just let him leave after what I had shared, and gave my father a soft smile. "I need to check on him. I'll be back."

No one stopped me, and they wouldn't have been able to. My magic was back inside myself, but every ounce of it craved to be with him. Every fiber of my being refused to let him out of my sight.

I entered the hall and heard the door to the back courtyard close. I followed the sound, and when I opened the door, I saw Evren standing in the middle of the courtyard with his hands on the back of his head as he stared up at the sky.

He paced, his anger driving his movement, and I quietly closed the door as I watched him.

But his gaze found me the moment the door latched behind me.

Pain shuddered over his face, and my chest ached.

"I'm sorry, princess. I just need a moment."

"Then take it." I nodded. "But you take it with me."

His gaze roved over me, and his eyes were so dark my heart rate spiked. "It is you I'm trying to stay away from."

My breath rushed out of me, and I searched his face. "Oh. I can go back inside."

I reached for the door, but it was his next words that stopped me in my tracks. "It is you who I can hardly look at without guilt eating me alive. The things my brother did to you." He swallowed hard and shook his head. "I will never forgive myself for it."

I turned back to face him, and he dropped his hands as his gaze ran down my body.

"It is you I want to leave my mark on until no one in this world or the next is confused about who you belong to. For them to have no confusion about my devotion to you."

"You do not need to mark me for them to know." I pushed away from the door and stepped toward him. There was so much possession in his eyes, his desire drowning him. "But if that's what you need, then take it. I will wear any mark you give me."

"You should go back inside, princess." His teeth were bared, and chill bumps ran down my spine. "I have no control when it comes to you."

"I'm not going anywhere." I shook my head. "I want you." I reached out, wrapping my fingers into his shirt, and the heat of his skin burned into them.

He bent down and whispered harshly in my ear, "I can't be gentle."

My breath caught in my throat as his strong arms embraced me, and I shivered as his familiar scent filled my senses. His gaze was intense, searching for something in my eyes.

When I didn't pull away, his hands moved to my lower back, pressing me firmly against him. I could feel how badly he wanted me as his arousal pressed against my stomach. Moisture pooled between my thighs as his fingers dropped to my bottom, and he lifted me. His head lowered into my neck, and he let out a sigh as I responded in kind, locking my legs around his waist.

He moved us quickly, not stopping until my back hit the stone of the palace wall, and his teeth scraped against my neck.

A whimper passed my lips, and his hips surged forward against me. Tortured pleasure coursed through my body. My thighs tightened against him, pulling him more firmly against me.

My hands gripped the material of his shirt, and I pulled him closer. His mouth left my neck, and he growled against my ear. "Princess."

The word on his lips sent a shot of ecstasy through my body, and he thrust against me again. I whimpered as my magic snaked through me, desperate to get to him.

"Evren," I moaned as it consumed me, and his face lowered to mine, his lips trailing over my jaw, so close to my lips, but he denied me what I wanted. He denied me his kiss as his nose ran down the length of my jaw, and I whimpered at the gentle pleasure until he replaced it with pain.

His teeth scraped against the sensitive skin of my neck, rougher than they had just moments ago.

I let my head drop back against the palace wall, and his hands moved beneath my dress until he was cupping me. His fingers dug into my skin as his teeth moved harder against me, and I cried out even though I couldn't focus on either sensation without being overwhelmed by the other.

"Will you let me?" His words were muffled with his mouth against my skin, but his teeth scraped even harder, driving his question home. "I want to erase every trace of him. When you wake tomorrow, I want your body to ache with memories of me and me alone."

I nodded my head against him, the feeling in my core driving me crazy with need.

"Say it, princess." He pressed his lips over the skin he had just ran his teeth across. "Tell me you want it too."

"I want it." The last word had barely passed my lips when his teeth sank into my neck.

A cry left me, and my body convulsed. Every inch of me was on fire, drowning in pleasure and pain. He gripped my bottom and ground against me harder and harder. I could feel the wetness between my legs as he moved, and my legs weakened, still wrapped around his waist.

The pain in my neck seeped away, slowly morphing into the kind of agony that would make me beg him on my hands and knees. There was an inferno burning through me, awakening every inch of my body and reminding it exactly who it belonged to.

And there were no doubts in my mind that this man before me was mine.

That fact radiated through every part of me, begging me to take every part of him. My fingers dug into his shoulders and the back of his neck, holding on to the feeling with everything I had.

Evren let out a low growl against my neck just before he slowly pulled his teeth out of my skin. His tongue gently caressed the marks he had just made, sending a delicious shiver down my body.

He dropped his hands from my ass, the movement so quick I had no choice but to let my legs fall from around him and press my feet back to the ground. Evren dropped to his knees before me, and there was no hesitation as he wrapped his hands around my thighs and spread my legs apart.

He pushed my dress up my stomach, and I bit my lip at the sight of his burning gaze roaming over me. Heat flared in his gaze, and his eyes were darker than I had ever seen them before.

"Evren," I whispered and reached forward until my hand tangled in his dark hair.

"I'm going to taste every inch of you." His fingers tightened, and when I looked down, I saw his black magic leaking from his fingertips with his lack of control.

He moved those fingers, burying them in the sides of my undergarments before he ripped them down my legs. I stepped out of them quickly, leaving me completely bare before him, and the smile on his face turned wicked.

He wasted no time as he leaned forward and pressed his lips against my pussy. He ran his tongue through the length of me, and I gripped the strands of his hair between my fingers.

He gripped my thigh in his hand, lifting it and laying it over his shoulder. I felt completely open in front of him, and my stomach clenched as I looked down and watched him staring up at me as he ate from my flesh.

"You taste so fucking good," he murmured against me, and my eyes rolled into the back of my head as he sucked my clit into his mouth.

Pleasure exploded through my body, and my head dropped back against the wall behind me.

Evren ran his hand up the inside of my trembling thigh, which was barely holding me from falling, and when he reached the apex of my thighs, he lifted me off the ground completely until both of them rested on his shoulders.

He tilted my body back, and my pulse raced through me as I felt like I might fall. My upper back and head were the only things touching the wall, everything else completely under his control.

My legs shook, and my fingers pulled on his hair as his dug into me. He tugged my hips even closer to his mouth, and a whimper escaped me. The sight of this god of a man kneeling between my thighs with nothing on his mind except chasing my pleasure was enough to drive me mad with need.

My hips rolled against his mouth, silently begging him for more, and he growled against me.

He pulled away, and I moaned at the loss of his mouth. He grinned with my wetness coating his lips, and he moved one of his hands toward my center.

His gaze never left mine as he pushed two fingers inside me. I arched my back, my body already knowing exactly what it needed from him, and he gave it to me immediately.

He worked his fingers in and out of me, each thrust hard and deep, and he walked a line of pleasure and pain that made me feel as if I would shatter into a million pieces.

But I didn't care. He could destroy every part of me, and I would be asking him for more.

He continued working his fingers in and out of me as he brought his mouth back to my pussy, and as soon as he sucked me back between his lips, every bit of pleasure crashed into me.

"Evren!" I cried out his name, and the rough stone of the wall scraped against my back as my hips moved against his mouth.

"Please." I didn't care how desperate I sounded. I only cared that he didn't stop.

He sucked harder, and his fingers hit somewhere inside me impossibly deeper, and I could hold on to that high no longer.

Pleasure coursed through every part of me, and I cried out over and over as he slowed his movements and coaxed every drop of my pleasure with his tongue.

My body trembled and my fingers tightened in his hair as I stared down into his dark eyes, which swirled with his magic. He pulled away from me slowly, but his hands were still firm on my body.

He dropped my thighs from around his shoulders, and his hands moved to my lower back as he slowly pulled me until I was straddling his lap.

He rested his head in the crook of my shoulder, his lips brushing over the spot where he had fed from me, and my body vibrated against him.

His length was hard beneath me, and even through his trousers, it brushed against my sensitive center and sent a shock wave of pleasure through my body.

"I need to be inside you," he moaned against my neck, and his hips surged up against mine. "I need to fuck you until I forget everything but you and me."

I rolled my hips against his as I tried to catch my breath, and he growled before lifting me off his lap and turning me until I was on my knees before him. His hand moved under my dress, dragging the fabric up as he went, and he groaned as his fingers skimmed my wetness between my thighs.

He spread it around, making sure it coated every inch of me, before he pressed his other hand against my upper back and pushed me down until my elbows pressed against the ground.

"You are so fucking wet." His breath was ragged and filled with his desire. "Taste it."

His body leaned over mine, his chest pressed against my back, and he fed his fingers into my mouth. I tasted myself on him, and I shouldn't have been so turned on by that fact.

But my pleasure belonged to him, every part of me did, and I licked it from his fingers greedily.

"Gods, you're such a good fucking girl." He pressed his fingers deeper into my mouth until I worried I would choke on them before he slowly pulled them from my lips.

He moved behind me, the sound of his trousers dropping like a drug that was teasing me as it sat just out of my reach.

My fingers dug into the ground, and my heart raced as he pulled me back just enough to line up his cock with my entrance. He rubbed himself up and down my slickness, my body on fire from the movement, and he positioned the tip right at my sex.

He slid into me slowly, and I gasped at the way he filled me. I hadn't realized how badly I needed this, how much I missed this, but something deep inside me settled as he thrust inside me as far as he could get.

His fingers trailed down the length of my spine as he began moving in and out of me slowly. His body thrummed behind me, his control vibrating as if it were about to snap, but he was still being so careful with me.

He was tempting me with his cock, the pleasure his body brought mine overwhelming, but it wasn't what I wanted.

He needed to lose control inside me. He needed to use my body to feed the overwhelming possession that haunted him.

And I wanted every second of it.

"Please, Evren," I whimpered and stretched my arms out in front of me, pressing my cheek against the cold stone of the floor. "I need more."

He stilled for a moment, and I worried that I had said something wrong. I started to lift to look back at him, but his hand came down hard against my upper back, and he pressed me harder against the floor as he slowly pulled out of my body.

I didn't have time to think of what he was doing before he slammed into me so roughly that my own magic sparked in my vision.

His other hand dug into my hip, holding me in place as he fucked me roughly, and I reached my hands out farther. I dug my fingers into the stone before me, pain slicing through the tips, but I didn't care.

I needed this as badly as he did.

I needed him to destroy the ghost of anyone else until I had no choice but to remember him and him alone.

"You are so perfect," he growled from behind me, and my pussy clamped down around him. "The gods made you for me. Made your body for me to worship."

I squeezed my eyes closed, and my breath shook heavily from my chest.

"Mine," he growled, and I hadn't realized how badly I needed to hear the words as tears filled my eyes.

I needed him to claim me like this. I needed him to love me in this way that only he was capable of.

"You are mine," he groaned as his body slammed into me again and again.

He reached forward, his fingers digging into my ribs, and he lifted me easily until my back was pressed against his chest. His knees widened between mine, forcing my legs farther apart, and he felt impossibly deep in this position as he continued to thrust up inside me.

His fingers moved to my sex, and he thrummed them against my sensitive clit. I cried out and wrapped my arm around the back of his neck.

"This is mine." He slammed into me again, and he pinched my clit between his fingers. Pleasure bombarded me, and I cried out. "My beautiful girl." He ran his teeth along my neck. "My perfect fucking mate."

His other hand lifted, his fingers wrapping around my throat, and he pressed firmly on the sides of my neck as he thrust into me harder and harder.

I couldn't catch my breath. I couldn't hold on to my pleasure as it raced through me. I was in Evren's hands, and every part of me was his to control.

I could feel myself slipping over the edge, and he played my body perfectly. He was so in tune with my pleasure, and his hands on my clit and my throat became harsher as he helped me chase it.

"Give me what's mine, Adara," he murmured against my ear before his teeth ran along the shell. "Come for me."

My body tensed around him, and I moaned his name over and over as he raced toward his own climax.

"Fuck." The word was murmured against my neck as he thrust hard, and I felt him come deep inside me.

His hand softened on my throat, and I drank down breath after breath as I tried to calm my racing heart. He pressed a kiss against my neck before lazily moving to my shoulder. His hand rose, pressing against my jaw and turning me to face him.

His lips met mine, a slow, languid kiss, and some piece that Gavril had stolen seemed to slip back inside me. "I love you, princess," Evren murmured against my lips, and I could feel wetness coating my cheeks as tears rolled down my face.

"And I love you."

"We're okay." His hands moved over my face gently. "We're together, and we're okay."

I nodded even as the fear of our future started to creep its way into my thoughts. "But he's not going to stop."

Evren swallowed hard as he watched me. "I know, and we must prepare for this war that he'll bring."

That word from his mouth sent a chill down my spine.

"I've requested aid from the old fae kingdom across the sea, and our people are prepared to fight."

"Is it true that Gavril's men attacked the kingdom after I went with him?"

Evren hesitated for a long moment. "They did. The blood of ninety-four of our men and women will stain my brother's hands for all eternity."

As they would mine. I couldn't stop the way guilt flooded me. Guilt that I hadn't been here to help protect them, that I was the reason Gavril had come here in the first place.

"I'm sorry, Evren."

He pulled me into him and pressed his lips gently against mine. "There is nothing for you to be sorry for. We were unprepared for his power and his cruelty, but we won't make that mistake again."

"Do you think the old fae will come?"

"I'm unsure." He pushed my hair over my shoulder. "But our people will fight to their very last breath if that's what it takes."

"As will I."

Evren's gaze darkened as he watched me. "I want to protect you at all costs, but I won't stop you. But you must promise me that you will cling to your power. Never give it up again. You will never sacrifice any part of yourself again to protect me."

I nodded even though it was a lie. I would give up everything to protect him, even if I had to relive every bit of hell with Gavril, but I knew that Evren and I were stronger together.

If we were to defeat him, we would need to stand together to do so.

"Promise me, Adara." There was a low growl in his voice.

"I promise."

He pulled me closer to him until his lips pressed against mine. "I won't lose you again, princess. I'm not strong enough to do so."

"You won't lose me."

He searched my face, committing every inch of me to memory before his lips met mine again. He pulled me from his lap and stood before reaching down and helping me to my feet. "Come on. I need you to myself for a bit longer before Thalia really does try to steal you away."

15

EVREN

There was a soft knock at the door, and I groaned as I buried my face in Adara's back.

She was so warm and soft in front of me, and I didn't want to move. I didn't want to lose the safety I felt just having her in my arms.

But that insistent knocking started again.

I ran my nose along the length of her neck, and the way she arched back into me combined with the soft moan that left her mouth was enough to kill me.

And what a wonderful death it would be.

I pressed my hardening cock against the edge of her bare bottom, and her hands dug into the pillow in front of her. The smell of her in my bed was intoxicating, everything about her was, and my chest felt lighter than it had in a long time.

I ran my lips along her shoulder, the skin smooth beneath them, before scraping my teeth over that same sensitive spot.

The craving to taste her again was overwhelming, and it had nothing to do with the power she possessed.

"Evren," she whispered, arching into me further, and my hand snaked up her stomach until I cupped her breast in my hand.

"Yes, princess," I purred against her skin, and she laughed softly.

"You really should get the door." As soon as she said the words, another knock sounded against the wood.

"Damn it," I growled before pulling away from her and grabbing my trousers from the floor. "I'm coming," I called out before shoving my legs into the pants and pulling them up my hips.

I looked back down at her as she stretched out before me, completely bare and begging for my touch, and she smiled.

"The door, prince." She nodded toward it with a smirk, and I turned away from her as I ran my hand down my face.

I didn't want to let anyone in. I didn't want to face any part of the world outside this room.

It was her and me, and that was all I needed. It was everything.

I was at the door within seconds, but my hand didn't move to open it. I took another moment to try to pull myself together and adjusted myself in my trousers.

I cracked open the door, expecting to see Mina, but it was my best friend who leaned against the frame with a wicked smirk on his face. He twirled a dagger in his hand as he grinned at me, and I felt the need to pull it from his hand and kill the smug bastard.

"What do you want?" My voice was gruff and showed my annoyance at being interrupted with Adara, and Sorin only smiled.

"Apologies for disturbing you, my prince." Sorin bowed his head, and the urge to smack him was overwhelming. "Your presence has been requested in the library."

"I'm a little busy with my mate right now." I glanced back over my shoulder to see Adara sitting up in my bed, the covers pulled around her body, but it was clear to anyone who saw her that she was naked beneath.

I narrowed the door even more.

"She's needed too. Get dressed. We'll meet you there." He pushed off the wall and tucked the dagger back into his side.

"We'll meet you there shortly." I pushed the door closed with a click, and I heard his snicker of laughter on the other side.

"Don't make me come back after you all. I'll break down the door if I have to."

I rolled my eyes and turned back to Adara. She was grinning, the look on her face genuine happiness, and my chest ached with the need to never allow that look to fall.

She had moved to the edge of the bed, and I rushed to her side as she tried to reach for her dress. I knocked it out of the way before she could grab it and watched as it fell to the floor.

"Hey." Her nose wrinkled as she looked up at me. "I was about to put that on."

"Not yet." I shook my head and pressed my knees to the bed

in front of her. She spread her legs just enough to accommodate the width of me, but she clung to the sheet against her chest.

"You heard, Sorin. They are waiting for us." She pushed against my bare stomach, and her lips turned down into a pout when I didn't budge.

"And they can keep waiting." I pushed my fingers into her hair and tugged at the base of her scalp until she was forced to look up at me.

She bit down on her bottom lip, and I could see her warring with herself. She wanted me, but she also didn't want to keep them waiting.

She was such a good fucking girl, and she deserved to be rewarded for it.

"What if it's important?"

I leaned down until my face was level with hers, and I took a moment just to breathe her in. She smelled of sweetness and sin, and when I looked down in her eyes, all I could see was the warrior that I loved burning inside her.

"There is nothing in this world more important than you." I brushed my lips against hers so lightly that it didn't feed the need inside me. It only made it deepen.

Every part of me burned with my desire for her.

She leaned back from me, tugging on my hold, and her gaze darkened as she peered up at me. "He said he would come back."

My knee nudged against hers, forcing her thighs farther apart, and a rush of breath escaped from her lips. "Then we should make this quick."

I pressed my lips against hers again before pulling back as she went for more. I moved lower, kissing her jaw, then gently down her neck.

Her hand was still fisted in the sheet, her knuckles turning white from her hold, and I slowly rolled my tongue over them before dropping to my knees before her.

Her thighs tensed, an involuntary movement, and I could scent how badly she wanted this. It didn't matter what she said; her need for me was as bad as my own for her.

There was nothing that could keep me from her.

"I can smell me on your skin," I murmured against her as I ran my nose along her stomach. I slid my hands beneath her thighs, wrapping them around until my fingers dug into her flesh, and I spread her open before me. "Drop the sheet, princess. Let me taste you."

She let out a soft whimper, her thighs jerking in my hands, but her hands didn't move away from the sheet. I leaned forward, pressing my face against the sheet that still lay between me and her pussy, and I ran my nose against it before giving her the briefest of kisses.

"Drop it, Adara, or I'll rip it away." I turned to the side, dragging my tongue against her supple thigh, against my mark on her beautiful skin. My hands clenched, spreading her farther, and I was rewarded by one of her soft moans.

"You wouldn't dare."

I looked up at her, and her eyes were hooded as she stared down at me. Her chest heaved as breath rushed in and out of her. She wanted this as badly as I did, but she wanted to play.

My beautiful, strong girl wanted me to prove to her that I

was the one in control, and I would give her exactly what she needed.

It would be my fucking pleasure.

I nipped at her inner thigh, knowing she loved that edge of pain, and she hissed even as her hips surged forward toward my mouth. I didn't give her time to adjust. I lifted my head and used my hands to jerk her forward until she hung precariously on the edge of the bed.

She still clung to the sheet, but her breasts peeked out from the fabric. I growled as I took in the view of her before me, and the surge of desire that rushed through me made my already hard cock strain painfully against my trousers.

I gripped the sheet in my hand near her hip before pressing my knee into the bottom of it, which draped on the floor, and I pulled it taut against her body. I could see the outline of her perfect pussy beneath the fabric, and I stared up at her as I slowly lowered my mouth.

She was watching me, her gaze not straying from mine for even a moment, and I held that gaze as I breathed her in. I slid my tongue against the smooth fabric of the sheet, and her body lifted from the bed, chasing the feeling.

"If you want to hide from me, then you can hide," I murmured against the sheet again before pressing my tongue firmly against her clit, which lay beneath. Her hips jolted off the bed, pressing hard against my mouth, and I rewarded her by sucking the sheet and her body between my lips.

"Evren," she whispered and dropped the sheet as her hands tangled in my hair.

"Hold the sheet, princess," I growled against her. "You drop it, and I stop."

Her hands stalled in my hair, and her breath rushed out of her. "What?"

I turned my head, kissing the edge where her thigh met her bottom. She squirmed against me, but her hands didn't move from my hair.

"Do as I said." I nipped at her skin and felt her hands drop from my hair. I looked up at her, and she was staring down at me with both hands clinging to the sheet. A smirk graced my lips, and I pulled the sheet tighter against her sex.

She moaned, her hips jerking beneath me, and she spread her legs wider as I lowered my head between them.

"That's a good girl." I scraped my teeth against her before swiping against her pussy with my tongue.

The sheet was soaked with her want and my mouth, and it drove both of us crazy for me to be so close yet so far away from her. It was the most delicious kind of torture.

Her whole body was strung tight, waiting for more, and the sight of her like that pushed the animal inside me to the surface.

I jerked her even closer to me, her body almost completely off the bed now, and I reached forward, snatching the sheet from against her.

Her pussy glistened in front of me, her want for me dripping down her body, and the growl that ripped from my throat was liable to be heard throughout the castle.

This was my mate, my future wife, and the sight of her before me was the most powerful I had ever felt in my lifetime.

"Gods, I could worship you forever." I pressed my lips gently against her clit, and she jumped.

She bucked against me, and I knew she was close to her orgasm. I had barely touched her, yet she was so ready to fall over that edge.

I lapped at her, my tongue sliding against her slick pussy, and she moaned above me. I spread her wider with my hands, and I dove into every inch of her.

Her breath came out in pants as she clutched at the sheet. "Evren..."

"Do you like that, princess?" I demanded with a growl.

"Yes. Oh gods. Please." Her words were a breathless plea, spurring me on, and I dropped my hold on one of her thighs. Her words gave me power. They fed me in a way that nothing else ever would.

I ran my fingers through her, meeting my tongue as it flicked against her clit, and she bucked against me.

"Evren." She rolled her hips against my mouth.

I slid two fingers inside her as I sucked her again. She cried out, her pussy clamping down around my fingers, and there was another knock on the door.

I felt her tense, her body going rigid beneath me, but I didn't stop.

An entire army could be outside that door, and I wouldn't stop.

"Evren." My name left her lips in a hissed whisper, and I sucked her harder into my mouth.

She cursed under her breath, and I grinned against her as I

slid my fingers in and out of her. Her wetness was dripping down my fingers and covering my hand.

"It's your choice, princess," I said against her sex. "You can clamp those pretty lips closed while I suck your pleasure from you, or whoever is on the other side of that door can hear you come against my mouth." I sucked her into my mouth again to drive my point home, and the deep moan that fell from her lips made me smile. "Your pleasure belongs to me either way." I glanced up at her, and she lifted onto her elbows so she could stare down at me. I held her gaze as I pumped my fingers into her harder and curled them inside her.

Her sex milked my fingers, and her gaze widened as she pressed her thighs firmly against the sides of my head.

She was so close, so damn close, and I selfishly wanted her pleasure.

I needed it.

I sucked her clit harder, deep, slow pulls, and she cried out, the sound guttural and ringing throughout the room.

There was no mistaking that whoever was on the other side of that door could hear her, and even though it made my jealousy flare at the thought, I couldn't bring myself to stop.

I slowed my movements, easing every drop of her pleasure from her body, and when her legs finally relaxed around my shoulders, I pulled back and looked up at her.

She stared at me as I pulled my fingers from her soaking-wet pussy and slid them into my mouth. I groaned even though I had just been tasting her, and her cheeks reddened as she watched me.

"You are so addicting." My voice was rough, giving away my own lack of restraint, but my words only made her blush deepen.

My cock was hard and pulsing against my trousers as I stood, and her gaze fell as she stared straight ahead at it.

She reached forward, running her soft fingers over the length of me through my trousers, and I hissed at the feel of her.

"I want to taste you," she said softly, and it was almost enough to make me come right then and there.

I reached forward, wrapping my hand behind her neck, and I tugged her forward until my lips could meet hers. I kissed her roughly, and she tasted herself on my tongue. My hand was rough against her, but I was struggling to find my control.

She whimpered as I pulled away, but if we didn't leave this room now, we wouldn't be leaving.

"Later," I reassured her and lifted her in my arms as I carried her to the washroom. "Right now, we're needed elsewhere."

ADARA

Evren followed me down the hall as we headed toward the library, and I couldn't stop myself from giggling when his hand gently ran over my bottom.

"Be good." I pointed at his chest as I turned to face him. I walked backward as he grinned, and gods, I just wanted to go back to the room and get lost in him forever. "You were the one who said we needed to leave."

"Technically, I said we were needed." He ran his hand over his mouth, that same mouth that had just been all over my body. "But surely they can find someone else, right?"

I smiled as his dark gaze dropped to my breasts, which were encased in one of his shirts. "You are the crown prince. I think it would be pretty hard to replace you."

"Pretty hard?" He cocked a brow. "But not impossible?"

"I don't know," I teased, and the smile dropped from his face. "I haven't seen everything this kingdom has to offer."

He shot forward, reaching out for me, and the predatory look on his face made me squeal and run before he could get a hold of me. I stepped through the library doors just as he wrapped his arms around my waist and lifted me from the ground.

Three sets of eyes turned in our direction, and I let out another laugh as Evren buried his face in my neck.

I shot my elbow backward, trying to get him to stop, but he only tightened his hold on me. He blew a raspberry against my neck, and the snort that escaped my lips was far too unladylike.

"Do you two need another moment?" I heard Jorah's voice, but my feet still hadn't hit the floor.

I elbowed Evren again, and he finally set me back on the ground before lifting his face from my neck. But his hands were still pressed flat against my stomach, his hold on me strong and sure.

"Sorry." He pressed an almost unnoticeable kiss to the back of my head, and my stomach dipped. "Adara needed to be taught a quick lesson."

My elbow shot back once again, this time connecting with his stomach, and a laugh shot out of him as his hands loosened around me. I stepped out of his hold, pushing my wild hair back out of my face, and I zeroed in on Thalia's smiling face.

I headed in her direction immediately. "What's going on?"

Even through my happiness, there was a tendril of fear that crept through me. I tried my hardest to block out memories of

Gavril, of the fae kingdom, and when it was Evren and me alone, it was easy to do so.

But then reality would come crashing back in.

"Where's everyone else?" Only Thalia, Sorin, and Jorah sat around the library with a few candles lit and a small fire roaring in the hearth.

"Asleep, I assume." Thalia smiled up at me before holding up a deck of cards in her hands. "We're having game night."

A laugh bubbled up my throat as I looked from Thalia back to Evren. He walked up behind me, once again wrapping me in his arms, and that fear from a moment before dissipated.

"You made us get out of bed to come play a game?" Evren grumbled behind me.

"Not just any game." Sorin lifted a large bottle of wine in each hand. "We're playing drinking games."

"For gods' sake," Evren cursed under his breath, but I couldn't stop smiling.

"Are we on teams?" I pulled out the chair next to Sorin, and Evren finally released his hold on me long enough for me to sit. He helped me into my chair, pushing me up to the table once I was settled, then pulled the chair next to me as close as he could get it to me. "Are you trying to cheat?"

He wrapped his arms over the back of my chair as he settled back in his own, and he looked so relaxed. So content. "How am I supposed to cheat if we're on teams?"

"Because I'd pick Thalia as my partner." I looked across the table, and my friend was grinning like a fool.

Evren softly pinched my side, and I squirmed and shot a look back in his direction.

"What? We already beat you and Sorin once before."

"This is true." Thalia laughed as she began shuffling the cards. "You can't break up a winning team like that."

"No teams." Sorin popped the cork on one of the bottles of wine before setting five glass mugs on the table.

"Every man for themselves." Jorah leaned back in his chair as he smiled up at Thalia. I didn't think I had ever seen him look so relaxed. "But watch out for Thalia. She really is a bit of a cheat."

She scoffed and smacked at his chest. "I am not!"

Jorah caught her hand against him and lifted it to place a soft kiss against her knuckles. "Of course not. How dare I accuse you of such a thing." He winked at me dramatically, and I couldn't stop myself from laughing.

But when I looked back at Sorin, at the wine he was pouring, his gaze was burning into Jorah's hand on Thalia's. I knocked my knee against his under the table, and he blinked as if he hadn't even realized he had been doing it.

He lifted his hand, and with a small flick of his fingers, the mug slid in front of me, so full that a little sloshed over the edge before he used his magic to push one in front of Thalia. I had never seen him use his magic before, but I was too distracted by the look that ghosted over his face to ask him about it.

This man, who was always so full of himself, so full of nonsense, looked so unsure, and when I looked up at my friend, that same look passed over her gaze as she looked at him before quickly glancing away.

"What are the rules?" I asked my question to cut the tension, but I wasn't sure that anyone felt it besides me. But gods, it felt as if it might snap between my two friends at any moment.

Jorah launched into the rules, a simple game of cards, as Thalia dealt.

"And whoever loses has to drink from the bottle."

"Of wine?" I laughed as I lifted the mug to my mouth and took a sip. I sighed around the sweet fruity flavor and decided then that losing at this game wouldn't be so bad.

"Nope." Sorin popped the word before pulling another bottle of alcohol from his side. "Of this."

The bottle was filled with a dark brown liquor that I imagined burned when going down, and I wrinkled my nose.

"Just don't lose," Evren said from beside me as he leaned forward in his chair and collected his cards. He arranged them in his deft dark fingers, and I watched his face morph into one of concentration as he studied the cards before him.

"That's a very good strategy, prince. Thank you." I lifted my own cards as Sorin laughed at my words.

One of Evren's hands came down against my thigh, and he trailed his fingers along the seam of my trousers before squeezing my knee.

"It works for me." He shrugged. "I always beat the hell out of these three."

"Oh, here we go." Jorah rolled his eyes as Thalia narrowed hers.

"As record would have it, I stand the reigning champion in cards and the co-reigning champion in silvers. I wouldn't get too arrogant there, Evren." She arched a brow at him, and the smile that lit up his face was enough to take my breath away.

I lifted my cards in my hands, but from what I could tell, I didn't have anything good. I had only seen the men in my village play cards a few times, but I had never known the rules. What I had understood of the game came from eavesdropping.

But I had seen the way they fooled each other into believing that they held a better hand than they did. And that I could do.

"You haven't held that record for long." Evren moved his cards around in his hand. "But let's not forget who won the last ten games before that."

"That's ancient history." Thalia rolled her eyes before turning to Sorin. "How many?"

"Two." He slid two cards face down in her direction, and she dealt him two more.

"Adara?"

I looked through my cards and pulled the two lowest numbers. I pressed them face down on the table just as Sorin had before me.

"Would you like me to help you until you get the hang of it?" Evren moved toward me, making to look at my cards, and I hurriedly pressed the remaining three against my chest.

"Shoo." I grabbed the two cards from the table that Thalia had just dealt me and placed them with the others against me. "You're not going to cheat off me."

Everyone laughed, but Evren narrowed his eyes in my direction as he ran his hand along the back of my neck. He gripped me there, just enough pressure to make me want more, and he pulled me toward him until my lips met his.

"I don't cheat," he said against my lips, and Sorin snorted a laugh.

"Yeah, sure." Sorin's voice dripped with sarcasm. "Adara, don't let him fool you with his charms."

Evren's lips formed into a smile against my mouth, and I found myself leaning into him, more interested in his kiss than anything that was happening at this table. "Is that what you're doing?" I asked as I blinked up at him.

Evren's hand tightened on my neck, a bite of pain that did nothing but promise pleasure before he slowly pulled away.

"I need three, Thalia." He placed his cards on the table, and Thalia quickly dealt three more in his direction.

She turned her gaze to Jorah, and he shook his head, not even looking at his cards. I narrowed my eyes on him, trying to read his expression, but he simply smiled at me.

"I'm taking two." Thalia dropped her own cards to the table before grabbing more.

Sorin laid his cards on the table, and I snorted when I realized that his hand looked worse than mine. He narrowed his gaze on me, but I quickly dropped my cards beside his.

He knocked into my shoulder with a grin. "I hope you're ready to drink."

"I hope you all are." Evren dropped his cards on the table, and even though I didn't really know what his cards meant, Thalia cursed under her breath.

"I fold." She threw her cards face down on the table.

Evren leaned back in his chair and pressed his hands to the back of his head as he stared over at Jorah, waiting for him to show his hand.

Evren was so handsome, his body relaxed and his face filled with nothing but amused confidence. His eyes locked on mine, capturing my gaze, and I found myself unable to look away. My eyes drowned in the softness of his, my heart hammering in my chest at how good this felt, but even here with our friends, there was a coil of worry deep in my gut for what was to come.

For what Gavril would be willing to take from me. Especially after what I had taken from him.

I dropped my gaze from Evren's and stared down at my hands. They were clean, not a trace on them, but they felt as if they were still coated in Queen Kaida's thick, sticky blood.

Evren must have noticed because he ran his fingers over my knuckles softly before grasping my fingers in his hand and slowly bringing them to his mouth. He pressed a kiss along them as he peered at me. I tried to focus on that look, on this feeling of being whole in his presence.

He lowered his eyes from mine, and I turned my attention to the table, only to see that he had lost.

A slow smile spread across Jorah's lips as he pressed his cards to the table, and Thalia laughed at the sour look on Evren's face.

"Drink up." Jorah laughed as Sorin pulled the heavy cork from the bottle of liquor. He took a long drink of the liquid before pushing the bottle in my direction.

I grabbed it and brought it to my nose. My nose wrinkled, and I pulled my hand away quickly as Sorin laughed.

"That's rule number one." He held up one finger in my direction. "Never smell your drink. It always makes it worse."

"For once, I actually agree with Sorin on this." Thalia laughed. "But it's still pretty bad on its own."

Sorin grinned at her before looking back at me. "Get on with it."

Evren wrapped an arm around the back of my chair as he spoke. "It's not as bad as Thalia makes it sound. Just take it down in one go."

"You're not giving me much confidence here." I swirled the liquid before I lifted the bottle and pressed it to my lips. The deep woodsy taste of the spirit hit my tongue instantly, but it was the strong burn in my throat that had me coughing as I wiped the liquid away from my lips. "That's horrible."

Evren took the bottle from my hand and swallowed down the drink as unbothered as Sorin had been, and I reached for my wine to chase away the taste.

My head swam with the feeling of the spirits, but it was the way Evren laughed at my side that made me feel lightheaded.

"Come here." He passed the bottle to Thalia before he took my arm in his hand and pulled me until I was sitting in his lap. He moved me until my back was pressed against his chest, and he settled back into his seat until we were both relaxed.

His hand trailed up my arm before he laced his fingers in my hair and played with it mindlessly.

And made me squirm against him.

Sorin dealt the next hand, and I did my best to keep my cards hidden from Evren. But it was no use. He won that hand and the next, and by the time a few more hands were dealt, I was playing worse and giggling from the way the liquor was making me feel.

"I think Adara might have had enough." Evren grinned up at me as I took another sip of my wine, and I turned in his lap until my legs lay across him and hung over the arm of the chair.

"I think she has not." I lifted my glass and took another drink.

"Agreed." Thalia laughed and gave me a lopsided grin before she lifted her glass in my direction. A bit sloshed over the side, but she didn't seem to notice. "We're just getting started."

"When did Thalia become such a lightweight?" Sorin grumbled, but when he looked at her, his gaze softened. He rested his head on the back of his chair, and he stared over at her with hooded eyes and a soft smile on his lips.

Even with the dizzying effects of the liquor, it was easy to see that the way he looked at her was much more than Thalia tried to make it out to be.

"You're so adorable, Sorin." I sighed, and Evren stiffened beneath me.

"Excuse me?" Evren asked, and his hand wrapped around my hip.

"Look at him." I waved my hand in his direction, and a bit of wine sloshed out of my cup and into Evren's lap. "Oops." I giggled and wiped at the wet spot, even though it didn't do any good.

"He is handsome." Thalia laughed, and I looked up at her.

"Yes! See?" I pointed toward my friend. "And the way he looks at you." I bit down on my knuckle playfully, causing Thalia to snort.

Sorin only grinned, and I knew the man loved the attention

he was getting. "If only she'd give me a chance, Adara." He pressed his hand over his heart, and Thalia rolled her eyes.

But there was such a light there. A playful look on her face that made the heaviness in my chest lighten even more.

"Don't let him fool you. He's had plenty of chances." Thalia took another sip of her wine, and Jorah leaned forward and collected the cards from the table.

There was a look on his face that I couldn't quite place. Not quite jealousy, but he looked uncomfortable with our conversation.

I cocked my head to the side as I studied him.

Evren tightened his hands around me, and I turned my head to look back at him.

He shook his head once, a warning for me to leave the thought alone, and I lifted my hand that was wrapped around his back and pushed my fingers into his hair. The strands were so soft, so silky between my fingers, and I dug my fingertips into his scalp.

He leaned his head back, closing his eyes against the feeling, and there was such a calmness to him. A contentment that made my chest ache.

It made me never want to leave his side ever again.

"I can't wait to marry you." I thought I whispered the words, but Evren's gaze popped open, and I heard Thalia giggle again from across the table.

Evren's fingers dug into my side, pulling me closer to him, and he grinned as his lips pressed against my cheek. "I think you might be drunk."

"Just a little." I sighed and tugged on his hair until he was forced to look back up at me. "But this has nothing to do with that." I searched his dark, heavy gaze, and gods, I was so in love with him.

My stomach tightened as he watched me. Here he was in my hands, and I still somehow felt like I couldn't get enough of him.

Even with my hands digging into his scalp and his body against mine, I couldn't stop thinking about how badly I had missed him. How I never wanted to miss him again.

"I want to marry you."

Evren's gaze darkened, and he lifted his hands until they were pressed against my cheeks. He pushed my hair out of my face, and his hands held me firmly yet like I was the most precious thing he'd ever touched.

"You have no idea how badly I want to make you my wife." His voice was quiet and rough, and my stomach tightened at the sound. "I think of it night and day. I want to claim you in every way this world will allow, and even then, it wouldn't be enough."

My wineglass pressed between us as he kissed me, the movement slow and deliberate, yet it felt like desperation.

"Oh shit!" I heard Thalia laugh hysterically from behind me, and I looked away from Evren long enough to see Sorin catch her just before she fell to the ground. "What did you put in that wine, Sorin?"

"Oh yes. Blame it on me." He rolled his eyes playfully before lifting her into his arms as if she weighed nothing. "It couldn't have anything to do with the ten pulls of liquor that you and Adara both took."

She waved her hand as if he was being foolish. "Semantics. But you brought the liquor too, so either way, it's your fault."

"Agreed!" I pointed to my friend, and she giggled. "Thalia is innocent."

"You do realize we just watched you both drink like fish, right?" Evren laughed beneath me, and I swatted at his chest.

"Pick a side, Evren, but I'm on Thalia's."

"Yes!" Thalia leaned her head back from where she was held in Sorin's arms. "We will have each other's back until the end. You can't break us."

"Exactly." I climbed from Evren's lap and moved toward my friend. I felt shaky on my feet, but I didn't let that stop me.

She grinned as I approached her, and she looked like a dead weight in Sorin's arms. "I love you," she said it so nonchalantly, so easily, but it stabbed into my chest and took hold.

I pressed my hand against my stomach as tears filled my eyes. "I love you."

I pushed forward and hugged her, and Sorin's deep grunt sounded around us. "I think it might be time to get these two to bed."

Thalia's hands just tightened around me and mine on her. "They are trying to kill our moment."

"They just can't handle us."

"Oh, I will handle you just fine." I squealed as Evren wrapped his arms around my middle and pulled me away from my friend.

Sorin laughed but looked down at Thalia as soon as she swatted at his chest.

"Good night, Thalia," Evren said as he cradled me against himself.

I dropped my head back as I looked at Thalia while upside-down. "I love you!"

"Good night!" She craned toward me, and Sorin looked like he might drop her.

We passed by Jorah, who held our used mugs in his hands and a solemn look on his face. "Good night, Jorah."

"Good night, Adara." He smiled softly, and I studied his face as Evren led us from the room.

I ran my hand over Evren's chest, tracing the buttons of his shirt. "Jorah seems sad."

"He's fine."

"Are you sure?" I peered up at him. "I think he might be a little bit in love with Thalia too. Not that I blame him."

Evren snorted out a small laugh. "I think he's been in love with Thalia for as long as I can remember, but that's for him to do with what he will. You're meddlesome when you're drunk."

"Who said I was drunk?"

"The way you're looking up at me with one eye closed is a good indicator." He laughed and shifted me in his arms as he opened the bedroom door.

"I just love your friends." I sighed and pressed my head against his chest. "They make me feel like I'm home."

Evren's body went tight beneath me before he laid me down gently against the bed.

"They are your friends too, and this is your home." He kissed my forehead, and I smiled. "I am your home." He pulled the blanket up over my body before kissing me again. "You need to get some sleep."

He turned from me, heading in the direction of the washroom, and I caught his hand in my own.

"You can't be serious right now."

"I'm sorry?" He looked back down at me with a laugh.

"I'm not going to sleep." I climbed on the bed until I was sitting up on my knees. "You promised that we would continue what we started later. It's later."

His gaze darkened as he stared down at my lips. "And you're drunk."

I shrugged, and his lips twitched with amusement. "I want you."

His hand reached out, cupping my cheek and rubbing his thumb along my bottom lip. "There hasn't been a moment since I met you that I didn't want you, princess." His finger pressed harder against my lips. "You are everything I have ever wanted."

"I want to taste you." I clung to the lapels of his shirt and pulled him closer to me until my chest pressed against his. "I want to make you feel as crazy with need as you do me."

"It doesn't take your mouth for that, princess." He pressed his thumb against the opening of my mouth, and he slowly slid it inside. I widened for him, enjoying the fullness of his touch, and my eyes closed as I silently begged for more. "But I think of your perfect mouth wrapped around my cock often, stretched out before me, begging me with these beautiful fucking eyes."

He pushed in farther until his thumb reached the back of my throat, and I hollowed my cheeks around him, sucking him into me.

"Fuck." He let out a long sigh, his eyes never leaving my face. With a gentle, deliberate motion, he pulled out of my mouth. His hand left an imprint of warmth on my chin as he wiped away the trace of saliva.

I moved off the bed before he could stop me, and I slid to my knees before him. My head still swam, but it no longer had anything to do with the liquor and had everything to do with the man standing before me.

I slowly ran my trembling fingers along the front of his trousers, my heart a flurry of anticipation, and I could feel how hard he was beneath the fabric. His warm, calloused fingers slid beneath my chin and traced along my jawline, and I shivered with pleasure as he laced them through my hair.

I looked up at him as I slipped my fingers against the button of his trousers and carefully undid them. I pulled them down slowly, my fingers shaking and fumbling, but he didn't rush me. He simply ran his thumb back and forth in my hair, comforting me, spurring me on.

His cock fell out in front of me, and I licked at my lips as I wrapped my fingers around the thick length of him.

"Fuck, you're beautiful."

I swallowed against his words, and my hand tightened around him. He groaned low and heavy, and I couldn't wait another moment before tasting him.

I slowly lowered my head, and I stared up at him as he watched me. I slid my tongue against the head of him, causing him to hiss, before I opened my mouth and sucked him into my mouth, my tongue running along the underside.

I didn't stop until my lips hit my fist, which still gripped him around the base of his cock.

"Princess," he growled, and I moaned at the feel of him on my tongue.

I pulled back as my tongue lapped at him, covering every inch of him with my saliva. I pressed my thumb against the underside, and he hissed until his hand tightened in my hair with the most delicious kind of pain.

"You're making me lose every bit of control I hold, princess." His other hand moved to my face, his thumb rolling over my bottom lip just below his cock.

I shivered, my skin flushed and warm, as I took him back in my mouth. I took him as far as I could get him, and I gagged slightly when he hit the back of my throat.

Then I watched as he lost that control he had just been talking about. His hands tightened on me as he jerked against the back of my throat; then he slowly slid out as I watched him.

I wasn't prepared for his next move, but moisture pooled between my legs as he slammed back inside and started fucking my mouth. I flattened my tongue and pressed both of my hands into his bare thighs as I held on to him.

My nails dug into his flesh, and he cursed as he thrust into me again.

"So fucking good." His words were slightly muffled, but they fueled me as I hollowed my cheeks and sucked him harder.

I closed my eyes and focused on the way it felt to have him in my mouth.

"Touch yourself, Adara," he demanded, and I glanced back up

at him. "Bury your hand in your pussy and show me how much this turns you on."

I whimpered against him and did what he said. I let my hand fall away from his thigh and slid it into my trousers as he had demanded. I tensed against him as my fingers met my sex and found the waiting moisture there.

I was so wet, so desperate for anything he would give me, and my other hand dug into him as I ran my fingers over my clit.

My hips jerked forward, and he pushed into the back of my throat. I couldn't stop the deep moan that I let out, but the sound was muffled by him inside me.

I rubbed over my clit harshly, following the pace of his cock thrusting into my mouth, and it had only been a few moments, but already I felt myself falling apart.

"Come for me, princess." He pulled out of my mouth and ran his cock over my swollen lips only long enough for me to catch my breath. "I want to watch you come while my cock is buried deep in your throat."

He thrust back inside me, and I clamped my eyes closed as I chased the feeling I desperately craved. Even though it was my fingers working me, Evren controlled my pleasure.

He fueled my need.

I couldn't help the small choked moans that fell from me as he picked up his pace. I tried to suck him into me, tried to keep up, but he was fucking me with a desperation that overwhelmed me.

My fingers moved harder as I watched him, and when his hand lowered to my neck and pressed firmly against it, I couldn't hold myself back any longer.

I cried out around him as pleasure coursed through me. He held me up, his hands still buried in my hair and on my throat. His movements slowed, but they were no less harsh, no less desperate.

He fucked my mouth hard as I caught my breath, and only then did he slam into the back of my throat as his seed spilled into my mouth. I swallowed it down quickly, eagerly, and his roar of pleasure erupted around us.

He slowly pulled out of my mouth, and his thumb pressed against my lips, collecting the moisture there.

"You are so perfect." His voice was rough and laced with his pleasure.

He reached down, pulling my hand from my trousers, and he bent, sucking my fingers into his mouth. His gaze met mine, and he didn't look away from me as he licked the evidence of my pleasure away from my fingers.

"That belongs to me." He finally dropped my hand before helping me to my feet. He pressed his lips against mine as soon as I stood before him, and my legs shook beneath me. "Now it's time for some sleep."

SORIN

I pushed through Thalia's bedroom door as she laughed. I had no idea what she was still laughing about, but I couldn't help smiling as I looked down at her. Her nose scrunched as she smiled, and she was breathtaking.

I almost tripped over her shoes as I made my way to her bed, and that only made her laugh harder.

"Don't drop me!"

I set her down, her body bouncing softly against her mattress and her curls framing her face.

She leaned back against her pillow, and I reached forward and tugged her boot from her foot before quickly grabbing the other. "How many nights have I had to carry you home after a night of too much drinking? I've never dropped you once."

"There's always a first time." She sighed and lifted her hips as I reached for her trousers. I tugged them down her legs, revealing her beautiful thighs, and bit down on my lip to stop myself from groaning at the sight of her.

I was used to this torture.

I had been Thalia's friend for more years than I could remember, and I had craved her just as long. I had become a professional at keeping those thoughts to myself.

I loved to tease her, but that was as far as it ever went.

I could feel my heart pounding in my chest as I looked down at her. My desire for her grew with every second that I was in her presence, and I needed to leave her room.

I reached for her blanket and gently laid it over her body before pushing her hair out of her face.

"Good night, Thalia," I said softly before straightening.

"Stay with me." She looked up at me, her eyes pleading.

"That's not a good idea." I shook my head even as my cock jerked in my trousers.

She frowned, and a pout formed on her full, perfect lips. "Why not?"

"You know why," I said, my voice tight.

But she didn't respond. She simply grabbed my hand in hers and tugged me toward her. "Please stay."

Her gaze softened, begging me, and I couldn't deny her. I kicked my boots from my feet before I climbed into the bed beside her and lay on top of the covers.

She giggled as she curled up against me, her head finding a spot on my chest.

The heat of her body radiated through me, and the scent of her overwhelmed me. It was my favorite smell in the world, vanilla mixed with something that was uniquely her. It reminded me of home.

I gently stroked my hand down her back, and she shifted, her body melting into me.

She looked up at me, her eyes heavy with longing, and I knew I wouldn't be able to resist her.

"I really should leave."

"I want you to stay," she purred, her voice thick with her want.

"You're drunk," I reminded her and myself of that fact.

"How long have we known each other?" She cocked her brow as she leaned forward and ran her fingers over the seam of my lips. "It doesn't matter how much I've had to drink. I still know what I want."

"Thalia." I groaned and ran my hand down my face, and I could feel her retreating from me.

"Fine." She pushed off me and leaned against her pillow. "Leave."

I watched her for a long moment, but she refused to meet my gaze in the dark room. Moonlight filtered in through her window, illuminating her enough that the sight of her drove me crazy, and I huffed as I stood from her bed.

"Sorin." She said my name on a moan, and when I looked back down at her, she had her eyes clamped shut and her lips parted.

Then I saw her hand as it began to move beneath the blanket.

"What are you doing?" I growled, and her other hand reached up, cupping her breast. I could feel my arousal increasing with each passing second as I watched her silently touching herself.

Her breath rushed out of her as she mewled, then she opened her eyes to look up at me. "You said you were leaving." She looked to the door before her gaze fell back on me. "But that doesn't stop me from wanting you. If you don't want to touch me…"

I shot forward and clamped her wrist in my hand as I leaned over her. She moaned softly, and I ran my nose along her jaw. "You think I don't want to touch you?" I moved her hand away from her breast and replaced it with my own. My hand was rough and greedy, and I pinched her hard nipple between my fingers as my cock strained painfully against my trousers. "You think I don't dream of all the things I would do to your perfect fucking body, Thalia?"

She gasped, pushing her head back into the pillow, and I pressed my lips against her exposed neck.

I lapped at her skin with my tongue before I moved to her mouth and pressed my lips against hers. I kissed her softly at first, hesitantly, but when she opened her lips, moaning into my mouth, I lost every bit of my control.

I deepened the kiss, my tongue chasing hers, my teeth nipping at her lips, and she moaned as my hand left her breast and moved down her body.

Her hand was still pressed between her thighs, still rubbing small circles against herself, and I wrapped my hand around her wrist before I lifted it between us and sucked her fingers between my lips.

I groaned at the taste of her and burned it into my memory. I had imagined what she would taste like a million times over, but my imagination had done her a disservice.

I pulled her fingers from my mouth before dropping her wrist, and she watched me as I lowered my hand between us and slid my fingers through her wetness.

She was soaked. I slid my fingers into her undergarments and over her clit. I lowered them until they met her entrance. I stared into her eyes, waiting for her to tell me to stop, but there was no hesitation there.

"Are you sure?"

She nodded eagerly as she bit down on her lip, and I sank two fingers into her pussy as I watched her eyes flutter closed.

"Sorin," she moaned as I moved my fingers in and out of her.

It was enough to bring me to my knees.

I curled my fingers inside her as I lowered myself down her body and breathed her in. I pulled my fingers from her body, and she whimpered at the loss.

I wrapped my fingers around her undergarments, tugging them down her legs before I used my hands to press on the inside of both of her thighs until she was open before me.

She gasped as I lowered my head and kissed her softly on her pussy. I felt her body quiver beneath me as I ran my tongue through her before centering my efforts on her small clit.

I flicked my tongue against her before sucking it into my mouth, and she pressed her hand against her mouth as she cried out in pleasure.

"This is how much I want you, Thalia. I have dreamed of

tasting you. I have fisted my cock and thought of nothing but you as I imagined how good it would be."

I sucked her harder into my mouth, and her thighs clamped down around my head as her hands tangled in my hair.

I looked up at her and met her dark gaze as she watched me. "It didn't compare." I slid my fingers back inside her, and her pussy clamped down around me as another shudder coursed through her.

Thalia's grip on my hair tightened as I curled my fingers inside her. I flicked my tongue against her clit over and over as she moaned and moved her hips against my face.

Her pleasure was consuming her, driven by the ecstasy on her face, and she called out my name again as her hips finally slowed, and I pressed a soft kiss to her sex.

She tugged on my hair, lifting my head until my gaze met hers. "I want to fuck you," she said softly, and I almost came right then and there.

I groaned as I moved my hands under her thighs and lifted her up. She wrapped her legs around me, clinging to my chest as I stood.

She grasped my face between her hands, and for a moment, we just looked at each other, the intensity and desire emanating from both of us before she leaned down and pressed her lips against mine.

My chest heaved with need as I shifted her weight in my arms until I set her against the bed on her knees. She nipped at my bottom lip before pressing a kiss against it one last time and letting out a breathy laugh as she released me.

I stepped back, pulling off my shirt while Thalia kneeled on the bed in front of me. She moved until she was on all fours before me, an inviting look passing over her face as she met my gaze again.

The hunger that had taken me over was palpable, and I couldn't help but kneel on the bed behind her.

I freed my cock from my trousers before I pressed my length against her. I ran it back and forth through her sex, through her moisture, and she mewled as she leaned back into me, rocking against me, her body begging me to give her something I had craved for years.

I pressed into her slowly, inch by inch, until I was fully seated inside her tight core. She moaned loudly as I rocked my hips against her and began to move as her body responded to me.

My fingers dug into her bottom as sweat formed on my skin. I pushed into her over and over as she tightened around me. I ran my hand up her spine until I reached her neck, and my body thrummed with my lack of control.

I leaned down, pressing my lips to the small of her back, before I wrapped a hand around her body and lifted her into me.

Her back pressed against my chest, and I continued to roll my hips, to thrust into her as she cried out.

I tugged on the shirt that covered her body, lifted it up and over her head until she was completely bare in front of me, and I felt like I couldn't breathe.

I brought my left hand around her body, pressing my fingers firmly against her clit, and I continued to push inside her, but it was my lips, which moved along her arm, that caught her attention.

I kissed along her skin, along the many scars that Gavril had given her, and I felt her tremble beneath my movements.

"You are so beautiful," I groaned as my pleasure spiked inside me. I was so close to coming, but I didn't want this to end.

I never wanted to stop touching her.

"Sorin, please," Thalia begged, and I thrust into her hard as I pressed my fingers more firmly against her pussy. Her body tensed, and I couldn't hold back a second longer.

I groaned loudly against her back as I came inside her, and she cried out as her body shook and moved against me. Together we flew over the cliff into a pleasure we had craved from each other for years, and we clung to each other as our breathing calmed.

I pulled out of her gently before I lay against her bed and pulled her down with me. She smiled as I tucked her head back against my chest, and her fingers trailed over my stomach.

They slowed until they were a ghost of a touch, and even as my mind raced with a million thoughts about what we had just done, I felt her calm against me.

"Good night, Sorin." She looked up at me before leaning forward and pressing a gentle kiss to my lips.

"Good night, love." ☾

EVREN

"You mean to tell me that out of all these years you've lived, you've never seen the ocean?" Adara's father looked over at her, and she laughed.

"No." She shook her head. "Mom and I never left the village. I think she was too scared that the fae would come for me, and I wouldn't be there."

The muscles in his jaw tensed, and his mouth tightened into a thin line. His hands clenched into fists, and his eyes flashed with pain as he opened them wide, but Adara kept talking as if nothing was wrong, her voice unwavering and light.

"I used to pretend like I was a siren, though." She laughed at herself, at her memories, and I collected them inside myself with a desperation to know every part of her. "I would swim in the small creek just outside town, and I would braid little flowers into my hair."

She smiled, and my chest burned.

"When any of the boys in town were cruel to me, I would pretend like I had a siren's song and could lure them to their death if I so choose."

"The boys were mean to you?" I leaned forward in my chair, and she rolled her beautiful eyes.

"Calm down. It was a long time ago, and I didn't know you then."

Yet I had been waiting my entire lifetime for you.

"I even managed to convince a couple of them that a siren song was a part of all this." She waved her hand toward her face, toward her star marks. "They were scared of what I was capable of and didn't mess with me after that."

"Good," her father grumbled as he leaned near the fireplace. "Serves them right."

The man was still frail, a type of feebleness that only came from years of not taking care of himself, or in his case years of abuse.

His shoulders carried too much weight, and the light in his eyes had almost gone out, like a candle with a dying flame. But he was slowly coming back to life. You could see it in the way he smiled at Adara, in the way his cheeks were just a bit less hollow than they had been the day before.

I had been the one responsible for handing this man over to Queen Kaida, but even I hadn't known what she had done to him. I believed the man to be dead days after he arrived in the fae kingdom.

The fact that she had been able to keep him a secret, that she had been able to keep Gavril's mate a secret, was alarming. And it made me question so many other things I thought I knew.

They claimed I had been the traitor in their kingdom, but they were just as treasonous as I was.

More so.

"Adara." As soon as I spoke her name, she turned to me, and the smile that still rested on her face took my breath away. This woman was my mate, and she was soon to be my wife.

And I didn't deserve either.

"Yes?"

"Do you care to go grab Thalia for me? She was supposed to meet me over an hour ago, and we both know her hungover ass will be much nicer if you're the one to wake her."

She wrinkled her nose as she laughed and stood from her chair. "This is true." She moved toward her father, and there was such a hesitation in her movements. She was still so unsure around him, scared to make the wrong move.

But she wrapped her arms around his frail frame for a small hug before moving to me. She leaned down, dropping a kiss against my lips, and if her father hadn't been in the room, I would have deepened it. I would have demanded more from her than I ever should have.

And she would have given it to me.

She pulled away from me, smiling as she walked away, and

I waited until she had stepped outside the door before I turned back to her father.

He watched me carefully, and I didn't know if he simply didn't trust me or if he didn't trust anyone.

"Sir." I stood from my chair and moved closer to him. He still stood by the fire, and my hands were soaked in sweat from my nerves and the heat. "I know we haven't had a lot of time to talk since you arrived here, but I wanted to talk to you now. To ask you something."

He nodded his head, encouraging me to go on.

"I love your daughter." I stated the fact, the one I hoped he could already see.

He crossed his arms, but he didn't argue against what I had just said, so I continued.

"I plan to keep her here in the Blood kingdom if this is where she wants to be, and I would like for you to stay as well. She loves you, and I never wish for her to be parted from you again."

There was a bit of shock in his eyes, but he quickly recovered. "Are you asking me to stay?" He laughed softly, and I felt a bit foolish.

"What I'm trying to ask you…" I rubbed my hand down the back of my neck. Why was I so nervous? I knew Adara's answer without asking her father's permission, but for some damn reason, I wanted it. I craved it. "Is for your blessing in marrying your daughter."

Her father stared at me for a long moment, and with every passing second, my chest tightened.

"I understand why you wouldn't give it to me." I ran my hand through the back of my hair, but he cut me off.

"I didn't say I wouldn't give it to you." He shook his head softly before his gaze met mine again. "I know that my daughter loves you. Hell, I hardly know her, and even I can see that clearly."

"And I hope that you can see how much I love her."

"I can." He shifted on his feet. "But I also see your world. I see what you're surrounded by, and I need to know that she's going to be safe. All I have ever wanted is for her to be kept safe. Even though I failed at doing so."

"I want that too." I nodded and couldn't get the knot in my stomach to stop tightening. "I want to promise you that I will always keep her safe and happy, but I think she would hate me for that." I laughed softly. "Your daughter is so strong, and even when I can't protect her, I know that she can protect herself. But I will do everything in my power to make sure she keeps a smile on her face. I will do my best to make sure she wants for nothing, and I will love her with everything I have until I'm taken from this world and even then. I would give up everything to do so."

He nodded his head, but I had no idea if he believed my words, if he could see how serious I was.

"I know it was my hand that led you to a life you've been forced to live, my hand that took you from her, and I can't explain to you how badly that fact has haunted me. I didn't know what they were capable of then, but I still did it. I am still responsible." My chest tightened to the point I almost couldn't breathe as I thought of what I took from her, from him. "I will never forgive myself for what I took from her. It will haunt me for the rest of my days, but I didn't know that the queen still had you or Gavril's mate. I had no idea." I shook my head and let out a shaky breath. "I don't know what I would have done if I did, but I'm not the same man that I was then. I have always known that your daughter would be the one to change our world, but I didn't realize how much. I didn't know then how she would change me."

"You have my blessing." He searched my gaze, and relief flooded me. "Although I don't think you need it." He laughed, his voice deep and rough. "Adara doesn't seem like the kind of girl who needs anyone's permission to do what she wants."

"She isn't." I laughed alongside him. "But I'm still honored to have it. I can't tell you how much." I bowed my head in his direction, showing this man who had been my father's prisoner the respect he deserved.

"Sir." The sound of one of my guard's voices had her father and me both looking in his direction as he pushed through the door. "You need to come."

I looked back to her father before storming from the room and in the direction the guard had just walked in. I followed him to the main entrance of the castle, and I searched the halls as we passed them, my body tight with the need to find Adara to make sure she was safe.

But I stopped short as soon as I hit the entryway and saw Sorin covered in blood. He was carrying someone in his hands, but I couldn't see who it was as I moved toward him.

"What's going on?" I demanded, and Sorin looked up at me with a solemn, heavy gaze.

He laid the body on the ground before me, and I stopped short when I noted the blood caked on the side of Adara's mother's face. I would never forget the face of the woman I watched hand over her daughter so willingly. Her eyes were closed, and I couldn't tell if she was breathing.

But it was the parchment that was staked into her stomach that drew me to a stop.

A mother for a mother.

"Is she?"

"Dead." Sorin nodded and lifted his hands. They were covered in her blood, along with his shirt, and dread and rage filled me.

I turned to look behind myself at the sound of approaching footsteps, but it was Adara's father who now stood there, staring at the body of the woman he once married.

"Where was she?" I asked Sorin, and my muscles tensed as he answered. I could feel my jaw clench and my fists tighten as the heat of my anger filled me.

"On the front steps of the palace." He slowly met my gaze, and my entire body tensed. "Whoever brought her here did so without any of us noticing, without being caught."

"Where's Adara?" I turned on my heel, storming toward the hall to Thalia's room, but stopped short when I heard her laughter.

"We're coming. Thalia tried to hit me at least three times, but I finally forced her out of bed." She stopped short when she saw my face. "What's wrong?"

"Don't come in here." I held up my hands, and she craned her neck to look past me.

I wouldn't lie to her about what my brother had done, but she didn't need to see. She didn't need any more nightmares to haunt her dreams.

"What happened?"

"Someone from the fae kingdom was here." I said the words softly, but both she and Thalia froze. Thalia's hands shifted to the dagger at her side, and black smoke dripped from Adara's fingers.

"Was it Gavril?"

"I don't know." I shook my head and steeled my spine for what I was about to tell her. "But they left your mother." I looked at her. I stared into her eyes as I told her the horrible truth. "She's dead."

She didn't say anything for a long moment. She just stared at me, her gaze searching mine, and I wished I held the answers she was searching for. I wanted to protect her, to shield her from this pain, but I couldn't do so.

She shook her head back and forth as her hands trembled at her sides, and she walked toward me until she was passing by me completely.

I reached out for her, taking her hand in mine. "Princess."

"Don't stop me," she pleaded, her voice quivering and tears shimmering in her eyes.

I didn't drop her hand. I tightened my hold on her as I turned to face the way I had just come. I lifted her hand to my mouth as we started walking together, and I pressed my lips against her knuckles.

Her gaze roamed over those standing around the entryway, and I noted my own mother, the queen, standing there with her hand covering her mouth.

The smell of earth, death, and sweat bombarded us. The smell of blood and magic.

Adara pushed through the few people blocking us from getting to her mother's body, and my chest hit her back when she stopped completely. She stared down at her mother, at what was left of her in this world, and she was so still that I worried she had quit breathing.

"He did that to her?" Her voice was weak and pleading, and I hated that I couldn't take this away.

I moved closer to her, forcing every inch of space out from between us, and her body trembled against me.

"This was him."

Her eyes skated over every inch of her mother, and I knew the moment she saw the note Gavril had left for her. Because there was no mistaking his intentions. He did this to hurt her, but he also did it to haunt her. To make her face the things she had done to his mother and pay for those sins.

But she had already paid more than enough. And I was tired of watching her sacrifice.

If I wasn't already prepared to kill my brother, then the look on my Adara's face now would have sealed his fate. I didn't care what kind of magic he possessed. I would kill him and my father.

"Oh my gods." Adara stumbled backward, but I was already there. Already holding her and trying to give her the only support I had to offer.

She turned into me, digging her fingers into my chest, and she let out a harsh, ragged breath against my neck. I wrapped my arms around her, pressing her into my body as tightly as I could get her, and I breathed her in as I stared at the people around us.

"Sorin." I simply said his name, but he was already nodding.

"I've got it." He met my gaze, and I could see the truth lying there. "Go take care of her."

I tightened my arms around her and lifted her into me, and she didn't stop me. She only clung to me harder as I pulled her away from the space, away from the horror, and my gaze met her father's.

He too looked haunted by what he had just seen, but there was so much concern there. Concern for his daughter, who he had lost so much time with.

I left him there, along with everyone else, and I moved us until the sounds of their voices were drowned out behind us. Adara didn't say a word as we left them, but I heard the way she tried to stop herself from crying, the way she tried to hold it together.

And it made me feel helpless.

I pushed through our bedroom door and kicked it closed behind me. I wanted to burn the memory of the way her mother looked from my brain, but I knew that she never would. This would be something that would stay with her forever.

And I would never let her carry that burden alone. I would carry it for her if I could.

I climbed into the bed, still holding her against me, and only when I leaned back against the headboard did she allow the first sob to rack through her.

She grasped my shirt as if it was the only thing keeping her in this world, her nails digging into my chest underneath as she buried her face against me.

I ran my fingers over her hair and down her cheek, trying to reassure both of us that she was okay. Tears poured down her face, and her breath hitched in her lungs, the oxygen intoxicated by her emotion.

"I've got you, princess." My hands tightened around her, and she buried her face harder into my neck. I didn't know what else to say, if there was anything I could say that would take even an ounce of this pain away from her.

But I knew that I wouldn't leave her.

So I did the only thing I could. I held her and ran my hand slowly up and down her back until her sobs calmed and the tears stopped rolling so fiercely down her cheeks.

She had become so still I thought she had fallen asleep, but her hands tightened against my neck just before the words slipped from her lips.

"I feel..." She hesitated, and I continued to run my hand along her skin, encouraging her. "I feel so guilty." Her voice was hoarse from her tears, and she stumbled over her words.

My hand stalled against her back, and I pressed my palms into her upper arms until I could pull her away from me far enough that I could see her face. I needed her to see how serious I was when I spoke.

"There is nothing for you to feel guilty for. You didn't do this."

"But..." More tears seeped down her face. "But I did kill the queen, and he took my mother's life for it."

"The queen deserved her death, Adara. If it hadn't been by your hand, it would have been by my own. Her blood on your hands should bring no guilt."

She wiped at the tears on her face as she gently shook her head. "I haven't even thought of her."

"The queen?"

"My mother," she admitted quietly. "I have barely thought of her once since you arrived in my village to take me. I have hated her."

I wasn't surprised by her admission. From what I knew of her mother from her deal with my father and Queen Kaida, she was cruel in the worst of ways. She used Adara, raised her for slaughter for my family, and then she pretended to hold back tears as she so easily gave her away.

She knew what the king and queen had done to Adara's father, or at least what we all thought, but still, she gave her only daughter to those very people, and she was paid handsomely for it.

I had delivered many of the coins myself.

Her daughter was the Starblessed that was promised, and she lived her life bleeding every bit of those advantages dry.

When I first met Adara, I had that same vision of her in my mind, but I was wrong. She wanted no part in being the Starblessed. If she could have simply ripped those marks from her skin, I had no doubt she would have.

But her mother wouldn't have traded her blessing for anything.

"And you are not to feel guilty for that either." I pressed my hand against her chin, lifting her head until her remorseful gaze met mine. "You are still allowed to mourn her, Adara. You can be sad about the death of the woman who didn't treat you well. She was your mother, whether she was good at it or not. But you don't owe her anything. Not in life and not in death."

She blinked her eyes closed as another tear streaked down her cheek. I leaned forward and pressed my mouth there, letting my lips taste her sadness, and my hands tightened against her.

"When I was young, I was so confused about who I was supposed to love," I said softly.

"What?" She blinked up at me with confusion clouding her beautiful eyes.

"I loved my mother so much, but then she told me of the prophecy. I knew very early on that I was going to be a pawn in this game of kingdoms, and she made me hate my father. Before I even knew him, I hated the man."

She pressed her chin against my chest, relaxing into me as she watched me with rapt attention. It made my heart hammer in my chest because this wasn't something I talked about with anyone, but I wanted to share it with her.

I wanted to share everything with her.

"When my father came for me, I was prepared. I knew the day would come when he would rip me away from my mother, and I tried my hardest to hold on to that anger when he took me back to the fae kingdom. I was only ten years old." I adjusted myself in the bed, lying down until she rested on top of me completely.

I put one arm behind my head, resting it there while the other held on to her. The weight of her body brought such comfort to me. It bled into my skin, coaxing every memory out of me, and she sighed against my chest.

"What happened?" Her fingers ran over the base of my neck, slowly moving back and forth, and I stared up at the ceiling.

"When I got there, I expected this ruthless king that I had

been told of, but he was just my father. Here was the man I didn't know, who I had spent years missing out on, and even though I had been taught that he was the enemy, he was my father."

I felt her eyes glance up at me as I spoke.

"And for a long time, that was the only way I could see him. He slowly erased the things my mother had told me about him, and he made me question this kingdom, my kingdom. I was their pawn, but I no longer knew what team I played for."

"What changed?" She reached up, running her fingers over my jaw, and I caught her hand in mine, bringing it to my mouth. I pressed a kiss there, remembering what I had.

"He would tell me the worst things about my mother. He and Queen Kaida both would."

She shivered as I said the queen's name, but I kept going.

"It wasn't until I saw how cruel Queen Kaida was that I realized they had been trying to mold me into exactly what they wanted. I worked my way through the ranks of the guards just like my father wanted me to, and with every day of training, my head became clearer. By the time I made captain, I had become her personal soldier for her agenda."

I swallowed hard as I tried to block out the memories of everything she had made me do over the years, of all the men I had killed in her name.

"I had been doing her work for decades when you were born. When I took your father, when I saw him fight to the death to save his daughter, I knew that my mother had been right. Queen Kaida heard of your birth within days of your parents having you, and she watched you always. When your father refused to promise your hand to her son, the mask she held on to so easily crumbled, and I saw so clearly who she was for the first time."

"And your father?"

"He calls himself a king, but he's nothing more than another one of her puppets. He does exactly as he's told, and she's so manipulative that most of the time, he doesn't even see it happening." I lifted her hand to my face and pressed my lips once again to her palm. "But the blood you have on your hands, princess, it was justified. Mine?" I held them out in front of her. "Mine are stained with so many innocent lives. So many that should have never been taken. All because of her."

"I'm sorry, Evren." She settled in closer to me as if our bodies could mold together.

"Don't be." I cupped her face in my hand and stared down at her. "When you took the queen's life, you did it for you, for everything she had taken, but I can't tell you how breath rolled into my lungs at watching her fall. She had caused me so much pain in my lifetime, and it was at my mate's hands that she fell."

"She'll never hurt us again," she whispered and pressed her lips to my mouth softly.

"She'll never hurt anyone again, princess. And I will do everything in my power to make sure her son is to never hurt you again either."

Her eyes shuttered, and I hated that he still had so much control over her.

"I have failed you. I am still failing you, but I will spend the rest of my life trying not to fail you again."

"You didn't fail me." She shook her head, but she was wrong. She was so damn wrong.

"I have done nothing but fail you, princess. I failed you when I broke your trust. I failed you when I let you go with my brother, and I failed you again when I allowed him to get so close to you that he was able to lay your mother on our doorstep."

"Stop," she whispered and gripped me tighter. "Please, stop."

"I don't deserve you, princess, but I will also never let you go. I am not strong enough to let you go."

It was the truth. Even though I knew she was probably better off far away from me, I would never be strong enough to let that happen.

"I don't want you to." Her chest heaved, and I could see her trying to rein in her emotions. "There is no one else I want at my side. No one else I want."

"I have waited an entire lifetime for you." I pressed my lips against her forehead.

She tightened her hold on me, and I wrapped my arms fully around her until I could reassure myself that she was here. That she was safe.

We stayed like that for a long time, until her breathing evened out and her eyes fluttered closed. I continued to hold her while she slept and every bit of tension bled from her body.

She was mine, and I would protect her at all costs.

ADARA

It had been three days since Gavril had infiltrated our kingdom and discarded my mother's body on the steps of this palace. Three days that everyone had been on edge since someone had been able to get so close without anyone noticing.

Evren seemed to be bothered the most by that fact.

Whether it was Gavril himself or not, he was able to infiltrate our kingdom, our safety, and it stoked our fear.

Evren had barely let me out of his sight, not that I was complaining, but he took too much responsibility for the acts of others. If they were to come to our kingdom again, to bring this war to us, then we would have to be ready.

And as I had watched my father light the flame beneath

my mother's dead body, something steeled inside me that I would be.

The Blood kingdom had become my own. It was my home, the place my mother's ashes were now scattered, and the land I never wanted to leave again. It was on this land that I would marry Evren, and I would protect it no matter the cost.

I would protect its people. My people.

"The shop lady was very nosy, but this was the best I could find with Sorin watching my every movement." Thalia hung the dress on her closet door, and I moved off her bed to look at it.

The dress was so white it almost looked translucent, and it was covered in the smallest beads, which bled together to make it shimmer. "It's perfect."

I ran my fingers down the fabric and turned back to my friend. "And the creek?"

"It's already being worked on." She pushed her hair out of her face and smiled. "Are you sure you want to do this so suddenly? You haven't even told Evren."

I laughed and moved the fabric of the dress until it shifted in the light.

"I've never been more sure about anything." I let the dress fall and moved to the small desk, where I had been trying to tame my hair.

Thalia moved behind me, and she began pinning up the pieces of hair I had missed, and she smiled.

"You know that he asked your father for your hand, right?"

"What?" I spun around to face her, and she grinned wider as she nodded.

"And what did my father say?"

"Well, I hope that he gave him a bit of hell, but he gave him his blessing."

I scoffed, and she laughed, but a nervous joy took flight in my stomach. "Do you know where he is?"

"Your father?"

"Evren."

"He was in the throne room when I snuck back in. I'm sure Sorin is in there now telling him all about his spying trip."

I couldn't help but laugh at her as I stood. "He wasn't spying. He was protecting you."

"And I don't need his protection." She put her hands on her hips, and I rolled my eyes playfully.

"I can think of a few things you need from him, but from what I heard from Evren, you've already been getting it."

Thalia swatted at me, but I quickly moved out of her reach and headed toward the door.

I pulled the door open, and she followed behind me wordlessly as we made our way to the throne room. There were two guards who followed us from her room to the hall and two more who guarded the doors.

I walked past them all and pushed the throne room doors open until I could see inside. I let out a sigh of relief when I only spotted Evren and Sorin standing with their heads together and their words hushed.

"I hope the two of you aren't gossiping. You all have a bad habit of that."

Evren's gaze sought me out immediately, and I watched him swallow harshly as he looked upon me.

I was wearing nothing but the robe that Thalia let me borrow. The silky lilac material was buttery soft against my skin.

"Are you going somewhere, princess?" Evren cocked his head to the side as he studied me, and I could feel the heat in his gaze even from several feet away.

"Your wedding." I raised my chin as I crossed my arms. "You have two hours' time to get yourself ready."

There was shock in his eyes as he watched me, but his lips formed into a smirk that made my knees feel weak beneath me.

"My wedding?"

"That's what I said." I nodded, and he grinned harder. "I don't care what is still to come. I want you to be my husband before we face any of it."

His body went rigid for only a moment before his feet moved and carried him in front of me. He thrust his hand in my hair, messing up all the work I had just done, and he slammed his lips down against mine.

"I want nothing more than to make you my wife."

"You asked for my father's blessing?" I wrapped my arms around his neck, and he smiled down at me.

"And you said that Sorin and I were the gossips?"

I couldn't stop the small laugh that bubbled up my throat because he was right. "Thalia's not a gossip."

"With you, she most certainly is." He leaned down and kissed me again. "She used to be my most trusted friend, but not around you."

I smiled against his lips, and he tightened his arms around me.

"I wanted you to have a grand wedding." He whispered his

confession for only me to hear. "I wanted you to have everything you could have ever wanted."

"I do." I slid my fingers into his hair and pressed my forehead against his. "You and I are all I need, all I want. Our friends, this kingdom, it is all more than I could have ever asked for."

His hands clung to me, and I knew that he felt the same. I wasn't marrying Evren for some grand show. I wanted it to be nothing like what Gavril tried to force me into. I wanted it to be us.

"Meet me down by the creek," I murmured before slowly pulling out of his touch. "I'll be the one wearing white."

—

My hands trembled as my nerves raced through me. I could hear the voices of most of the people in town, all of them gathering at the last minute for our wedding, and I tightened my grip on my father's arm.

"Are you ready?" he asked, and I leaned forward and picked a piece of lint off his pressed shirt.

"I am." I nodded. I had never been more ready for anything in all my life.

I was Evren's mate, but I desperately wanted to be his wife.

Music flitted through the air, the sound of a light fiddle dancing around us, and I let the rhythm settle deep in my chest.

My father took a step forward, taking me with him, and my grip on his arm was so tight I worried I would hurt him. But I couldn't force myself to let go.

I had never imagined this day with him, with the honor of

him giving my hand away, and tears clouded my vision as he led me toward the aisle.

I could see dozens of people standing before the makeshift altar, and they all turned in time to watch as my father and I headed toward them. Candles and flowers of every color covered the small space, and the flames flickered and shone off the dress that clung to my skin.

We moved toward the aisle as people gasped and looked upon me as if I were something more than what I was.

The sheer fabric of my dress curved around my breasts before it clung to my ribs. It ran down to the ground, lying against my body in a simple silhouette, but the fabric billowed behind me in soft translucent layers that dragged on the moss and the earth.

I searched the end of the aisle, and my breath caught in my throat when my gaze met Evren's. He was wearing all black, his usual attire, but he wore the leathers of a warrior.

He looked fiercer than I had ever seen him before, and I knew that he would raze the earth for me if it was ever demanded of him.

His dark hair was pushed back out of his face, and his full lips parted as he took me in. With every step we moved closer to him, my heart rate slowed, and the anxious feeling in my gut settled.

He was my mate, and it was him I needed above all else.

It was only him.

My father and I made our way to him before he gently slipped my hand from his to Evren's. My magic swirled inside me at his touch, and I let him pull me forward until I stood before him and could see no one else.

The priest began speaking, but I couldn't look away from Evren. His words became a blur, and I barely managed to speak the words he asked of me.

But Evren was steady and sure.

He was the rock against which I crashed, and he held me firm in his gaze as he lifted a simple gold band in his fingers and slipped it over one of my own.

He handed another to me, and I repeated the act on him with trembling fingers and a full heart.

"You are bound in this world and the one beyond." The priest spoke as Evren wrapped his hand around mine. "An unbreakable vow bound to you forevermore."

Evren pulled me toward him, not waiting for the priest to finish his words, and his lips crashed against mine. The kiss was desperate and far too inappropriate for the crowd of people who watched us, but I did nothing to discourage him.

I kissed him back with as much vigor and every bit of love that thrummed through me. Tears streamed down my cheeks, tears of pure happiness, and when Evren finally pulled away, I saw his own tears swimming in his gaze.

The priest reached his hands forward, and I watched as he handed Evren a small golden crown that matched the one that sat upon his head. The gold metal was curved into intricate stars and crescent moons, and jewels encrusted much of its surface. Evren licked his lips as he looked at me, and he bowed his head softly in honor.

I dropped to my knees before him and bowed my head in return.

Evren placed the crown upon my head, the weight of it far heavier than I would have ever imagined, and the kingdom around us cheered as I lifted my head and looked back up at my mate. My husband.

He helped me back to my feet, and he didn't drop my hand again. He pressed my knuckles to his lips, and he kissed the ring that now decorated my finger.

Butterflies danced through my stomach as I stared up at him. He was so handsome, so honorable, and I didn't deserve him.

But I would never give him up again.

ADARA

I clung to my husband as we pushed through the door, and I giggled when his hand slid under my dress and pressed against my thigh.

He was carrying me in his arms, and I wasn't sure that I had ever seen him so happy.

Because I knew that I hadn't been.

There were a few guards and staff walking around the palace, but they all scurried out of our path as Evren carried me toward his room, our room.

"I can walk."

"Do you really think I'm going to allow my wife to walk on our wedding night?" He *tsk*ed, and my head swam lightly with the feel of him and all the wine we had shared. "I plan to do nothing but worship you tonight. And every night after."

His fingers tightened on my thigh just as we approached the door, and he was forced to shift me in his arms to grab the handle.

I laughed when he almost dropped my legs, but he caught me just in time and grinned. He took us into the room before kicking the door closed behind him, and he didn't stop until we reached the small desk in the corner of the room.

He set me atop it, my back pressing against the mirror, and he sat in front of me with his shirt slightly unbuttoned and his hair a mess from my exploring hands. He grinned up at me as his fingers grazed over my calf lazily.

"No bed tonight?" I grinned as I cocked my brow at him.

"Oh. We'll get there." He ran his hand over his mouth as his other slowly dragged my dress up my legs. "But first I'm going to see if you taste any different now that you're my wife, then I'm going to fuck you in front of this mirror with your dress still on."

I swallowed harshly, and the smile on his face deepened.

"I want that memory burned into my mind forever. My wife, with your perfect fucking wedding dress hiked up over your hips while I take you from behind."

"Evren," I whispered as my stomach tightened and moisture pooled between my legs.

His hands were barely touching me, teasing me in the most maddening way, and I needed him.

"Yes, wife?" He arched a brow, and gods, he was so handsome. This man before me. My husband. My mate.

"Please."

His fingers dug into my hips, and he tugged me harshly to the edge of the desk until my center pressed against his chest and my bottom felt like it might fall off the edge.

"I love hearing you beg." His fingers dug into me, the edge of pain burning through me, and I pressed my hands against his shoulders. "I love everything about you."

He caught my lips against his, searing me with his kiss, and I couldn't stop myself from rocking my hips against him, desperate for him to give me more.

He growled against my mouth before biting down on my bottom lip, and a soft whimper left me.

"Hands back," he demanded.

I did exactly as he said. I laid my hands against the desk behind me and rested against them as he lifted my dress even higher on my hips.

"So perfect." He ran a gentle finger against my undergarments, and my hips surged off the desk. "So eager." He leaned forward, his gaze meeting mine, and I watched him as he pressed his lips against my center through the fabric. "Lift your hips."

I pressed my feet against his thighs and lifted my hips off the desk as he laced his fingers into my undergarments and dragged them down my legs. He didn't stop until they were off me completely; then his hands pressed against my inner thighs as he spread me as far open as I could go.

For a moment, I felt self-conscious in front of him like this, but he erased that feeling so easily. "I cannot believe that I get to taste you for the rest of my life." He leaned forward and kissed the inside of my thigh. I clamped my eyes closed and let my head fall back as anticipation of his next move coursed through me.

Chill bumps broke out against my skin, and I could feel my magic buzzing.

I needed him to touch me, to taste me, to do whatever he wanted until I could handle no more.

He was now my husband, and I wanted every possible thing he could give me.

"You smell like heaven." He ran his nose against my center, and I gasped just before his tongue met my flesh. "And you taste even better."

He didn't give me time to adjust, to settle into the feeling he was giving me. He dove into me as if he had never been so starved in all his life, and I cried out as my body tensed and trembled against him.

He ate at me, a mixture of his tongue lapping at my skin before he sucked me into his mouth, and I wanted this damn dress off so I could see him better. I wanted there to be nothing between us.

Evren lifted my thigh, positioning it over his shoulder as he sucked my clit into his mouth, and I felt his fingers move against me. His fingers slowly slid inside me, stretching me, and I moaned.

"Fuck, princess. You are so fucking wet for your husband."

My hips surged toward him. Hearing him call himself my husband while he worked my body with his hand and his mouth would be my undoing.

"So fucking wet." His fingers curled inside me, and I could feel myself so close to the edge. Pleasure coursed through me, raced through every inch of my body, and I tried to hold on to any bit of control I had.

But Evren ripped it out of my grasp.

"I could do this for the rest of eternity, princess." He curled his fingers inside me and started pumping harder and deeper. I gasped for breath as I stared down at him, and he held my gaze. "I want to worship every inch of your body. I want to possess it."

He sucked my clit back into his mouth, and I could no longer hold it back. Pleasure shot through me, pushing me over the edge, and I couldn't look away from him as my thighs clamped around his head and my hips surged off the desk.

I ground against his mouth as my vision swirled, and he coaxed every drop of pleasure from my body.

I let my body fall back to the desk, exhaustion hitting me, but Evren stood with a growl and lifted me in his hands. My feet pressed against the cool floor, and he turned me quickly until his chest pressed against my back.

"I'm dying to be inside you." He kissed the back of my neck gently before working his mouth along my shoulder.

"Please." My voice was barely audible as I stared in the mirror at him standing behind me.

I could hear the rustle of fabric, him lowering his trousers, and I reached behind me and pressed my hand against his stomach.

His gaze jumped up to meet mine in the mirror, and it was filled with such darkness. His hand lifted to my neck, and I watched as his power seeped from his fingers. His fingers wrapped around the back of my neck, and the black smoke surrounded his hold.

He looked so powerful standing behind me, like a god, and I would kneel before him for the rest of my life.

I would worship him unlike any god I had ever been told of before, and even then, I wasn't sure it would be enough.

He pressed down on my neck until I was forced to bend in front of him and my elbows dug into the hard wood of the desk. He lifted my dress and groaned as I felt the cool air against my skin.

His hand slowly slid down my neck, down my spine, until it met my bottom. He rubbed gently against my skin before his fingers dug into me. He pulled my hips backward until I almost came off the desk completely, and he continued to caress me.

His thumb ran down the seam of my bottom, and I tensed against his touch. "I cannot wait to take you everywhere." He stared down at where his body met mine, and I could feel his hard cock pressed against me.

I wanted it. I wanted every part of him.

And my chest ached with how willing I was to let him have any part of me he wanted in return.

He ran his cock through my moisture, running it through my center from my clit to my entrance, and I pressed my head against the desk as aftershocks from my pleasure coursed through me.

He settled against me, the head of his cock pressed against my entrance, and he groaned long and hard. "Look at me." His words were a demand, and my gaze snapped back up to meet his. "Watch me as I fuck my wife." He ran his hand over his mouth before it settled back on my hips.

"Gods, please," I begged him and pressed my hips back into him. He slid into me only an inch, and I whimpered.

"So impatient." He groaned and his hands moved against me. His thumbs pressed on either side of my center, and he spread me open as he stared down at where he entered me. "You are mine, princess."

I nodded my head, and he looked back up at me.

"Say it." He licked his lips. "Tell me you're my wife."

"I am your wife." I let the words fall from my lips, and a chill ran down my spine at the way his gaze darkened. "I am your mate. I am anything you want me to be."

He growled and his magic grew around us. He was barely holding on to his control as he slammed inside me, and my chest hit the desk.

I cried out and stared at him in the mirror. He looked absolutely ruthless behind me. I arched my back and tilted my hips further as he dragged himself out, only to thrust back into me again.

His fingers dug into my hips, holding me in place with a pinch of pain, and I found myself craving more.

And he didn't make me wait for long.

He pushed into me harder, and his magic slid over my back. It was a whisper of a touch, testing me and drawing chill bumps against my skin.

His black magic wrapped around my neck as he watched me, and I bit down on my lip as he thrust into me so hard, I shot forward on the desk.

His magic pressed into me, holding me in place and stealing my breath at the feel of it.

I opened my mouth, and a silent plea escaped my lips. Evren's hand slipped around me, pressing against my clit, and my body shook around him as a sheen of sweat formed along my body.

"I have never wanted anyone more," he growled, and I could feel myself slipping. "You were made for me, princess, and I for you."

He rubbed his fingers more firmly against me, and his magic tightened against my neck.

He watched me, his eyes dark and wicked. I panted, my arms shaking as I held myself up.

My gaze was trapped in the mirror, watching him sink into me, while his magic continued to wrap around us. It pressed into me more firmly, and I whimpered, the moment so thick I could choke on it.

My breath rushed in and out of me quicker as each of his thrusts pushed me harder against the desk. My fingers gripped the wood, and I tried to brace myself the best I could.

But then his hand came down hard on my center, his fingers slapping against my sensitive clit, and I screamed as his magic tightened around me even further.

My vision blurred, the pleasure racing through me too intense and all-consuming. Evren roared behind me, thrusting into me over and over, and I felt him come inside me.

He slowed his movements, his hips still moving inside me gently, and I trembled beneath him as I slowly came down from the high he gave me.

He pulled out of me slowly, and I felt moisture drip down my thighs. I didn't have the strength to lift myself off the desk, so I turned my head to look at him in the mirror.

His magic still hovered around me as if it was as hesitant to leave my skin as he was.

Evren stared down at where he had just fucked me, and his fingers pressed against my center. I surged forward, still so sensitive, but his fingers were gentle. He gathered the moisture there, the mixture of him and me, and he slid a finger back inside me.

I whimpered and watched as his chest rose and fell harshly.

"I love seeing me drip out of you." His gaze didn't move away from where he was touching me, and he slowly slid in and out of me. He slipped his finger from my body, and I felt hollow without his touch almost instantly. "Taste us." He brought his finger to my mouth, and even though I felt like I should be ashamed, I opened my lips and let him slip his finger inside. "Taste how fucking good we are together."

I shivered when I felt his finger slide against my tongue, and I closed my eyes. I could taste him, his power, and there was no doubt in my mind that I belonged to him.

"Gods, you're so good," he praised me, and I sucked the taste of him from his finger eagerly, my body heating again with the taste of the two of us mixed on his skin. "I am so fucking enamored with you."

I opened my eyes and met his gaze in the mirror.

He pulled his finger from my mouth and slowly brought it down along my back. His fingers worked at the lace of my dress, and he pulled me up until I was standing before him once again as the fabric fell from my body and pooled around my feet.

I was completely bare before him, my body, my soul, and I had never felt more alive than I did in that moment.

This prince behind me, the man I was destined to find, he was everything I had ever wanted, and I couldn't help but love the feeling of being claimed by him.

He tugged on my hair gently, turning me until I was forced to look at him over my shoulder. His mouth was mere inches from mine, and I could see his possessiveness still swimming in his eyes.

His dark magic still swirled around us, as potent as he was, and I could feel need stirring inside me again.

"I'm never going to tire of you," he murmured against my lips before he kissed me, the move possessive and demanding, and I reached for him, digging my fingers into the side of his neck. "I will never tire of fucking you."

He wrapped his hands around my hips and turned me fully until he could lift me into his hands. He moved to carry me to the bed, and he made good on his promise.

EVREN

I sat at the head of the makeshift table we had placed in the throne room and looked around at those who sat at my side. My mother, the queen, sat to my right along with Sorin, Jorah, and Thalia, but I was missing Adara. My wife.

She was sleeping so soundly when I got dressed that I didn't want to wake her. We had spent most of the night worshipping each other's bodies, and even as the man before me spoke, I couldn't stop thinking about the way she had tasted, the way she had whimpered and cried out at my touch.

"If he doesn't attack, will you take the war to him?"

I blinked up at the man and ran my hand over my jaw to try to clear my head.

"I have no doubt that my brother will attack. He won't stop until he gets my wife or we kill him, and he will never touch my wife again."

King Drystan nodded, and I could see the weariness on his face from his travels. He and his army had marched through many days and nights when I put out the call for their assistance, and I felt honored that there had been no hesitation in him answering my call.

Because I didn't know what we were to face.

His brothers stood behind him, all three of them the epitome of a warrior, but it was the deep black symbols that were inked on their skin that gave away what they were.

The old fae.

They had ruled this land before either of my parents and their parents before them, and although I had never met the brothers, I had heard legends of their father's ruthlessness.

King Drystan had to take his rule too young after his father's untimely death in the battle that lost him this land.

The fact that he was here now, that he had come to our aid, was shocking.

The double doors to the throne room opened slightly, and I couldn't stop the grin from forming on my lips when Adara poked her head inside. She wrinkled her nose when she saw everyone around the table, but her gaze softened as soon as it landed on me.

I nodded for her to come in, and she straightened and squeezed through the door opening. The door clicked closed behind her, and I felt like everyone's eyes went directly to her.

I understood why. She was so damn gorgeous, and I didn't want to look away from her. I never wanted to let her out of my sight again.

"King Drystan." He looked over at me as I said his name, and I nodded toward Adara, who was making her way over to me. "I'd like for you to meet my wife, Adara Achlys, princess of the Blood kingdom."

Adara's gaze flashed as I said her title, and the urge to pull her down into my lap and wrap my body around hers was overwhelming.

Drystan bowed his head slightly, honoring her with his respect, and Adara did the same. "It's nice to meet you, Adara."

"Likewise." She moved to my side, and her hand tangled into the hair at the back of my neck. "You should have woken me," she whispered only loud enough for me to hear, and my grin widened.

I looked up at her, her hair still a bit rumpled from sleep, and wrapped my hand around the back of her neck until she was forced to meet my lips. I kissed her gently, but just the taste of her caused a frenzy of want to race through my body.

If I didn't stop, I would end up taking her right here in front of everyone. My heart hammered in my chest, and I knew that fact shouldn't have turned me on, but the urge to claim her, to make sure everyone knew she belonged to me, was overwhelming.

She was my wife, and I was a possessive bastard.

I broke the kiss gently, but I didn't remove my hand from the back of her neck. "You looked exhausted when I left you, and I wanted you to get your rest."

"I still could have gotten up with you." She peered into my eyes.

I pulled her closer to me until my mouth pressed against her ear. "Then maybe I didn't fuck you thoroughly enough last night." I nipped at her ear, and she squirmed in my hold. "I won't make that mistake again."

Her breath rushed out of her mouth, and I finally let her go to face those that still sat around us.

"We should be ready for anything from my brother and my father." I let my hand run down Adara's arm and tugged on her until she took a seat on the arm of my chair.

Adara's face tightened in concern, and I wrapped my hand around her thigh.

Drystan leaned forward in his seat and pressed his elbows against the table. "Do they know yet of your marriage to the Starblessed?"

Adara tensed again, but I slowly dragged my hand along her leg to calm her, to make sure she knew that she was my utmost concern.

She always would be.

"No." I shook my head as I looked at him. "And that's how we'd like to keep it. We'll need to use any advantage we can have on him."

My brother didn't need to know she and I had already wed. It didn't matter that we had strengthened the bond between us or that he couldn't fulfill the prophecy without her.

That knowledge would only drive him crazy, make him more reckless, and we needed to be careful with every move we made going forward.

"His kingdom is already suffering at his hand, and it will continue to suffer until we stop him." I adjusted myself in my seat but kept my hand on her. "He will use any man, woman, or child in his fight to get her back, and we don't need to make him any crueler than he already is. We have no idea if he's killed his mate or if he still has her."

"Our soldiers are ready," Sorin commented in a stern voice that spoke of how seriously he took this.

"As are mine." Drystan nodded. "We've set up a perimeter around the edge of your kingdom, but we should be prepared if he uses his magic to bring his soldiers in."

"Ours will remain tighter around the palace." Sorin nodded. "We don't know the extent of his power, but Adara must be protected at all costs against him and his death magic."

"Can you fight it?" Drystan looked at me, and I knew what he was asking. He wanted to know if I was strong enough to take on my brother or if I was setting us up for a losing fight. I gave him the only truth I had.

"Not on my own." I lifted Adara's hand in mine and pressed my lips to her knuckles. "But together, my mate and I can. The nymph in the Onyx Forest told of Adara being the one to defeat him."

Adara's back straightened as the king searched over her carefully.

"Good." Drystan nodded as he shifted and stood from his seat. His brothers moved with him. "My men and I need to get some rest after our long travels. If you'll excuse me."

"I can prepare you all a room." I started to stand, but he waved me away.

"We'll sleep in the tents with my men." His hand rested on his sword on his side. "They traveled the same distance that I did. Your Majesty." He bowed toward my mother, and she bowed her own head slightly from where she sat quietly at my side.

My respect grew for the man as he left the room.

As soon as he left, Sorin turned to me. "Our defenses are up around the palace grounds. No one will arrive in our kingdom unnoticed."

I nodded and looked to Jorah. "The scouts?"

"No sign of any movement." He shook his head. "The forest edge has been quiet, too quiet, but they are still on the hunt."

"Good." I nodded and looked to my mother. "How many have evacuated?"

Fury and despair flashed in her eyes. She shook her head as she spoke. "Almost none." I could feel the heaviness of the situation pressing down on her. Despite her imperfections, my mother was a beloved queen, and our people adored her. "Our kingdom has decided they will fight at our side." Her gaze slid from me to Adara. "They will fight to keep their princess safe."

Her words sat heavily in my chest, the realization that these people loved my wife as much as I did, and I couldn't imagine the moment when she would become their queen.

"The children?" Adara asked, and my hand tightened around her.

"Most have been moved into the west wing of the palace. We have set up rooms, and the kitchen is preparing plenty of food. Some women have come too, but they are all prepared to protect our children and our palace."

I thought about the sweet faces of those children from the night before. How they had danced and laughed with Adara as they had celebrated our union. For them to be facing this now, so young, hardened something inside me.

I would protect them at all costs. I would protect everyone in this room, in this kingdom, and I would do so without hesitation.

"What can I do to help?" Adara turned toward my mother, and I could see the wheels turning in her mind. "I'll do whatever they need."

There was a flash in my mother's eyes, a respect for Adara that was growing, and she looked down to Thalia. "Thalia and I are going to head that way to make sure that everyone is settled and doesn't need anything. You are welcome to join us."

"Of course." Adara made to stand, but I pulled her back down to me.

"Kiss me first," I growled playfully, and she rolled her eyes. But she still brought her mouth down to mine, and I held her there until I was forced to let her go.

I didn't want to face this war. I didn't want to face anything other than my new wife, but we would face this together.

"I love you," I murmured against her mouth, and she laughed.

"And I you, husband."

Then she left the room to help the people of our kingdom.

ADARA

I closed my eyes as I counted, and if I wasn't careful, I was liable to fall asleep.

"Ready or not, here I come." I opened my eyes and was met with a stream of laughter from throughout the room. "Now where could you be?" I tapped my chin as I stood and looked around.

There was a set of blond curls poking out from behind the chair and ten little toes sticking out from one of the beds.

"You all are too good at this game." I moved around the room, and every time I came close to either of them, their laughter would ring out around me.

I couldn't stop myself from smiling. We had been in the west wing of the palace for hours, and the queen and Thalia were still working with the other women to make sure everyone had a space to sleep and food available.

We weren't sure Gavril would bring the war to us, but we wanted to be prepared for whatever came. And as I watched Queen Veda care for her people, I felt a sense of respect for her that I had never felt before.

But it was there now.

I had been put on the duty of entertaining some of the children whose fathers had stayed in the kingdom, and I took my role seriously. Even if they had run me ragged with their games.

"Is there anyone in here?" I tore the door to the small closet open, and I was met with more giggles when I found no one. "You all are sneaky." I huffed and closed the closet again.

The little blond that had been hiding behind the chair was now scurrying beneath the bed with his friend, and I smiled as I watched his little kicking legs scoot him farther under the bed.

"Got you." I gripped his tiny foot in my hand, and they both screamed in laughter as I gently pulled him from the bed.

"The monster's got me!" he yelled, and his friend reached out for his hand to help save him.

But I grabbed him too. I pulled them both out from under the bed, and their laughter was infectious.

"You all just thought you could get away from me." I dropped to my knees and pulled both of their little bodies in front of me as I tickled them.

They snorted in laughter and fought against my hold until I finally let up.

I leaned back away from them and looked up in the doorway. Evren stood there, leaning against the doorframe, and he was watching me carefully. There was a softness in his gaze that made my chest ache.

"How long have you been standing there?" I pushed off the ground, but he didn't get a chance to answer me.

Both boys were running toward him, and the little blond one wrapped his arms around Evren's leg.

"Prince Evren!" They squealed in delight at seeing their prince, and I grumbled even though my stomach tightened at the sight.

"How come he gets to be Prince Evren, but I'm the monster?"

Both boys squealed harder. "Save us from the monster, Prince Evren!"

I rolled my eyes playfully, and the smile on Evren's face only grew. He squatted down until he was eye level with the boys, and he spoke to them both quietly. "I'll tell you what. You two run off and get a snack before bed. I'll make sure to take care of this monster for you."

Both boys did as he said immediately, and Evren stood back to his full height. He smiled at me again, but it did little to hide the worry that was swimming in his dark eyes.

"Did something happen?" I straightened out my shirt and pushed my hair behind my back.

"Come here." He beckoned me forward, and I went to him immediately. He pulled me into his arms. His hands slid into my hair, and his nose brushed against my cheek as he placed a soft kiss there. "I missed you."

I wrapped my arms around him, my fingers gripping the back of his shirt. "It's only been a few hours at most."

"And that's a few hours too long." He moved his lips to my forehead.

"I've missed you too." I sighed and peered up at him. That same dark cloud of worry clouded over his face, and I tensed in his arms. "What is it?"

"One of the scouts has returned from the forest edge."

My breath rushed out of me as I searched his face. "And?"

"My father's army marches toward our kingdom."

"So he is going to bring the war here?" I balled my hands into fists in his shirt as I stared ahead at his chest.

"Well…" He pressed his fingers under my chin and lifted it until I looked back up at him. "The scouts have yet to see the king or the prince with his army."

"The cowards."

That brought a grin to his face. "Whatever we are to face, we shall face it tomorrow." He leaned forward and gently pressed his lips against my mouth. "Tonight, I want to enjoy my wife."

"We should be doing something…" I looked out the door to where kids were still running around and laughing, but Evren quickly turned my head back to him.

"There is nothing else to do tonight." He pushed my hair back out of my face before his hand caressed my cheek. "The morning is to come no matter how much we prepare."

"The children…"

"Will all sleep soundly tonight." He reached down and took

my hand in his before bringing it to his lips. "You have done everything you can tonight."

I nodded my head even though I didn't really believe him.

But a tiredness set deep in my bones as I looked around me and realized that maybe he was right. I needed to rest. I needed to be ready to face our enemy tomorrow even though at this moment, I tried to block him from my mind.

Because I wasn't sure I would ever be strong enough to face Gavril again.

"Okay." I nodded and squeezed his hand. "You're right."

Evren's eyes widened, and he grinned.

"What?"

"Nothing." He laughed as he shook his head and pulled on my hand until he led me from the room. "I just don't think you've ever admitted I was right before."

I rolled my eyes dramatically, and he laughed again. "That's because you're usually wrong."

"I was right about you." He kissed my knuckles as he led us down the hall.

"Don't try to charm me. You already got me to marry you." I started to roll my eyes again, but he jerked me into his body and dipped me backward.

His mouth rested against mine as he smiled. "And it was the best damn day of my life."

He kissed me then, soft and teasing, and when he finally pulled away, I could see his burning desire staring back at me.

"Come." He nodded his head toward the hall, and I followed him dutifully.

Once we left the west wing, the palace was quiet. There were a lot more guards throughout the grounds than I was used to seeing, but they were all alert to their posts. They glanced in our direction as we walked by and bowed their heads slightly before quickly getting back to their watch.

The sight of them should have comforted me, but fear coursed through me. Tomorrow was coming. This war was coming, and I wasn't ready for it. I selfishly wasn't ready to give up this time with Evren.

If I didn't love the people of this kingdom so much, I would have begged him to run away with me. Just me and him where no one else could ever find him.

But I couldn't do that.

I would never be able to leave Thalia, Sorin, or Jorah. I couldn't leave those children or their brave parents, who had stayed in the kingdom when they were offered the chance to run.

I would stand at their sides tomorrow, ready to fight, even if I did so with trembling hands. I would stand with them just the same.

Evren opened the door, and his fingertips pressed on the small of my back, guiding me into the room. His fingers were light, but I could feel the strength of him behind me. It should have reassured me, calmed my racing heart, but with every second we moved closer to tomorrow, my heart seemed to race faster.

An icy chill ran through my body, and my palms began to sweat as I scanned our room, and I prayed I'd be able to keep my fear from showing.

Evren's lips brushed against my neck, and he breathed me in as I tried to calm my own breathing.

"Everything is going to be okay, princess." He wrapped his hand around my arm and tugged me back just a step until his chest was plastered against my back. "We have each other."

"What if that isn't enough?" I let my biggest fear slip past my lips. I hadn't wanted to say it out loud for fear it would be true.

"I have searched for you through a thousand lifetimes, princess, and I will search for you through a thousand more." He pressed another kiss to my neck, and I let the feel of him settle deep inside me. "It is with you that I feel most powerful. It is you who strengthens every part of me."

His tongue traced over the back of my neck, and I shivered under his touch.

"It is you, princess, who will change our world."

His hand tightened against me, and he moved from behind me, pulling me toward the bed. There was such a fire in his gaze, a desire that threatened to burn me, and it became hard to think about anything other than him.

He backed me up until the backs of my knees hit the mattress, and his fingers slowly tugged the edge of my dress up my body. Cool air kissed the skin of my bare legs, and I took a sharp breath as his fingers grazed over my hips.

He peered down at me, his gaze moving from my lips back to my eyes. "It is you and I, Adara." I nodded, and he lifted my dress higher. "You are all that I need, all that I desire." He pulled the dress over my head swiftly, and I stood before him in nothing but a pair of boots and the undergarments that covered my center. "Tonight, I will think of nothing but you."

He stepped forward, his knee pressing between my thighs until I was forced back on the bed. He lifted my leg in his hand, just behind my knee, and he brought my foot up to his chest. He slowly undid my boot before pulling it from my foot and dropping it to the floor.

He lowered my foot back to the ground before he did the same with the other, and my body trembled with anticipation of his touch, of anything he was willing to give me.

He set my other foot back on the floor, and he moved between my thighs, his body forcing my legs to separate. He slowly undid his shirt as he stared down at my body.

Evren was so focused, so intent on me, and moisture pooled between my thighs as I watched him. This man before me was my mate, he was my husband, and my body thrummed with need for him.

I needed his body to make me forget, to make me remember. I needed him to reassure me that no matter what came, it would be him and me in this life and in the next.

He pulled his shirt over his head before pushing his trousers down his legs. He kicked out of them before straightening back up before me. "You are so perfect."

His fingers hooked into my undergarments, and he pulled them down my legs. The slow drag of the fabric drove me crazy, and when they finally fell to the floor, I widened my thighs in front of him.

Evren groaned before dipping his head and pressing his lips to my lower belly just above my sex, and I whimpered as the need inside me built.

"Evren." I pushed my hands into his hair, and I tugged on the strands as his tongue touched my sensitive skin.

"I love the way you say my name," he murmured against me, and his hands trailed up my thighs in a ghost of a touch. "I love every little thing about you."

His fingers met my center but grazed over it teasingly. I lifted my hips, desperate for him to give me more, and his tongue lapped at my skin once again.

"On your knees, princess," he growled against my stomach, and I looked down at him.

"What?"

He stood, pulling back from me slightly, and he gripped my hips in his hands. There was the smallest bite of pain from his hold before he flipped me on the bed until my stomach pressed against the mattress.

I couldn't stop the small giggle that left my mouth, but it was cut off when his hand came down against my bottom. I moaned, unable to stop myself as my stomach tightened in want, and he caressed the spot he had just slapped with his hand.

"On your knees now, Adara," he growled from behind me. "I need to taste you."

I did as he commanded. I climbed to my shaking hands and knees before him, and I looked back at him over my shoulder. He stood behind me, his body on full display, but it was the way he stared down at me that made my breath catch in my throat.

"I have thought of little else all day, princess. There is a threat to our kingdom, and my mind continuously drifts back to tasting you, to getting back inside this body that was made for me and me alone."

He lifted his hand and slipped two of his fingers into his mouth as he stared down at me. He pulled them from his lips before bringing them down to my center, and I moaned as he slid them inside me with no other warning.

"So fucking wet," he groaned and slowly pulled his fingers out of me before sliding them back inside. "So damn ready for me."

He leaned down and pressed a kiss against my bottom as he continued to move his fingers in and out of me. I let my head fall to my hands as I tried to control my breathing, but it was no use.

Evren dropped to his knees behind me, and he slid his fingers out of me. I whimpered at the loss, but then his hands were on me again, his fingers digging into my thighs and his thumbs spreading me open before him.

He groaned as my stomach tightened in anticipation. "Fuck, Adara." His tongue ran through me, and I shot forward, almost falling from my knees. "You taste so fucking good."

He spread me open farther as he dove into my flesh. There was no holding back, no teasing touches. He ate from me as if he was as desperate for me as I was for him, and I couldn't contain the cry that ripped from my throat as pleasure coursed through me.

His fingers moved, sliding below my body, and they pressed against my clit as his tongue tasted every other inch of me. I shook, my arms trembling beneath my weight, and I was so close to falling over the edge that I couldn't concentrate on anything else.

Evren lifted behind me, his hand still moving against my clit, as I felt the heat of his body against me.

"I could do this for hours, princess." His other hand caressed my backside, spreading me open and making me feel bare before him. "I could do it for a lifetime and it wouldn't be enough."

His hand skated down my back, over my spine, before it slipped into my hair. There was a bite of pain as he lifted me and brought me up until my back pressed against his chest.

He kissed my ear softly, so at odds with his hold in my hair. "I want you to fuck me." He bit down on my earlobe, and I moaned as my hips surged against his still moving fingers. "I want you to show me just how badly you need me."

"Please, Evren."

He pulled my head back farther, and his teeth grazed against my neck. My nipples pebbled, and my stomach tightened to the point of pain.

He dropped his hold on me, moving beside me quickly, and as soon as he lay on his back beside me, he reached out for me.

"Come here." He pulled me toward him, and I straddled his body as he gripped my waist. I watched his face as he adjusted me above him, and when my wet center pressed against his hard stomach, he let out a grunt.

I lifted myself just enough for his cock to slide against my pussy, and I whimpered as the head brushed against my opening. I dropped down slowly, enjoying every inch of him filling me up, and when I settled against him fully, I pressed my hands into his stomach.

"Fuck, you feel so good."

I pushed against him, lifting myself up before dropping back down, and the sound of my body sliding on his filled the room. I did it again and again before I dropped my head back and fell into a rhythm against him.

"So good." Evren's thumb touched my clit, and I came down hard against him as pleasure coursed through me.

I couldn't control myself or the way my body moved against him. I was desperate for everything he was giving me, and I ground down against him as his thumb moved more rapidly against me.

I rolled my hips, feeling him deep inside me, and I moaned as he thrust his hips up to meet me.

"You are mine," he growled, and his body moved beneath me until his chest pressed against mine. He wrapped one arm around me, holding me close with his hand on the back of my neck. "Tell me you're mine."

"I'm yours." The words slipped past my lips immediately, the truth of who I belonged to the greatest thing I had to cling to in that moment, and Evren's hips surged forward.

"That's right." He groaned and pressed his face into my neck. "You are mine, and I am yours."

His hot breath rushed out against my neck, and I was so close to coming. So very close to falling where no one could catch me but him.

"Come for me," he grunted against me just as his teeth sank into my skin, and I did as he commanded. His name left my lips on a cry, and when his thumb pressed against my clit more forcefully, I lost myself to the pleasure.

He lifted his hips, pushing into me over and over as he drank from my neck, and the pleasure that shot into me was overwhelming. It was too much yet I still reached out for more.

He groaned, his teeth sinking harder into me, and I dug my nails into his back as another wave of pleasure coursed through me as I felt his own pleasure spill inside me. My magic thrummed inside me, aching and desperate, and I was barely able to keep a hold of my control.

He pumped into me a few more times, riding out our pleasure, before I felt his teeth slowly retract from my skin. I whimpered at the loss, and he licked the spot, slowly caressing it with his tongue.

My magic still snaked inside me, and he tugged me tightly against his chest before moving his mouth to meet mine.

We kissed as if we couldn't get enough of each other, as if he wasn't still inside me with the proof of our need sliding down my thighs, but I didn't care.

I still needed him like I needed my next breath, and he gave it to me. He kissed me long and hard, and only when I felt my body ache with the need for him to move inside me again did he finally pull away.

He pushed my hair out of my face as he assessed every inch of me, and his gaze was so dark it reminded me of his power, which was so like my own.

"It is you and I, princess," he reassured me, and I nodded my head.

"You and I."

EVREN

The temperature around the kingdom seemed to drop even as the sun rose higher in the sky.

I had just finished meeting with King Drystan to make sure they were ready for whatever today was to bring. I couldn't tell him what we would face, but I could see from the stern look in his eyes that he would be ready just the same.

Two of the scouts had returned in the dark hours of the night, and they told of the army marching toward us. Men I had spent years training beneath me as the captain of my father's guard.

And now I was prepared to destroy them all.

"They'll likely reach the edge of the kingdom within the hour," Sorin said from beside me, and I nodded.

"Once we're all ready, we'll meet them at the boundary. I want this war as far away from my people as I can get it."

I wanted it as far away from Adara as well, but I knew that she would fight. And I would never try to convince her otherwise.

This was her fight just as much as it was mine, and these were her people.

And if the nymph's words were true, we wouldn't win without her.

"Is Thalia still sleeping?" I asked because her room was where I had found Sorin this morning when I went looking. I didn't know what was happening between them, but I knew well enough to keep my nose out of it.

"She was when I left her room." He checked his daggers at his side as we moved up the street and toward the palace.

Most of the kingdom was still sleeping, and I looked around, taking it in one last time before we faced the evil that was my brother. He would do what he could to see my kingdom destroyed.

But he had no idea what he would be taking.

I looked around me, and memory after memory flashed through my mind. Some from my childhood but others with Adara, with my friends.

"We won't let him destroy it." There was such a conviction in Sorin's voice, and I let it settle deep in my chest. He was right. No matter what power Gavril possessed, we would do whatever we could to stop him. "We will fight him to whatever end."

I looked back at my friend, at the man who had been more like a brother to me, and I bowed my head slightly. He was the greatest warrior I had ever fought with or against, and I knew his word to be true.

I would have him at my side no matter what happened, and I was thankful for that.

I turned back to the palace, and I watched as Adara and Thalia both stepped outside. Adara lifted her hand, blocking the rising sun from her eyes, and my breath caught in my throat as I watched her.

They were both dressed in all black. The trousers Adara wore clung to her body like a second skin, but it was the leathers that she now wore across her chest that made my heart race.

They were leathers that matched mine and every man's in my guard. They were leathers of a warrior, and even though I wanted nothing more than to keep her safe, I knew that she was one.

She had been a warrior since the moment I met her.

I headed in her direction, and she turned toward me and smiled. We were still dozens of yards away from her, but my hands itched to hold her in my arms, to reassure myself that we were okay.

But I never got the chance.

There was a loud crack through the sky, loud enough to wake the entire kingdom, and I started toward my Adara in a sprint before I could see what was going on. But my path to her was blocked.

Fae soldiers landed in a flurry of magic, their boots hitting the ground with a loud thud, and I saw the surprise in their eyes when they saw Sorin and me standing before them. But I didn't give them time to think.

My power shot out of my hands, and the few soldiers that were closest to us crumpled to the ground, but there were dozens and dozens more. And they all blocked the path to Adara. They blocked my view of her too.

I could no longer see her or Thalia. I could barely make out the palace through the wall of men.

Sorin slammed his blade into the man in front of him, and the soldier fell to the ground.

There were far too many of them for the two of us to fight on our own. I shot another burst of power and sent the fae soldiers flying back into one another. Some slammed against buildings while others crashed into the streets.

"Fuck," Sorin cursed through clenched teeth, but before I could question what he was cursing at, he slammed his sword through one of the soldier's chests.

He lifted his hand, and his power took out another, swiping his legs from beneath him.

I pulled out my blade, and I sliced through the man in front of me until I could see what Sorin was looking at.

The palace.

Anger burned through me as I watched flames lick up the side of the stone castle. I still couldn't see Adara or Thalia, and I felt like I couldn't breathe.

"Clear a path," Sorin growled as he swung and blocked the sword of one of the soldiers.

A loud horn rang out through the kingdom, the sound echoing over my land. It was the call of my people, of my soldiers to ready themselves for the war that was already at our doorstep.

I stared at the flames, and I knew it would only be a matter of moments before they swallowed the palace whole. I reached deep within myself, within the well of magic that felt wild and ready to destroy, and I pushed it out of me.

I had no idea how many men hit the ground before me, but I could move through them now. Sorin and I stepped over the bodies of the soldiers as we continued to fight our way to the castle.

I searched every face we passed, but there were no signs of my brother or the king.

And the unknown of where they were, of what they had planned, caused a fear deep in my gut.

I could not let him get his hands on Adara. Not again. Not ever.

My heart pounded in my ears as the fire raced up the side of the stone walls and onto the top of the roof. Smoke and ash filled the air, and my gut sank as I thought of the children who were probably just blinking open their tired eyes, thinking they were safe inside my home.

I couldn't get the image of the two boys who Adara had spent hours playing with the day before out of my mind. Where were they now? Were they safe?

I sliced through the last three soldiers who stood in my way and breathed a moment of relief when I stepped closer to the castle and saw my guards barreling toward the fae soldiers that remained in the streets.

"Kill them all," I demanded of my men who passed me, but they didn't need my order. There was already so much rage and hate on their faces as they lifted their swords and slammed into our enemy.

I spotted Jorah as I got closer to the palace. He was directing soldiers and townspeople alike as some ran toward the palace while others ran out.

My boots crunched on glass that littered the ground, and I covered my mouth with my arm as smoke filled my lungs. There were people screaming, crying for help, and as I looked out over the horizon, I saw the rest of my father's army breaking through the tree line toward King Drystan's waiting soldiers.

Ash rained down around me, and I turned in time to see magic of the deepest blue swirl through the air. It touched the flames, kissed them with the softest touch of power, and the flames bowed before it.

The flames withered and retracted and answered to the call of the magic.

And Thalia became their master.

She stood before the castle with both of her hands held high in the air, and I could see sweat beading on her brow as she controlled the massive flames that were destroying our home.

I had never seen anything like it, never seen her magic so strong, and when I looked to Sorin, he looked to be in awe of her as well.

"Where's Adara?" I yelled to Jorah, and he nodded toward the castle.

"Moving the children." His fingers wrapped around his dagger, and he launched it past me.

I heard the deep crunch as it landed in a soldier at my

and Sorin's backs, but I was already running toward the palace entrance.

"Any sign of Gavril?" Jorah asked, and I simply shook my head.

I would deal with my coward of a brother the moment he arrived, but right now, my focus was on finding Adara. I needed to see her face, to know she was safe.

I ran through my home, and my heart sank with every door I passed. The flames had not touched every piece of the palace, but there was an immense amount of damage.

And still the tamed flames ate at it, more slowly than before, but they destroyed just the same.

I stepped over ash and debris as I moved through the palace, and I spotted the queen, my mother, guiding people down the hall, her clothes covered in soot.

"Evren." She sighed my name in relief as a child passed by her, running toward the kitchens at the back of the palace.

"Where's Adara?" I growled, unable to keep the panic from my voice.

"She's still in the west wing." My mother coughed, and I could see how much the fire had affected her. "She's making sure every last one is out."

I didn't wait for her to finish her sentence. I ran toward the west wing, where the flames were still licking up the walls, and I searched every room I passed until I finally saw her.

"Adara!" I called out to her, and she turned in my direction immediately.

The leathers she wore were now covered in soot, and the

long braid of her hair was coated in ash. But it was the child she carried in her arms that caught my attention.

"What are you doing in here?" She moved toward me, and I noted the burns that covered part of the child's body.

"I came to find you." I reached out for the child to give her a break, but she held him closer to her chest.

"He needs a healer." She moved past me, her hands coated in blood, and I followed her step for step as we headed toward the other end of the castle. "You're okay," she whispered to the boy, but I didn't think he could hear her.

His little eyes were closed, but his chest still rose and fell with life.

I pressed my hand to his chest as we walked, and allowed my power to flow through his small body. I could feel his burns healing and his pain easing as we passed through the halls, both of us stepping on debris from the fire. Adara didn't stop until we reached the dining hall, where most of the others were now camped.

My mother rushed toward us, and Adara reluctantly handed the child over to her.

"I've got him," my mother reassured her as she took in my black marks on his skin.

I reached out for Adara's hand. She looked up at me, but I could see the hesitation in her eyes. She didn't want to leave them. Not these children she had grown to love in such a short time.

"Stay with them." *Stay where it's safe.* I looked to the side of the room where most of the children were huddled together, but Adara was checking the daggers at her side.

"Take him straight to a healer," she ordered my mother before looking back up at me. "Evren used his magic, but make sure he's okay."

My mother nodded, and Adara looked back to me.

"How many are there?"

"Hundreds." I looked her over, making sure there were no signs of injuries, but it was only exhaustion I saw lingering on her face. "But there are no signs of Gavril yet."

She nodded once before heading out into the hall, not waiting for me. She didn't stop until she had almost reached the main doors, and I caught her hand in mine to stop her.

It trembled against my hand, her body giving away her fear even when she wouldn't admit it.

"You stay by my side," I reminded her of the thing we had already talked about dozens of times already, and she nodded in understanding.

"Regardless of what happens, you stay." I reached forward and wrapped my hand around the back of her neck. My fingers were met with the soot and sweat that coated her skin, but I didn't care.

This was my wife, the woman willing to fight for my kingdom, and I had never loved anyone more.

My hands were steady against her head, even as my breath shook in my chest, and I pulled her forward until her lips met mine. She kissed me roughly, desperately, as her hands dug into my leathers and clung to me.

When she finally let go, when she pulled away, there was dread that filled my stomach. Dread and fear unlike I had ever known.

I wasn't scared for myself, but I was fearful of ever living in this world without her. Yet I would not cower, and I knew that she wouldn't either.

"I love you, princess," I whispered as I pressed my forehead to hers.

"And I love you." Her words were soft, but they ripped through every inch of me, steeling my nerve and readying me for the battle I was about to face.

We walked out of the castle hand in hand, and it was startling to see the number of bodies that already littered the ground of my kingdom. Most of them were fae soldiers who had made the wrong decision to attack my kingdom, but not all.

I allowed myself the briefest moment to mourn the men who had fallen before I looked to the horizon. There was red smoke there, red power, and Adara's hand tightened in mine.

"Gavril." It was one word, one simple name, yet I could feel her palpable terror.

The dread I had been feeling moments before suddenly became nothing in comparison to the anger that now spread through my body.

"No matter what happens"—Adara squeezed my hand in hers—"we do as we said. No matter the cost."

I nodded once and felt my power coursing through me. "No matter the cost, he dies."

Thalia moved to the other side of Adara, and I could see the same determination in her eyes.

"Sorin and Jorah are both there." She nodded to the battlefield. "Gavril took down the entire front line of King Drystan's defense."

I couldn't wait any longer. I squeezed Adara's hand in mine before dropping it to grab both blades at my sides. "You have her back," I told Thalia. It was an order, but one I knew I didn't need to make.

Thalia would protect her at all costs.

She bowed her head slightly with her hand over her heart before she pulled her own bloodied blades from her sides; then the three of us took off.

We passed by soldier after soldier battling with the fae, and when the first fae soldier raised his sword toward me, I was caught off guard when a black tendril of power slithered past me and stabbed straight into the man's chest.

I watched as his life drained from his face even as he clawed at her power, as if he could stop it.

But Adara was already passing him as his body fell to the ground, and the marks along her cheeks glowed as brightly as the hatred in her eyes.

More soldiers approached us, but each and every one was taken down by either her power or mine. Thalia used her blades, and I worried how much of her power she had drained containing the flames.

But Thalia was a warrior with or without the powers the stars had bestowed on her. She was a warrior forged from her past and led by her future.

And there was no fear in her eyes when I looked upon her.

There was only determination. Only strength.

My feet moved faster, and my body grew lighter as I sensed the pull of my power growing stronger with each soldier that fell at my hand.

Together, we claimed the souls of every soldier we passed. Only one landed his blade against me, his sword slicing through my upper arm, but I could hardly feel the pain when I ripped his soul from his chest with the thrumming power within me.

When we finally reached King Drystan's force, which mixed with my own, I realized that the fae soldiers were swallowing their line at a much faster rate than I expected.

They were trying to draw us out, to separate our forces, and even if we weren't outnumbered before, we were now.

And Gavril's army, which pushed through the front line, every one of them had a dead look in their eyes. A red hue shone around them, startling me.

"It's his death magic," Adara called from beside me as she wiped the sweat from her brow. "It's Gavril."

King Drystan and his brothers stood before their men, and they slayed every soldier that dared approach them. I didn't see them use their power. Instead, they fought with their blades and their hands, and as I watched King Drystan wrap his fingers around one of the soldier's heads and snap his neck, I ground my teeth and forced my way to the front line.

I could still feel Adara with me, although she was a few steps back, and I harnessed the feeling of her as I gathered my power deep in my gut before letting it flow out of me.

Black smoke poured through the fae soldiers, taking out more than I could count at once, and I could feel King Drystan's eyes on me.

"My brother?" I yelled, and he nodded beyond the soldiers before us.

I should have known that the coward would be hiding far beyond his front line, but it didn't matter. I would destroy them all until I could get to him.

Each of them became nothing more than a step in killing my brother, a step toward protecting my mate.

I slammed my dagger into the chest of a soldier as I stepped over another and blood sprayed out around me.

But as I raised my hand, ready for the next soul to strike, it was my own body that was thrown back as my dagger fell from my hand. I gasped for air as my back slammed into the ground and my head hit with a thud.

"Adara." I said her name even as I struggled to make out anyone that was around me. I needed to make sure she was with Thalia. I needed to make sure she was safe.

"Hello there, brother."

I looked up, and even though my head still spun from the impact, there was no mistaking Gavril before me. He looked so much different than he did the last time I saw him.

His eyes met mine, the familiar hue now clouded with the red ring of his power. It ate away at everything he was, and I wondered if any part of the brother I had once loved was left at all.

"I'm so glad you could join us." He squatted next to me, and he pressed his hand to my chest.

I was shocked by the power that bolted into me. It tore my breath from my lungs and forced a grunt from my lips.

"Did you bring my bride for me to collect?"

He let up just slightly, and I gasped for breath even as

I felt blood trickle from my nose. "Are you referring to my wife?"

I watched as his gaze flooded with the red power that controlled him, consumed him, and that same power slammed back into my chest.

"She is not your wife in my kingdom.. We don't recognize the laws of this barbaric land." He leaned closer to me until his mouth was close to my ear. "I suppose she will fuck better now that you have trained her as your whore."

I lunged for him with my power, and he laughed.

"Don't worry, brother. When I'm finished with her, she won't remember that you were ever inside her at all. It will be me and me alone that she prays to."

He pressed harder, and I could feel my ribs cracking under his power as red smoke surrounded us both.

"She is my mate," I growled, and Gavril *tsk*ed.

"Mates make you weak." Stronger and stronger, his power grew against my chest until I feared that I wouldn't look upon Adara's face again before he stole my life with the wicked power that coursed through him.

"Where is your mate? Where's Leda?"

His gaze shuttered, and for a moment, I thought I saw a trace of emotion hiding there.

I reached forward, wrapping my hand around his wrist, and my palm burned where we touched.

"You will never lay another finger on my wife. I do not care that you were willing to give up your own mate. You will never touch mine again." I hissed the words through my teeth as I let every bit of my power flow through me and blast into my brother. It drained from me so quickly that I didn't have time to catch my breath as the black smoke clouded my vision.

Then the darkness took over completely. ☾

24

ADARA

Evren's power blasted into me, blasted into every soldier that stood within a twenty-foot radius of him and Gavril, but I quickly climbed back to my feet and pushed toward him.

His body went limp beneath Gavril's hand, and I swallowed the scream that was clawing up my chest. I could no longer feel him, the spot in my chest that he filled going hollow, and my ravenous gaze slammed into Gavril's as he looked up at me with a sickening smile on his face.

Pain sliced through my arm, and I looked away from Gavril to the soldier before me. He had that same sickening red ring around his irises, and he snarled as he swiped his sword in my direction again.

I dodged it, just barely, and the man charged me. He was feral as he took me to the ground. My teeth came down hard against my tongue, and I could taste my blood filling my mouth.

I scrambled for my dagger, my nails digging into the dirt beneath us as he pinned his arm across my throat. My breath was cut off as I felt the edge of my blade against my fingers.

I stared up at the soldier, and for a moment, I thought it was going to be by his hand that I drew my last breath. But then the soldier was knocked away from me in a flash, and I pressed my fingers to my neck as I gasped.

I sat up, finally getting my hold on my dagger, but it wasn't one of Evren's guards who stood in front of me. It was the nymph from the Onyx Forest, Osiris, the one I had met before when I had tried to run from Evren, and her dark eyes were solid black as she crouched next to the soldier she had just killed.

"My queen," her voice purred, and my back straightened at her words. "We have come to serve."

She bowed her head in the slightest nod, and when I looked past her, I was overwhelmed by the number of creatures both like her and different that now fought against Gavril's army. Nymphs, who normally blended with the forest, along with creatures I didn't recognize, raised their hands, their claws, and took the lives of men who dared fight against us. Some had wings and tore through the sky while others were much smaller and scrambled through the men with traces of magic trailing behind them.

I climbed to my feet as I watched them, and my arm ached from the wound, which now leaked with blood. The nymph was still crouched before me as if she was waiting for my order, and I didn't know what to say.

"You honor me, Osiris." I bowed my head to her, my respect pure and unending.

She returned the small bow before she moved, quicker than any man who fought on the battlefield, and launched into another soldier.

I gripped my dagger in my trembling fingers and searched the battlefield. I could no longer see Evren. I couldn't see my friends.

My body hummed with fear and hatred, and I pushed forward, slicing my dagger through the neck of the closest soldier. He fell to the ground beside me, and I continued ahead.

My magic thrummed inside me, but I saved it for when I needed it most. Evren's body still lay limp on the battlefield, and I had to get to him. I refused to allow him to die.

The thought alone sent fear racing through me, robbing me of my breath, but I pushed on.

Gavril's men were still fighting, still coming from his line of defense, and I headed in that direction with only one thought on my mind. I was going to kill the Citlali prince and save my mate.

I would make Gavril beg for his life before I finally took it with my own hands.

A soldier hit me from the side, knocking me to my knees who screamed in pain as they connected with the hard ground. I slammed the butt of my knife into his temple, his gaze faltering with the hit as I scrambled to my feet before he could get a hold of me.

Every part of me ached, but I would not stop. Nothing

compared to the pain in my chest, to the hunger of my power, and I let it fall from my hands, taking out every soldier near me as I continued forward.

I searched for Gavril, looking for the coward through the ranks of his men, but it was a blond woman who caught my attention at the edge of the battle. She was surrounded by a row of soldiers, each of them watching for a threat, but her gaze was directly on me.

She looked sickly, her body worn and devoid of life. I didn't know who she was, but as my gaze met hers, chill bumps formed on my arms, and my gut told me that this girl was Gavril's mate.

I moved closer, another sword slamming into my thigh, but I fought through the pain as I took off in the direction of the girl.

"Hello, Starblessed." Gavril moved into my line of vision, blocking my view of the girl, and I bared my teeth as I slowed. "I've been looking for you."

"You've found me." I held my hands out to my sides, both covered in blood from his men.

"Come." He motioned me forward with his hand like the pet he believed me to be, and I ground my teeth together until I feared they might snap.

"I will never go with you again."

"Won't you?" He looked behind him, and two of his soldiers stepped near him, holding the limp body of my mate. My chest ached deeply as I watched him, and my magic thrummed, uncontrollable, raging to kill.

"Don't touch him," I growled, but that only made Gavril smile harder.

"I'm going to kill him, Starblessed. I'm going to torture and kill your mate until I break this fight inside you."

My power slithered through me, ready to strike, and I held on to that feeling as I looked beyond him to the girl. To Gavril's mate.

Her gaze was wide, but it was filled with a soul-deep exhaustion.

"You're such a pretty little thing." Gavril cocked his head to the side, and I gritted my teeth. "No wonder Evren wanted you so badly for himself."

There were hundreds of soldiers still fighting around us. The sounds of metal clanging, soldiers grunting in pain and power, and the creatures' animalistic cries their fight echoed around us, but my gaze went back to Gavril's mate.

"I am not something you want," I taunted Gavril as I glanced back in his direction, and his eyes grew heated as he stepped toward me.

Bile rose in my throat as he perused me as if I were a piece of flesh dangled in front of him for him to devour. Even in the middle of a battlefield, he saw me as nothing more.

"I want your power, Starblessed." His gaze fell down my body to my hands before slowly making its way back up. "I can see you have it back fully now."

"Is that what you wanted from her as well?" I nodded toward the girl, and a growl left Gavril's lips.

"Don't you dare speak of her." His eyes flared with his power, and I wondered if he would ever be able to do it. Would Gavril ever be able to kill his mate for the power he craved, or was there a part of him that still held a trace of humanity? Did he care for the girl he was slowly draining to her death in his own sick way?

I looked back to her, and she raised her chin even as tears streamed down her cheeks. She looked so lost, even in her show of strength, and every part of me ached to save her.

But then she mouthed two words that made my blood run cold.

Kill me.

"Did you get my gift?" Gavril licked his lips, and my hand ached as I clung to my dagger.

"If you consider my mutilated mother a gift, then yes."

His gaze fell to my hands, where my black magic trickled out uncontrollably.

"An eye for an eye, as they say."

I tried not to let him see me react, not to let him see his words were affecting me. "It's too bad Queen Kaida couldn't be here to see all her hard work."

"I will break you." The words slipped from his lips like a promise, and my back straightened as I noticed movement out of the corner of my eye. "I don't care if I have to take you to the brink of death. I will break every part of you until you are begging me to give you everything I've promised."

Sorin charged toward Gavril, his blade ready to launch in Gavril's direction, when Gavril caught sight of him, and his deep red power poured from his hands into Sorin.

Sorin fell to the ground as Gavril watched me, and I launched forward, heading for Gavril's mate before he could stop me.

I slid to my knees, slicing my dagger through one of the guard's shins before he fell forward. I climbed over his body, diving for Leda, and she clung to me with frail, brittle hands.

The other guards swarmed, but I let out a blast of my magic, knocking them back, if only for a moment. "I can save you," I told the girl, but she shook her head quickly as she reached forward and took the dagger from my hand.

"Don't let him live." She stared at me, and I reached forward for her hand. But she moved too quickly. She slid my blade against her neck, her deep red blood pouring from the wound rapidly, and my dagger fell from her hand as her body fell to the ground.

"No!" Gavril roared from behind me, and I scrambled for my dagger even as I let out another blast of my power.

I climbed to my feet as I pulled on my power, summoning it to do as it was told. It was ready to strike, not needing my command, and I unleashed it on Gavril as his wild gaze met mine.

He was expecting my magic, and his own slipped from his hand. Even with his mate dying on the ground before me, he still held his power.

Every bit of it was aimed in my direction, but I didn't stop. I poured my power out of me until I could feel myself weakening. It pushed through Gavril's power, slamming into his chest, and he faltered backward.

More of his men clamored toward me, fighting soldiers and creatures alike to stop me from hurting their prince, but none of them could get to me as the crash of metal and flesh rang out around me.

I didn't stop. I stepped toward him and continued to pour my magic from my trembling hands. I could feel my magic waning, reaching its limit, and I feared I wouldn't be able to defeat him on my own.

But then I saw her slip behind him. Thalia lifted her blade and wrapped it around Gavril's neck before he could dare fight her off.

Gavril's red power shot out from him again, pounding into me and knocking the breath from my lungs, but Thalia was unwavering.

Her blade pressed into his neck, his blood unearthly thick and so dark it reminded me of tar pouring from his skin. His eyes widened, shock filling them as he wrapped his hands around his neck to try to stop the bleeding.

But it was no use.

His blood seeped through his fingers as he fell to his knees, and Thalia circled around him, her blade still in her hand, ready to strike.

"Look into my eyes, prince." Thalia gripped his chin in her firm hold and forced him to look up at her. "Look at her." She turned his head until his gaze met mine, and more blood oozed from his neck.

His eyes fluttered, and I stared at him as I watched the last bits of his life drain away slowly. Thalia moved closer to him, her mouth near his ear to make sure he heard her, but I could hear her clearly from where I stood.

"You will die knowing it was at our hands your life was taken." His head began to loll, but she held him firmly in place until the last word passed her lips. "You will never take from another again."

Thalia released her hold on him, and Gavril fell forward until his face hit the dirt, which mixed with his blood that was already pooling there. The feel of his magic, the unnatural aura he carried, dissipated with his last breath, and I sucked in one of my own.

I desperately wanted to stay in that spot and watch until I could no longer see a single movement from his body, but my power pulled me forward, pulled me toward Evren.

I searched for him, finding him on the ground where Gavril's coward guards left him, and I dropped to my knees at his side. Gavril's army was fleeing the grounds as fast as they could now that their prince was no longer there to protect them.

I ran my trembling hands over Evren's body as tears pooled in my eyes. Gavril had hurt him. He had broken his bones and far more, but I would not let him die.

No matter the cost, I would not live in a world where he didn't exist.

Blood seeped from his mouth and oozed from his forehead. His chest was caved in. My fingers shook as I pressed them over the spot where I knew his heart lay, and his blood stained my fingers.

A sob tore through my throat, and I quickly wiped away the tears streaming down my face as I tried to form a single thought that would help me save him.

I lifted my dagger, my father's dagger, which I had carried with me through every kingdom until I found my home, and I sliced it across my wrist quickly. Blood ran down my hand instantly, and I raised my wrist until it fit securely over Evren's mouth.

"Come on," I begged him when nothing happened. Tears clouded my vision as my voice shook. "Please, Evren."

Thalia dropped to her knees beside me, and Sorin groaned as he limped to the other side of Evren. They were both looking him over with assessing eyes, and I hated the way Sorin's gaze shuttered in defeat.

"No!" I growled, even though he hadn't said anything, and I pressed my hand harder against Evren's mouth. "Take from me, Evren." I pressed my other hand to his chest, my tears clouding my vision, and I slowly let my power sink into him.

I could feel it curling and twisting throughout his body, begging him to stay with us, and I didn't let up even as minutes passed by.

Thalia slipped her hand onto my shoulder, and for a moment, I thought she was pulling me away. But then I felt a tendril of unfamiliar power. It flowed into me, strengthening my own power, which was waning, and I forced it into Evren's lifeless body.

"Please." Tears dripped down my chin, but I watched as Sorin pressed his own hand over mine. Another shock of unfamiliar power slithered through me and to my mate.

"Fuck." I heard one of the guards, but I didn't dare look away from Evren. "Is he?"

I didn't know who answered him, and I didn't care. The answer was no. Evren was still with me, still fighting, even though they couldn't see it. There was no breath in his chest, but I could feel it in the way my mating bond pulled tightly against me, begging him to wake.

He was still with me, and he would not die.

I refused to allow it.

I couldn't survive this life without him. I didn't want to. I needed him, his people needed him, and terror coursed through me at the thought of him not surviving this.

He had to survive this.

"Where is Jorah?" I looked up at Sorin. I didn't know what kind of powers he possessed, but I would take anything. I would do anything.

Sorin's gaze darkened, and he shook his head solemnly.

A sob broke from Thalia's lips, and I closed my tear-filled eyes as I focused on everything that flowed through me. I garnered it all, morphed it into something more than we were individually, and I pushed it into Evren with a prayer.

I would not lose Evren to this war.

If he didn't survive, this would all have been for nothing. Jorah's death would have been for nothing.

It was he who was to change our world. He who would forge kingdoms and heal its people.

It was he who the stars promised to a broken world, and those stars belonged to me.

I could feel my skin burning, the star marks that scarred me coming alive under my command, and I harnessed every bit of that into Evren. I didn't stop until I felt like I had nothing left to give, not until my body trembled and my soul felt weak.

Only then did my hand lift.

And I couldn't breathe as nothing happened. His body remained lifeless beneath me. Our magic hadn't been enough. It wasn't enough, and I pushed my fingers into my hair and pulled on the strands as a scream ripped from my throat as I pressed my other wrist harder against his mouth.

Evren's chest rose with a deep breath and an even deeper pull of my blood. His hand came down over my wrist, and he held it to his mouth as he drank three long pulls of my blood.

Then his dark eyes opened, and they found me instantly.

He was my mate, and even when facing the god of death, we would not cower.

EVREN

Adara's lips brushed over mine, and nothing else mattered. Not the ache deep in my chest or the way my head seemed to throb with every pull of breath I took. She was before me, and my hands trembled as I pressed them to her face.

"Princess." It left my lips like a plea, and the deep inhale I took after burned in my lungs.

"I'm here." She ran her own shaking hands over my face, pushing my hair away as she inspected me.

My head swam and I couldn't think clearly, but I knew her touch beyond everything else.

I pushed up off the ground, and every part of my body

protested in pain. But I didn't stop. The world around me shifted, and I remembered where I was as I saw the bodies slain along the battlefield.

I scrambled for my dagger and pulled Adara closer to me.

"It's over." She shook her head, and I could see the truth in her eyes. "It's over," she murmured again, and I looked around at the scene before me.

There were so many soldiers on the ground, too many of my own mixed in with those of my father's army. They had laid every ounce of their lives into this battle to protect our kingdom, our people, and I would be forever in their debt in this life and the next.

I stood fully, staggering slightly as I moved, but Adara held on to me firmly.

"Where's Gavril?" His name felt toxic on my tongue, as if I could still taste his cruelty inside me.

"Dead." Thalia moved beside me, and she nodded.

I turned to look, and there lay my brother, with blood still oozing from the wound on his neck. His eyes were open, staring into the nothingness of his future. My chest tightened as I looked down at him.

He was my enemy, but he had also been my brother. And for a long time, I had loved him as such. There was still a ghost of that love, a ghost of pain in my chest, at seeing him like this.

But I felt no guilt over his death. Not after everything he had done to my mate, to my friends, to my people.

He could have lived a life of greatness, of love, but instead he chose power. That lust, that craving for everything that didn't belong to him, was his final demise.

"My father?" I looked up just as Sorin reached us, and I hated the amount of blood that covered him.

"There has been no sign of him." Sorin shook his head. "Even as the last of his soldiers retreated, we never spotted the king once."

I shook my head and tightened my hold on Adara. "He always has been a coward."

"Do we pursue him?" Sorin asked with his hand resting on his dagger, and I knew that he would if that was what I asked of him. Even with exhaustion clouding his eyes and riddling his face, he would do whatever I commanded in the name of our kingdom.

"No." I shook my head and looked around us. "I think there has been more than enough death for today."

My men, who still stood on the battlefield, scoured the grounds, looking for survivors, and I let my hand fall from Adara's side as I began doing the same.

"Evren." Adara said my name, and I turned back to her, my gaze running over every inch of her to check for harm. Her lips trembled, and I hated the look in her eyes. "Jorah."

I pulled my gaze away from her to look for my friend, but when my gaze met Sorin's, I knew the truth before Adara could say it.

"He didn't survive the battle."

Tears streamed down Adara's face, and I swallowed hard as emotion clogged my throat. Jorah had been my friend for as long as I could remember, he had been my brother, and I would mourn the loss of him more than I ever would the one who shared my blood. ☾

"Where is he?" Guilt clawed at my still sore chest. I should have been able to protect him. I should have fought harder against Gavril so he never could have touched any of them.

But my failure cost my friend his life.

"We're moving his body to the palace." Sorin nodded toward me, and I knew that my friend probably had the same guilt fighting inside him.

I nodded once and reached out for Adara. I pressed my lips to her forehead and dug my fingers into her. I could feel her beneath my fingers, and I reminded myself that she was safe.

"He will have a hero's rite of passage into the next world." I swallowed hard and looked around me. "They all will."

ADARA

I climbed out of the bath and wrapped the towel around my body. I had been in there for far too long, until the water ran cold with time, but the heaviness of the day had weighed on me.

And I knew that it weighed harder on Evren.

He had been working tirelessly since he awoke on the battlefield, and it didn't matter that he needed to rest. He refused until he saw to everyone in our kingdom.

I had tried to stay by his side through it all, but I had finally given in to the exhaustion when my legs began to tremble beneath me. Evren had ordered Sorin to bring me back to our room while he finished what he was doing, and I didn't argue.

But now I wished I was still at his side.

Even as my own head felt heavy above my shoulders.

The deaths of those soldiers, townspeople, and Jorah tore at us all, and I wasn't sure that I would ever be able to escape the feeling.

I pulled the washroom door open, and I stopped short at the sight of Evren sitting on the bed. He watched me carefully, his gaze piercing and assessing, and the towel I wore did little to hide me from him.

There was such a heavy burden in his eyes, the weight of everything that had happened today bearing down on him, and I wanted to erase it.

I tightened my hand on my towel as I stepped toward him, and his gaze dropped to my bare thighs.

"You look exhausted." I stopped in front of him and ran one of my hands over his face.

"I am." He nodded as he closed his eyes and leaned into my touch.

"You should get some rest."

"There is still much to do." He turned his head and pressed his lips against the palm of my hand. "I just wanted to check in on you. I figured you'd be sleeping."

"You've done enough."

He lifted his head and opened his eyes, and he looked at me with such intensity that I felt my bones melting into nothing.

"So many of my men died today." His voice was rough and filled with guilt, and it killed me. "My friend died today."

"And they would give up their lives again to fight for this

kingdom, to fight for their prince, who has spent a lifetime fighting for them. Jorah would have given his life a hundred times over to fight for what he believed in."

He leaned forward and pressed his forehead against my stomach as his hands settled on my hips. He took a shuddering breath, breathing me in, and my body tensed under his touch. I pushed my fingers into his hair, massaging his head as they moved along his skull.

He was still wearing his leathers, his body covered in dirt and soot and gods only knew what else, but I didn't care.

"Stay with me," I whispered.

When he didn't answer me, I tugged on the strands of his hair and forced him to look up at me.

His dark gaze was almost black, and it made my stomach tighten with so much want for him.

"Stay." I closed the space between us and pressed my lips to his.

He kissed me gently, patiently, but I couldn't take my time with him right now. Every part of my body thrummed with my need for him, the need to remind myself that he was okay and that there was nothing that could take him away from me.

I chased his tongue with my own before I sucked his bottom lip into my mouth and moaned around it.

His hands tightened against my hips, digging the towel into me, and I pulled it away from my chest before he could stop me. The towel fell to my hips, bunching around his hands, and I pressed my hands into his shoulders before lifting my leg and straddling him.

"Princess," he groaned and shifted beneath me. The movement made a whimper slip from my lips, and I felt moisture pool at my core. "People need me."

"I need you," I said selfishly, but there was no way I was letting him walk out of this room. Not until I used my body to remind him that fate had chosen him because he was worthy.

He was worthy of his people, of his kingdom, of my love.

He had proven it to us all over and over.

"Please," I whispered as I pressed my lips to his. I kissed him quickly, not giving him time to think, and his hands moved from my hips to my back. He gripped me tightly, pulling me against his growing erection, and I moaned at the pressure.

I ground myself against his length as I pushed my fingers against the clasps holding his leathers against him. I fumbled as I undid them as quickly as I could, and he leaned forward and sucked my nipple into his mouth just as I finally pulled them from his chest.

"Oh gods." I threw my head back, and he rewarded me with his tongue and his teeth.

I moved harder against him, and my fingers clawed at his back, pulling his shirt up over his shoulders. He leaned away long enough to help me pull it over his head, then he continued his work against my breast.

I ran my fingers over every inch of his exposed skin, exploring, making sure that every part of him was fully intact.

The memory of him lying in that battlefield without a single spark of life in him flashed in my mind, and my fingers dug into his shoulders as I clung to him.

"Evren," I moaned his name, and he finally stopped his teasing of my breasts. He pulled his mouth from me, and I met his dark gaze. "Please remind me. Remind me that it's us."

The words were barely out of my mouth before he lifted me off him. My back hit the bed, and Evren stood before me, staring down at me like he had been waiting a lifetime for me. And I knew that he had.

He pulled his trousers down his hips, and his cock sprang free. He was so hard, so ready for me, and I trembled as I stared at him.

"You're so damn perfect." He wrapped his hand around his cock, and he fisted up and down the length of it as he stared down at my body before him. "Come here."

I lifted onto my knees and moved to the edge of the bed until my chest pressed against his. He was still working his cock, the head pressed against my bare stomach, and his hand wrapped in my hair.

He pulled me impossibly closer, his mouth pressing against mine, and he kissed me so roughly, so desperately, that I felt like I would fall apart from that alone.

"I love you, princess," he mumbled against my mouth.

"I love you too," I whimpered and wrapped my arms around his shoulders.

The hand in my hair moved down, gripping behind my back, and he lifted me higher in the bed until my head hit the pillow. He came down over me, only a few inches separating our bodies, and he ran his cock up and down my wetness as he watched where his body met mine.

I arched my back off the bed, desperate for him to get inside me, and he wasted no time. He coated himself in my want before he slid inside me, and I closed my eyes as he stretched me so deliciously.

"Gods, I've never needed anything more." He pulled almost all the way out before pushing himself back in. He shifted his hips and ground down against my clit, and I gasped for breath as every part of me felt like I was dying for him, for his touch. "I've never wanted anyone the way I want you."

I clawed at his shoulders, holding on to him and he wrapped my legs around his waist. "More."

His breathing picked up, and he groaned as he shifted his grip on me. He pinned my wrists above my head, and he started fucking me with so much force I worried that everyone in the kingdom might hear us.

But I couldn't bring myself to care.

I rolled my hips, matching his thrusts with my own, and I cried out his name.

I was so close to release, and I couldn't control it as it raced through my body. Every part of me wanted him: my body, my magic, my soul.

We craved him and every moment of his touch, and we chased the high he was giving us with desperation.

"You are mine," he growled. His words were like a drug, a reminder of how much I belonged to him. It was a reminder that I would give up everything for this life with him. I would go through every bit of suffering again as long as it led me to this.

"I'm yours," I moaned. He was mine, and I was his. And I never wanted to know a world where that wasn't the truth.

"Come with me," he roared and pushed himself into me roughly, his hips grinding down against my clit, and I cried out his name as pleasure shot through me.

He slammed into me again and again, and I felt him release inside me. Waves of pleasure coursed through my body, and he drew every ounce of it out of me until I felt myself shudder and shake, my body so sensitive that it felt like I was going to break.

Only then did Evren press his weight into me. He laid his head against my chest as he nestled himself between my thighs, and I combed my fingers gently through his hair as I tried to catch my breath.

We stayed just like that for a long moment until my body relaxed and I felt him do the same above me. His breathing evened out, slowly drifting, and even though I knew that we still had much to face, every part of me found comfort in the knowledge that we would face it together.

Come what may, Evren was my home, and I would do everything in my power to protect it as I knew he would.

My eyes drifted closed, and I was almost asleep when his whispered words floated over me like a prayer.

"The stars chose you, Adara Achlys. It was always you."

EPILOGUE

EVREN

I stared ahead at my mother even though I wanted nothing more than to get back to Adara. My desperation for her had only increased after the battle, and I never wanted her out of my sight.

"I think we both know that it's time." My mother rubbed her hand over her face slowly, as if trying to will away the fatigue. The crease on her forehead was more pronounced, and dark circles had taken up residence beneath her eyes. "The people of this kingdom love you. They trust you, and they need you."

My chest ached as I listened to her words. "They need you as well."

She nodded her head, but her gaze softened as she looked

over my face. "And they will still have me, but I'll be standing behind you as their ruler. You and Adara."

I couldn't stop the pride from swelling in my chest that she believed in me to rule this kingdom that she loved. That she was willing to step down and lay it before me.

"We are safe because of you." She swallowed roughly. "It is due to your sacrifice, and there isn't a person in this kingdom who doesn't realize that, who doesn't have the utmost respect for you."

I nodded once as words escaped me.

"If word of your father is to come, it is you who will continue to protect our people."

There had been little talk of my father. It was assumed that he was back in Citlali, but everything had been quiet, and that made me uneasy.

Though there hadn't even been whispers of him, my dreams had been plagued with the man I both hated and somehow missed the memory of. He had become my enemy, but he had once been nothing more than my father.

I hadn't told anyone of my dreams. Not even Adara. I couldn't burden her with that when the fear had just started to dissipate from her eyes.

We had already heard rumors of unrest in the old country, the land under King Drystan's rule and beyond, and the unknown was agonizing.

I wanted to keep her safe from any danger or worry, yet I knew that no matter how hard I tried, I could never shield her completely.

She had proven time and again that she was more than capable of protecting herself, but guilt still ate me alive at the memory of her having to do so.

"I'd like to talk to Adara before we decide anything."

"Of course." My mother nodded as I stood. "Although tonight might not be the night. I overheard Adara and Thalia talking about your plans to head to the Olde Vine tonight."

My chest ached at the thought. I had barely seen Thalia smile, let alone hear her laugh, since the battle—since we lost Jorah.

"I better go then. Who knows what those two are getting into?"

My mother smiled before I pushed through the door and made my way to them.

They were both huddled together near the door, whispering to each other as I walked toward them, and Sorin stood at their side with his gaze hardly leaving Thalia. He glanced up at me for only a moment as I approached; then his eyes went right back to her.

"The queen tells me that you two might be up to some trouble tonight."

Adara's gaze shot in my direction, and the smile that was already on her face widened until the corners of her eyes crinkled. "There you are."

She moved in my direction, and I wrapped my arms around her as soon as her body hit my chest. She pressed up on her tiptoes until her mouth was closer to mine, and I breathed in the intoxicating scent of her as I held her tighter against me.

"Have you already been drinking?" My words were whispered for only her to hear.

"You were taking too long, and Thalia was trying to back out of coming."

I looked up and stared at my friend as she leaned against the wall. Her gaze was glued to her feet, and I hadn't seen her look up at Sorin once even though he was still watching her.

"So you filled her with wine?"

"Exactly." Adara grinned, and my breath caught in my throat. "Sometimes you just need to forget."

"Okay." I nodded, even as worry for my friend stirred in my gut. "Let's go help her forget."

I pressed my lips against Adara's, and she let out the tiniest moan, which made me want to forget everyone else, haul her over my shoulder, and force her back to our bedroom.

But this was important. Adara was worried about Thalia, we all were, and I hated seeing that empty and unseeing look in her eyes.

Adara slowly pulled away from me, and I let her go before she moved to Thalia and wrapped her hand in hers. Thalia gave her a smile, a forced one, but Adara didn't let it stop her.

She never let anything stop her.

Sorin followed after them wordlessly as they headed out the door, and I caught up to him and walked at his side.

"She talk to you today?" I asked quietly so Thalia wouldn't hear me.

He shook his head, and his brow furrowed as he watched her walk in front of us. "I feel like I should be doing more. Doing anything."

"Our friend died, Sorin. Her friend died." I swallowed as the guilt over his death washed over me. "She just needs time."

"Yeah." He nodded even though I could see the doubt in his narrowed eyes.

Sorin was in love with Thalia. He had been for as long as I could remember, but so had Jorah.

And I had no idea what was running through Thalia's mind besides the blazing rage that radiated from her even though she tried to hide it.

The streets were bustling with people, and Adara waved and hugged everyone who approached her as we moved toward the pub.

My mother had spoken of my kingdom's respect for me, but they were all looking at her.

"Come to the Olde Vine." She held the hand of an older woman who had approached her before her gaze slid to mine for only a moment. "Drinks are on the prince."

I chuckled even as the woman's eyes lit up.

As we arrived at the Olde Vine, the sound of laughter and music filled the air. Adara led us to a table in the corner, and I pulled out her chair before pulling mine as close to her as I could get it.

I slid my hand on her thigh as Thalia called over the barkeep and ordered us all a round of drinks. Sorin sat at her side, as close as he could get, but she had yet to look at him.

Adara's brow furrowed as she watched her friend, but I slid my other hand around the back of her neck and pulled her to me.

"You look exceptional tonight. Are you sure we shouldn't just head back home?" I ran my nose along her cheek and breathed her in.

She laughed as she looked up at me. Her hand pressed against my chest, and I loved the way her fingers dug into the fabric, betraying her words. "No. We're here to distract our friends tonight."

"Fine," I grumbled, and she laughed harder.

"Come on, Thalia." She reached out for her hand, and I was forced to drop my hold on Adara. "Let's go dance."

There was a hesitancy in Thalia's gaze, and even though I thought she would deny her, she stood and followed Adara out onto the worn wooden floor.

Sorin tracked their movements, and I did the same.

Adara threw her head back in laughter at something Thalia said, and the smallest smile lit up Thalia's face.

Sorin sucked in a breath just as the barkeep set our drinks down on our table.

"Thank you."

He nodded once before getting right back to work.

Sorin grabbed his ale and downed the glass in one go, and I winced.

When I looked at Adara, all I felt was happiness. It raced through me and washed away every nightmare that wanted to haunt me.

But the nightmares were still there.

If I could change things, if I could stop Jorah from dying, if I could take away the ghosts in Thalia's eyes and the sorrow in Sorin's, I would.

I would take away every moment that burdened them and take the pain as my own, but I couldn't.

"Come on." I nodded toward Adara and Thalia where they danced, but Sorin shook his head. "I'm going to dance with my mate, and Thalia is going to be standing there all alone."

I stood and didn't wait for him to follow me.

Adara's gaze met mine as I approached, and she grinned as her hips swayed to the music.

"May I?"

"I don't know." Adara shook her head softly. "My husband's around here somewhere, and he's got a bit of a temper."

"Is that so?" I reached out and caught her hand in mine before pulling her toward me. Thalia smiled softly as she rolled her eyes at us, but I caught sight of Sorin stepping up and sliding his arm around her back. "Should we find ourselves some privacy within the shadows? I've heard legends of your husband."

"Legends? Really?" Adara arched her brow at me. "He already has an extraordinarily large ego. Please don't let him hear you say that."

My fingers dug into her back, pulling her more firmly against me as I buried my face in her neck. I ran my teeth over the sensitive skin there, and she whimpered even as she laughed at my warning.

"But you seem to like him."

"I do." She nodded against me, and I tasted her neck with my tongue as I moved us around the floor. "Unfortunately for you, he's just what my mate ought to be. Arrogant, handsome, filthy."

"You love that I'm filthy." I pressed my hips into hers, and the small gasp that left her mouth made me want to pull her from this pub and show her exactly how filthy I could be.

"That I do." She nodded. "I love everything about you."

"And I you." I moved my hand to the back of her head and gripped her hair in my hand as I forced her to look up at me.

But her eyes slid to our friends instead. I followed her gaze and watched as Sorin held Thalia firmly against him. Her fingers were wrapped around his neck as she stared up at him. I felt like I was intruding on something I shouldn't have been. Something that both of them desperately wanted even though they were too fearful to act on it.

"Do you think they'll be okay?" Adara asked as she looked back to me. "I need Thalia to be okay."

"She will be." I nodded. "We'll make certain of it."

"I sometimes feel guilty for feeling so happy." She ran her fingers through the back of my hair, and I groaned at the feel of her touch. "For having you."

"You have nothing to feel guilty for." I shook my head. "But I understand the feeling. I don't deserve you."

"Did I also tell you that my husband is far too good for this world?" She cocked her head to the side, and I couldn't imagine how I could ever find a greater happiness than this moment with her.

"And I will find you in any world?" I chuckled softly.

"Gods, I hope you do."

Thalia's laughter caught us both off guard, and we looked over to our friends as Sorin spun her around the floor.

He smiled down at her as he held on to her for dear life, and I watched as another man lost himself in a woman, blessed by the stars.

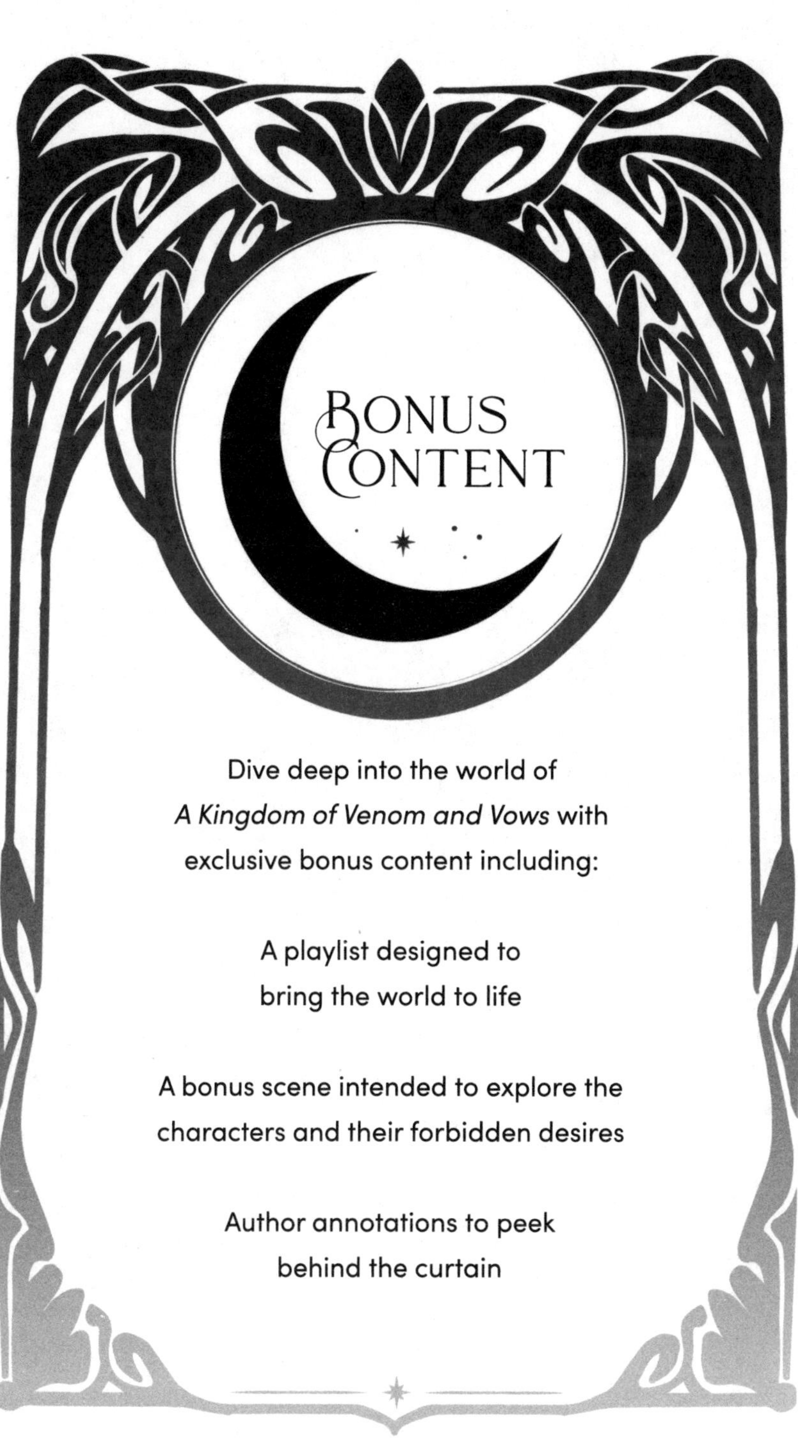

Bonus Content

Dive deep into the world of
A Kingdom of Venom and Vows with
exclusive bonus content including:

A playlist designed to
bring the world to life

A bonus scene intended to explore the
characters and their forbidden desires

Author annotations to peek
behind the curtain

Playlist

- "The Smallest Man Who Ever Lived" by Taylor Swift
- "Watercolor Eyes" by Lana Del Rey
- "Cosmic Love" by Florence + The Machine
- "Hurts So Good" by Astrid S
- "The Other Side" by Ruelle
- "Don't Forget About Me" by Cloves

Bonus Epilogue

ADARA'S POV

The tavern was alive tonight, a mixture of laughter and music filling the air. Candles flickered atop each well-worn wooden table, casting a warm, golden glow over the room, and the air was rich with the scent of freshly baked bread, roasted meat, and ale.

It smelled like home.

Our home.

Evren's hand slid along my waist as he navigated us through the maze of patrons and tables. His fingers spread possessively against my hip, a subtle yet unmistakable mark, as if anyone would dare touch me.

Yet, Evren's touch was a constant, as if he needed to remind himself that I was here, that I was his.

His lips found their way to my ear, and he pressed a kiss there before he spoke. "Did I tell you how beautiful you look this evening?" he murmured, his voice barely cutting through the chatter around us.

I leaned into him, letting his warmth steady me as we walked, his hand squeezing my hip and causing that same warmth to spread low in my belly. I looked up at him, and he was looking down at me with such adoration that I laughed.

"You know if you stare at me like that, people will start talking," I teased as we reached the old corner booth we always seemed to gravitate toward.

"You'll have to excuse me." His smile was a wicked promise of what was to come. "But I think they are all more than aware of who you belong to."

I arched a brow, settling into the worn leather of the booth. "I don't belong to anyone."

"Keep telling yourself that lie, Princess." He sat next to me, his thigh pressing against mine, his arm finding its way around my shoulders. I knew he needed this closeness. I needed it too.

I rolled my eyes, but my lips curved as I leaned into him. "You're insufferable."

"And yet you married me." He kissed me again, this time near my temple, before he flagged down the barmaid, ordering four mugs of ale, just as Sorin and Thalia made their way to us.

Thalia slipped into the booth first, sliding across from me with a grin on her face and a flush on her cheeks. She brushed back a lock of hair from her face and propped her elbows on the table as if preparing for battle. Sorin followed, settling beside her and tugging her body against his until there wasn't any space separating them.

"Settle a debate for us, Adara." She quickly winked at me, and gods, my friend looked so happy. She hiked her thumb over her shoulder in her husband's direction. "Who was more terrifying when you first met us? Me or him?"

Sorin let out a quiet groan, already reaching for his ale as the barmaid set them down on the table. "We've already settled this. We don't need to rehash it."

"Yes, we do." Thalia rested her chin in her hands, waiting. "I think it's obvious."

"Obvious that it was you?" I laughed.

She scoffed and kicked me under the table. "Me? He barely spoke to you. I trained you and showed you how to fight."

"That's called intimidation, my love."

Evren snorted beside me, and Thalia narrowed her gaze on him.

I grinned and leaned forward toward my friend. "I was scared of you and kind of hated you for how you pushed me when I first met you." I lifted my hand and pointed to Sorin. "But him? I thought he was just trying to get beneath my skirts." I widened my eyes with mock seriousness.

Sorin lifted his mug in salute with a devilish grin on his face. "That's called flirting, Adara. I'm sorry my friend here hadn't really mastered the art."

Thalia let out a light laugh as Evren's thumb brushed across an exposed sliver of skin at my shoulder. "My flirting landed me exactly where I wanted to be." He leaned closer, whispering so only I could hear. "Plus, I think you were far more intimidating than either of them."

I turned my head, my nose brushing against his. "You weren't intimidated by me."

"Another lie, Princess." He ran his hand along the underside of my jaw before he gently lifted my chin until my lips met his. "Everything about you was terrifying."

Sorin shook his head, smirking as he leaned back in the booth. "You still are if we're being honest. You terrify us all a little bit."

Thalia laughed, bumping her shoulder against his. "Speak for yourself. I find her delightful."

"Thank you, Thalia." I winked at her before turning my gaze on Sorin. "I'll deal with you later."

He raised his mug again with a grin. "And that, my queen, is exactly my point."

The table burst into laughter, the kind that felt easy now. The kind of laughter that came from surviving too much together and finally being allowed to breathe again.

The music shifted then, the soft strings picking up into a brighter melody. The rhythm was playful, inviting, coaxing people onto the small wooden floor near the hearth where a few couples had already begun spinning.

Evren's gaze flicked toward them before returning to me. That familiar gleam sparked in his eyes, the one that usually meant trouble for me.

"No," I said immediately, already knowing where his thoughts were headed.

His grin widened. "I haven't said anything."

"You're thinking it."

"Am I not allowed to think about dancing with my wife?"

I gave him a look even as my stomach fluttered. "Last time you nearly spun me into a table."

"That table was poorly placed." He slipped his arm from around my shoulders and stood, extending his hand toward me. "Come, Princess. Dance with me."

"Evren—"

"Adara." His voice lowered, and he couldn't stop the grin on his lips as his palm still waited.

Thalia waggled her brows at me from across the table, absolutely no help at all. "Your king has commanded it." She smirked before lifting her ale and taking a long drink.

"You're all traitors," I muttered, sliding my hand into Evren's.

The moment my fingers touched his, he pulled me to my feet and directly into his chest, his arm wrapping firmly around my waist.

His lips brushed my ear. "Don't worry. I plan on being on my very best behavior."

I snorted. "I'll believe it when I see it."

He grinned against my temple. "Dare to make a wager?"

I narrowed my eyes at him, already suspicious. "What kind of wager?"

Evren's grin deepened, his fingers lightly tracing circles against my lower back, just low enough to make my pulse quicken. "Simple," he whispered. "If I can keep my hands exactly where they're supposed to be for the entire dance, I win."

I arched a brow. "Where they're *supposed* to be?"

He feigned innocence, but my husband was far from it. "Respectable. Appropriate. Entirely kingly."

"I'm not sure you know what any of those words mean." It was a lie. Evren was respected by every one of his people. He was beyond respectable, and he was the greatest king any of us had ever known.

But tonight, in the golden light of the hearth, he was just Evren.

"Which makes the wager all the more interesting, doesn't it?" His eyes sparkled with a mischief that I loved. "If I fail, if my hands wander, even once, you win."

"And what do I get if I win?" I asked, unable to stop the smile tugging at my lips.

"Anything you want, Princess." His voice dipped, low and suggestive.

I hummed, pretending to consider. "And if *you* win?"

He leaned in until his lips brushed against my ear, the heat of his breath sending a shiver straight through me. "Then I'll get whatever *I* want."

I shot him a playful glare, but I could feel a flush creeping up my chest. "That's a very one-sided wager."

Evren only shrugged, entirely unrepentant. "I have strong motivation to behave."

I laughed softly, my heart already racing. "Fine," I agreed, pressing my palm flat against his chest. "But you're going to lose."

His grin was slow, wicked. "We'll see."

The music swelled around us as he pulled me into the dance, our bodies already moving in perfect rhythm. His touch was light, controlled, his hands resting properly at my waist. Exactly where they were *meant* to be.

For now.

His eyes gleamed as he spoke low enough for only me to hear. “You do realize I plan to torture us both with this.”

“I’m sure you do.” I smiled sweetly, though my pulse skittered with anticipation. “But I’m very much looking forward to watching you struggle.”

“Not nearly as much as I’m looking forward to winning.”

He spun me out and back again, never losing his hold, never letting his hands wander. But I could feel the tension humming beneath his restraint. I could feel the way his fingers flexed as though desperate to travel lower.

Every step, every breath between us was a battle of wills.

And gods, I loved every second of it.

The music wrapped around us like silk—smooth, intoxicating, and far too easy to get lost in.

Evren’s eyes stayed locked on mine, dark and hungry, even as his hands remained steady. His jaw flexed as my hips brushed against his, and his fingers dug into my flesh.

He spun me again, this time bringing me in until my back pressed against his chest, and I wasted no time in pushing my ass against him as we swayed to the music.

He inhaled sharply before a curse passed his lips. He slid his palm just a fraction lower, a hair’s breadth away from breaking his own rule. I felt the tremor of his restraint, the battle waged in every bone of his body, and it thrilled me to my core.

“You’re enjoying this far too much,” he murmured as he recovered quickly, steadying me against him, steady himself, and turned me to face him.

"Oh, I am," I whispered back, breathless. "I can practically feel your suffering."

His lips hovered near mine without touching, his voice a wicked rasp. "You think this is suffering, Princess?"

I arched my brow even as an ache started between my legs. "Isn't it?"

He pulled me tighter against him, so close that I could feel his heartbeat beneath my hand. The heat of his body pressed flush to mine, his breath warm against my cheek as his mouth ghosted near my ear. "You're cruel."

I let out a shaky laugh that betrayed far more than I intended. "This is your wager."

"Gods, you're going to be the death of me." His voice dropped, rich and thick as honey. "When this dance ends, I'm going to make you pay for that."

His fingers never strayed, never faltered, as I smiled sweetly up at him, even as my pulse raced out of control. "You have to win first."

His grin was pure sin. "Oh, I will."

He pulled me effortlessly into another step, his hands tightening at my waist just enough to make my stomach flip, but still not daring to slip lower.

It was maddening. Deliciously maddening.

Around us, the world blurred. I couldn't hear the laughter of the tavern anymore, couldn't hear the scrape of chairs or the clink of mugs. There was only him. Only the press of his body, the warmth of his touch, the way his gaze devoured me with every breath.

He spun me once more, letting the motion pull me away before dragging me back into his arms as the song faded around us.

His hands were still firmly planted at my waist, and I cursed under my breath.

He chuckled darkly, pulling me closer. "Admit it. I was right."

I glared up at him, my chest heaving, and I wondered if there would ever be a time when I didn't want him like this. "I'm not admitting anything."

He kissed the corner of my mouth, smug and utterly insufferable. "You're meant to be a queen. Not a sore loser."

I growled softly and ran my fingers through his dark hair until I could tug on the ends. "You're pushing your luck, Evren."

He had the gall to look amused, teeth flashing as he guided me toward the bar.

"Luck has nothing to do with it," he whispered, brushing his lips against my jaw as I leaned against the bar top. "I just want to hear you tell me how right I am, how good I am, while I collect my winnings."

Evren flagged down the barkeep, already grinning like a man who had far too many sinful thoughts running through his head.

"Two shots," he said to the bartender, his voice smooth as silk before he looked back in my direction. "And if you do as you're told, I'll make sure you know just how good of a girl you're being as well."

The barkeep set two shots of dark liquor down in front of us, sliding the small glasses across the worn wood.

Evren pushed one toward me, his fingers brushing mine as he leaned in close. "First," he rasped, and I squirmed against him.

"Get my wife a little drunk." His lips grazed the shell of my ear. "You're always so perfectly dirty when you've got a little liquid courage warming your blood, Princess. A little louder. A little messier. A lot needier."

Heat flushed up my throat, my knees nearly giving out beneath me.

"You're incorrigible," I whispered, barely able to keep my voice steady.

"And you love me for it." He pulled back just enough to meet my gaze, his eyes burning. "Don't you?"

I swallowed hard, my pulse hammering. "I do."

He lifted his glass in silent toast, and I mimicked the motion, my fingers wrapping around the cool glass.

But I didn't drink.

Instead, I watched as the man I loved so much swallowed his shot of liquor before his brow arched, playful suspicion blooming on his face. "Backing out already, Princess? That's not like you."

I bit my bottom lip, savoring the impending shift that was about to wreck every filthy plan he had brewing. "I can't drink that."

His eyes narrowed slightly. "Oh?" His voice was all dark amusement. "What would you prefer then?"

I shook my head, heart pounding as I smiled up at him. "No, Evren." I laced my fingers through his. "I can't drink it because I'm pregnant."

Everything froze around us. For a moment, the music, the laughter, the jostling warmth of the entire tavern receded into a hush.

Evren stared at me, his lips parted, the endless wit of his suddenly nowhere to be found. His hand tightened fractionally in mine, the only sign that he'd heard me at all.

I watched the realization dawn slow and blinding as the sunrise. I watched it steal the air from his lungs and fill him with wonder.

"You're…" He glanced down at my stomach, then up again into my eyes. "You're serious?" he whispered before a sudden laughter broke out from him, sharp and bright.

"I'm serious." I nodded and watched as that sinful grin of his returned, softer now, full of something far more dangerous than lust.

His hands found my face, trembling as he cupped my cheeks, and he kissed me with so much possession.

"Fuck," he said, when he finally let me breathe, voice thick. "Fuck, Adara. You…you…"

I pressed my lips against his palm. "Tell me you're happy."

He laughed, and it broke in his throat. "I've never been happier in all my years."

His words felt like the first time he said he loved me, like the first time he called me his wife, like something so much bigger than we were. They slammed into me, expanding in my chest, and I wondered if there would ever be an end to this kind of happiness.

He kissed me again, softer this time, and I felt the remnants of his laughter on my lips. When he finally pulled back, his eyes stayed locked on mine with a fierceness that was almost tender. "How long have you known?"

"A few days," I admitted, and bit my lip as I watched his face shift through a hundred emotions, each more wondrous than the last. "I wanted to be sure."

"You are so damn beautiful." He brushed his thumb across my lower lip and my stomach flipped at the pure awe in his voice.

His thumb lingered at my lip for a moment longer before he dropped his hand to my stomach, spreading his fingers over the slight curve that wasn't visible yet somehow felt real beneath his palm.

"You're carrying our future," he whispered like it was a prayer. "You've given me everything I never knew I wanted, and then somehow even more."

My throat tightened, but I managed a breathless smile. "You're going to be unbearable, you know."

"Oh, I intend to be." He bent forward, his voice rough and reverent as his lips brushed against my stomach. "You hear that, little one? Your mother's going to have to live with me being insufferable for the rest of her life."

I laughed, tears threatening to sting my eyes.

His hand found mine again, threading our fingers together. "I swear, Adara…" His voice broke again, quieter this time, like a vow just for me. "I will spend every breath I have making sure you both always know how loved you are."

I stared up at him, at the man who had once stolen me away from my home, who had become my king, my mate, my everything. "You already do."

And then his grin returned, wicked and beautiful. "Although…" he leaned in closer, voice dropping into that sinful rasp that never failed to undo me, "this doesn't get you out of the wager, Princess."

"Evren." I swatted at his chest, but he simply caught my hand in his.

"Pregnant or not, you still owe me your part of the deal." His lips brushed mine again, full of promise. "And tonight, when I finally get you home—"

"*No!*" Thalia's voice cut through as she and Sorin finally reached us at the bar, both grinning like fools. "Whatever you're about to say, Evren, I swear to the gods, save it for your chambers."

Sorin chuckled, slapping his hand down on Evren's shoulder. "I'm fairly certain half the tavern already knows exactly what he's about to say."

Evren only laughed, sliding his arm possessively around my waist as he looked back and forth between our closest friends. "Let them hear it. I've waited years for this life."

"Years of being an absolute menace," Thalia added with a grin.

"Years well spent." He winked down at me. "And now, it's only going to get better."

I leaned into him, my heart so full I could hardly breathe, and I realized that this was it.

The war. The pain. The fight. The falling. The choosing. All of it had led here—to us, standing in the center of the only home we'd ever truly needed.

Surrounded by family.

Surrounded by love.

And the promise of everything still to come.

PROLOGUE

Paragraph begins with: My steps echoed against the old, damp space as I made my way into the dungeon.

> **Holly:** Writing a chapter from Gavril's POV was one of my favorite and least favorite things at the same time. He is one of my characters that I hate the most, but I also loved seeing inside his head.

Paragraph begins with: "Don't touch her."

> **Holly:** Gah! Thinking about this guts me every time.

Paragraph begins with: "Don't fight me, love."

> **Holly:** I want to SCREAM at him for calling her love. How dare he?

Paragraph begins with: The power I would gain from killing my mate.

> **Holly:** HOLY SHIT.

CHAPTER 1

Paragraph begins with: I had given her every reason not to, but she still chose me.

Holly: This is one of my favorite things about this series. They have every reason not to choose one another, not to be together, and still, they choose each other.

Paragraph begins with: She made herself powerless, and I couldn't stop my fury.

Holly: Angry Evren is one of my favorite Evrens. Especially in the name of his girl.

Paragraph begins with: She was our hope, but we were her destruction.

Holly: This is one of my favorite lines in this entire book.

Paragraph begins with: I would go to whatever end.

Holly: He has spent his entire life fighting and suffering for his kingdom, and yet he would give everything up for her. SWOON.

Paragraph begins with: He had become that greed.

Holly: I love the idea that Gavril hasn't always been this evil person. He was born and bred by two greedy parents who poisoned him with their hatred and molded him into exactly who they wanted him to be.

CHAPTER 2

Paragraph begins with: Because everything he did was for someone else.

Holly: I wanted to make sure that it was clear that Adara understood this about Evren. Even though she could have been angry with him, she knows that everything he has ever done was in the service of someone else.

Paragraph begins with: They thought I was their savior, but I would be no such thing.

Holly: Yes, girl.

Paragraph begins with: Gavril followed my gaze, and a dark laugh fell from his lips.

Holly: The way I would love just five minutes with Gavril. Just to have a little talky talk.

Paragraph begins with: "You're so responsive."

Holly: Your Honor, I hate him.

Paragraph begins with: "The Blood kingdom is my home."

Holly: Gah, I wanted to cry when I wrote this. Adara has never truly had a home, and she finds it not only in Evren, but in the others as well. Thalia is her home. Sorin is her home. Jorah is her home.

CHAPTER 3

Paragraph begins with: His loyalty to me then meant nothing now.

Holly: Evren earned the loyalty of both armies, and I couldn't imagine the strength it would have taken for him to suddenly fight against people who fought at his side.

Paragraph begins with: She had a vicious look on her face.

Holly: Have I already mentioned that Thalia will forever be one of my favorite characters?!

Paragraph begins with: I rolled my head as his words coiled around me.

Holly: ON MY KNEES FOR THIS MAN.

CHAPTER 4

Paragraph begins with: I stopped in front of them, but I didn't dare bow before them.

Holly: Sassy Adara is my favorite Adara.

Paragraph begins with: "You will not speak of my mate in such a way again."

Holly: QUEEN BEHAVIOR.

Paragraph begins with "Cling to that word, Starblessed."

Holly: Every time I think I hate Gavril the most, she shows up and proves otherwise.

Paragraph begins with: "What could I have done, Your Highness?"

Holly: Oh, snap.

CHAPTER 5

Paragraph begins with: I would get her back.

Holly: When I first started writing Evren's character, I knew I wanted Evren and Adara to start as enemies but that he would become a simp as soon as he fell for Adara.

Evren has no problem showing his love and devotion to his mate, and that is one of my favorite things about him.

CHAPTER 6

Paragraph begins with: "Ah, Thalia."

Holly: I hate that he even says her name.

Paragraph begins with: "You made me bleed."

Holly: An eye for an eye, Gavril. Although I don't think there is anything Adara could do to truly make Gavril pay for all that he has done.

CHAPTER 7

Paragraph begins with: His mate was all I could think about.

Holly: Me too, girl.

Paragraph begins with: "I don't know."

Holly: The idea that she's caged in the very palace they are in makes me sick to my stomach.

Paragraph begins with: "I get it from my father."

Holly: Yes, Adara. Show her that fire.

Paragraph begins with: She was resolute, but her words were like glass being crushed underhand.

Holly: The rage I just felt for Gavril goes right back to her.

CHAPTER 8

Paragraph begins with: "Don't leave her."

Holly: I love Adara's father for this.

CHAPTER 9

Paragraph begins with: He pulled a small dagger from his side…

Holly: Me too. I know that Eletta works in the palace, but in this moment, I hate her as well.

Paragraph begins with: Because nothing would ever feel the same as him.

Holly: Never ever.

Paragraph begins with: But it was the thought of Thalia that I clung to as we walked through the double doors when someone announced our arrival.

Holly: Yes, girl. Channel your inner Thalia.

Paragraph begins with: "Do you think the bastard has ruined her?"

Holly: I hate them all.

Paragraph begins with: He arched a brow at me, a challenge, and I slowly let my arms fall away from my chest and lifted them as he held the shirt in my direction.

Holly: These softer moments of Gavril are what I hate the most. It gives a glimpse of who he could have been.

CHAPTER 10

Paragraph begins with: Her words made a chill run down my spine.

Holly: Mine too.

Paragraph begins with: "You do not need me."

Holly: SCREAMING, CRYING, THROWING UP.

CHAPTER 11

Paragraph begins with: My life over Evren's death.

Holly: I miss writing these characters so much. I felt so connected to both Adara and Evren when writing them, and I felt so bittersweet writing this book.

Paragraph begins with: "The true heir of your kingdom."

Holly: Defend him to the end, girl.

Paragraph begins with: "Did you send men to massacre my kingdom?"

Holly: You heard her correctly. MY kingdom.

Paragraph begins with: "Get your hands off my mate."

Holly: DADDY'S HOME.

Paragraph begins with: "Princess."

Holly: I never thought I would like the pet name Princess until I read it coming from Evren's mouth.

Paragraph begins with: I didn't have time to think about my next move before Gavril's dagger lodged in his mother's chest.

Holly: The way I was waiting for three whole books to finally write this scene.

Paragraph begins with: The surprise of the embrace stole the air from her lungs, and she dug her fingers into my back as we clung to each other.

Holly: I know that the romance will always be the star of the show, but Adara and Thalia's relationship will always be one of the most important relationships I think I've ever written.

Paragraph begins with: Evren shook his head as he pulled me forward.

Holly: This was important to me. I wanted Adara to save herself and for her love for Evren to be completely separate from that.

CHAPTER 12

Paragraph begins with: Evren's guilt bled out of him…

Holly: When writing this, I could visualize it so clearly in my mind. Evren's guilt felt like such a tangible thing to me.

CHAPTER 13

Paragraph begins with: "Of course."

Holly: Mina reminds me a lot of my mamaw, and subconsciously, I think I was thinking of her when I wrote her character. It's probably a big reason why she is one of my favorites.

Paragraph begins with: I would have waited a hundred lifetimes to get to her.

Holly: The way this man has me WEAK.

Paragraph begins with: "I want you," she whispered.

Holly: This part broke me. This desperation of wanting to forget everything that happened to her.

Paragraph begins with: "You have me."

Holly: I don't know how I'm ever supposed to get over him.

CHAPTER 14

Paragraph begins with: He was my family, but he was also a stranger.

Holly: When I first started writing this series, I knew that Gavril and his parents took her father, but I didn't realize how big of a role he would play in the story.

Paragraph begins with: "Queen Kaida's death would have come sooner or later."

Holly: Rereading this made me so emotional.

Paragraph begins with: I reached for the door, but it was his next words that stopped me in my tracks.

Holly: Poor, broken Evren. God, I just want to take away his pain.

Paragraph begins with: "Gods, you're such a good fucking girl."

Holly: Funny story: One of my sisters, Kenie Marie, is quite shy, and a lot of times readers will comment or tell me that Evren has the dirtiest mouth/they love his dirty mouth. I love to remind her that means that I have the dirtiest mouth because I wrote him. Lol. SHE HATES IT.

CHAPTER 15

Paragraph begins with: "Apologies for disturbing you, my prince."

Holly: Make him cocky and funny, and I'm going to fall for him every time.

Paragraph begins with: "It's your choice, princess."

Holly: Giggling and kicking my feet.

CHAPTER 16

Paragraph begins with: "Because I'd pick Thalia as my partner."

Holly: I loved every single second of writing this scene. Found family is one of my favorite tropes, and these people are Adara's family.

Paragraph begins with: But when I looked back at Sorin, at the wine he was pouring, his gaze was burning into Jorah's hand on Thalia's.

Holly: I have no clue how Thalia could possibly resist a pining Sorin.

Paragraph begins with: Thalia's hands just tightened around me, and mine on her.

Holly: I just want to have a girls' night with Thalia and Adara. I can just imagine the trouble we would get into.

CHAPTER 17

Paragraph begins with: I pushed through Thalia's bedroom door as she laughed.

Holly: Yessssssssssss!! This is the moment I have been waiting for since I met them.

Paragraph begins with: "Good night, love."

Holly: Writing this chapter made me so amped for writing *A Kingdom of Fire and Fate*.

CHAPTER 18

Paragraph begins with: A mother for a mother.

Holly: Writing this scene gutted me. Adara's mother was never good to her, but she was the only mother she had. And our girl has already been through so much.

Paragraph begins with: "And you are not to feel guilty for that either."

Holly: This hit me hard because it's so true.

CHAPTER 19

Paragraph begins with: "That's what I said."

Holly: Their engagement felt forced at first. They were choosing each other, but they also had a kingdom to save. This? This was only for them and no one else.

CHAPTER 20

Paragraph begins with: "Oh. We'll get there."

Holly: Excuse me, sir?! *blushes*

Paragraph begins with: "Yes, wife?"

Holly: I love a *good girl*, *princess*, even *baby*, but *wife* ?! That name has me weak in the knees.

Paragraph begins with: "Fuck, princess."

Holly: Eek! And now we get *your husband* thrown in there?!

Paragraph begins with: "Watch me as I fuck my wife."

Holly: *Stands up and salutes*

CHAPTER 21

Paragraph begins with: His brothers stood behind him, all three of them the epitome of a warrior.

Holly: The way I am dying to write their story.

CHAPTER 22

Paragraph begins with: "Nothing."

Holly: I needed this playful banter between them before such heavy moments that were to come. Their banter is one of my favorite things about them.

Paragraph begins with: "I have searched for you through a thousand lifetimes, princess, and I will search for you through a thousand more."

Holly: I fell in love with Evren while writing his character. I fell in love with his love for Adara.

Paragraph begins with: "It is you, princess, who will change our world."

Holly: *Chills*

CHAPTER 23

Paragraph begins with: I looked back at my friend, at the man who had been more like a brother to me, and I bowed my head slightly.

Holly: I was teary-eyed writing pretty much this entire chapter.

Paragraph begins with: I couldn't wait any longer.

Holly: Even reading this part back, it gets to me. "You have her back." Four simple words, and they tear me apart.

Paragraph begins with: "She is not your wife in my kingdom."

Holly: LET ME AT HIM!!!

Paragraph begins with: Then the darkness took over completely.

Holly: Noooooo!!!!

CHAPTER 24

Paragraph begins with: "My queen."

Holly: Yesss!!

Paragraph begins with: But then she mouthed two words that made my blood run cold.

Holly: Out of all the characters in this series, my heart breaks the most for Leda, for what she has been through. I think about her story often, how it started, who she was…

Paragraph begins with: But then I saw her slip behind him.

Holly: I needed to give Thalia this moment. After everything she has been through, it is hers and hers alone.

Paragraph begins with: Sorin's gaze shuttered, and he shook his head solemnly.

Holly: God, I broke my own heart with this one.

Paragraph begins with: It was he who the stars promised to a broken world, and those stars belonged to me.

Holly: I was basically a puddle at this point. I will never recover from it.

CHAPTER 25

Paragraph begins with: He was my enemy, but he had also been my brother.

Holly: Evren mourns Gavril even through his hate, and I can't imagine anything that could show the truth of his character more.

Paragraph begins with: Tears streamed down Adara's face, and I swallowed hard as emotion clogged my throat.

Holly: My heart! Why did I have to do this to Jorah?!

EPILOGUE

Paragraph begins with: "Come to the Olde Vine."

Holly: I didn't realize it at the time, but I think I poured a lot of myself into Adara. She feels like one of my oldest friends, and as much as she changed the world in the Stars and Shadows series, she changed my life as well.

Paragraph begins with: "I do."

Holly: The things we should all look for in a man lol.

Paragraph begins with: "Gods, I hope you do."

Holly: I miss them terribly. Rereading this series now makes my chest ache but also brings the biggest smile to my face. This series changed my life, and I will forever be grateful for these characters.

ACKNOWLEDGMENTS

Thank you to all the readers who have loved, shared, and screamed about this series. I am forever in your debt. I hope that Evren and Adara mean as much to you all as they do to me.

Thank you to my husband and children for your unending support. Hubie: Without a love like you've shown me, I would have never been able to write a love like this. A lifetime with you will never be enough.

Nolan and Millie: On the long nights and moments when Mama was locked away at her computer telling stories of love and triumph, thank you for letting me steal away that time. I have never loved anything the way I love the two of you.

To Brandi and Kenie Marie: Thank you for believing in and taking a risk on your crazy little sister. I am thankful for the both of you every single day.

To Lauren Cox, my baby angel: Finding you was fate. I could simply thank you for everything you've done at my side for my books and my business, but it would never be enough. You are one of my closest friends, and I will cherish you always.

To Amber Palmer: For simply being the kindest, most genuine friend I could ask for. You are stuck with me forever and always.

To Rachel Brookes: For your endless support, help, and love for my book babies, thank you.

Thank you to my entire team, who I couldn't do this without, Lauren, Savannah, Regan, Ellie, Rumi, Cynthia, and Valentine. Thank you, thank you, thank you.

ABOUT THE AUTHOR

USA Today bestselling author Holly Renee brings readers a pinch of angst, an indulgence of heat, and the perfect amount of heart in every book.

Born and raised in East Tennessee, she is a married mom of two wild children. When she's not writing, you can find her reading, pretending to be a dragon for the hundredth time that day, being disgustingly in love with her husband, or chilling in the middle of the lake with her sunglasses and a float.

Website: authorhollyrenee.com
Facebook: authorhollyrenee
Instagram: @authorhollyrenee
TikTok: @authorhollyrenee

A KINGDOM OF STARS AND SHADOWS

BETRAY A KINGDOM OR BETRAY MY HEART.

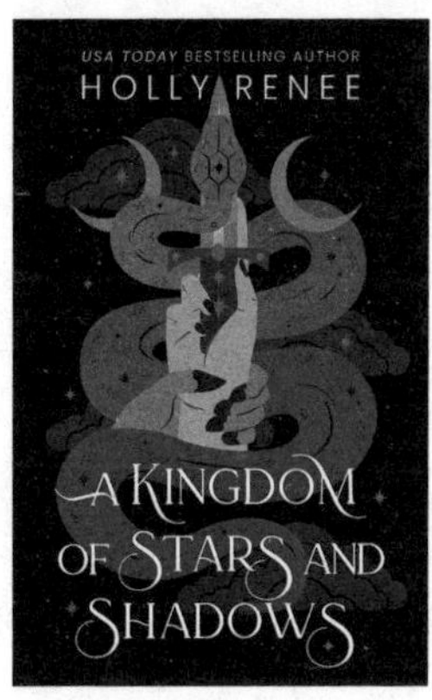

My union with the crown prince will determine the fate of the kingdom, but it isn't my betrothed who haunts my dreams: it's the half-fae bastard who stands at his side.

He is darkness and sin, and when he whispers wickedness in my ear, I crave a man I can't have. Every thought I have is treasonous. The way my hands ache to touch him deceitful. Even my dreams make me a traitor to the kingdom I am sworn to protect.

But when our kingdom is attacked, I am forced to make a choice...and face a bitter truth. For our lies and deception are entangled in the shadows and stars, and as they unravel, so shall my fate.

For more info about Sourcebooks's books and authors, visit:

sourcebooks.com

A KINGDOM OF BLOOD AND BETRAYAL

A FATE BOUND TO TWO PRINCES—
ONE BORN OF BLOOD, THE OTHER OF POWER.

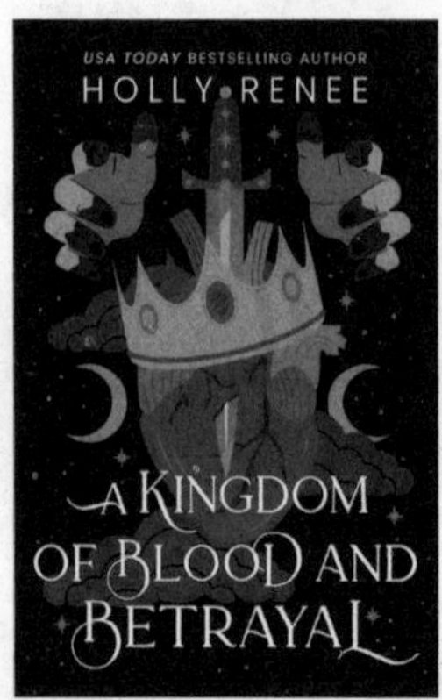

When the dark prince offers me a bargain that will save his people and my life, the cruelly intoxicating fae gives me no choice. Our union is his revenge, and I am his sacrifice.

His lies are unforgivable. His wicked touch bathes me in sin. He is my mate, and he is tortured by a curse to protect his people from his own family—from my allies. I can now see him for exactly who he is. So why can't I get his alluring touch out of my head?

I am the key to saving his kingdom, but he alone has the power to ruin me.

A KINGDOM OF FIRE AND FATE

PASSION IGNITES,
TORN BETWEEN DESIRE AND DUTY.

Love and loyalty collide in the aftermath of war, where Sorin consumes my every thought. But destiny takes a wicked twist. When news arrives that the human king, now allied with Evren's father, has invited Starblessed contenders to compete for his hand in marriage, I embark on a perilous journey into enemy territory. My goal: to uncover the enigmatic ruler's hidden secrets, with Sorin at my side.

In a world where trust is fragile and danger lurks at every step, we confront choices that shall shape our destiny. Will we betray our hearts in the name of duty, or plunge into the flames of an all-consuming love that could set realms ablaze?

MOONCURSED

SHE WAS NEVER MEANT TO BE CHOSEN...
COMING SOON FROM SOURCEBOOKS CASABLANCA.

They say madness dwells in the ocean's depths—and in the eyes of the Drowned King. Cursed to take a human bride and doomed to break her mind the moment she sees his face, the Drowned King spends his life in torment, waiting. Watching.

Louisa was never meant to be chosen. Now, blindfolded and bound in marriage to a man she must never see, she's thrust into a life of ancient gods and unraveling fate...and unspeakable desire.

THE VEILED KINGDOM SERIES

A NEW SERIES FROM HOLLY RENEE,
COMING SOON FROM SOURCEBOOKS CASABLANCA!

In a world where love and hate are two edges of the same blade, the missing daughter of a despised king finds herself caught in a delicate dance between forbidden desire and her looming destiny.

Book One: *The Veiled Kingdom*
Book Two: *The Hunted Heir*
Book Three: *The Rivaled Crown*